"The character development is lacking. Everyone always dies."
THE 5AM ZOMBIE PODCAST

"I have a bone to pick with this set of stories."
SIR SKELETAL OF YONDER TOMBSTONE

"I put a curse on his artwork. See for yourself."
LOCAL PORTLAND WITCH

"Not to be too on the nose, but I howled with laughter at how bad it all was. No Werewolf representation at all."
AN OVERLY HAIRY SHIRTLESS GUY

"I wish Rip Graven would wrap up his career."
NEWLY EXCAVATED MUMMY FROM EGYPT

"Somehow we got pulled into this mess too."
HAUNTER'S MONTHLY

"I foresee much time wasted."
MADAME BUDAGO'S ONLINE PSYCHIC SERVICE

"This book makes me want to sit in the sun."
COUNT VLADIMIR VON SHOOKTON

RUNNING CHILLS

A Collection of Haunted Horror Tales

STORIES & ARTWORKS BY

RIP GRAVEN

THINK DEEP PRESS

Think Deep Press
thinkdeeppress.com

Copyright © 2023 by Rip Graven

For information about special discounts for bulk purchases, or to book the author for your live event, please contact Think Deep Press at: **info@thinkdeeppress.com**

Manufactured in the United States of America

First Edition

2 4 6 8 10 9 7 5 3 1

Library of Congress Cataloging-in-Publication Data has been applied for.

ISBN 979-8-9887230-4-2 (Nightmare Edition Hardcover)

ISBN 979-8-9887230-5-9 (Nightmare Edition Paperback)

ISBN 979-8-9887230-2-8 (Midnight Edition Paperback)

ISBN 979-8-9887230-3-5 (Midnight Edition Ebook)

ISBN 979-8-9887230-0-4 (Color Hardcover)

ISBN 979-8-9887230-1-1 (Color Paperback)

For my bride, Steph, who always encouraged me to chase my dreams.
And for the best writing companion one could
ask for—my loyal pug Bartholomew.

I love our little family.

Contents

A Word of Warning

Running Chills pairs tales of horror with artworks created by the author, Rip Graven. These artworks are a combination of ambient surrealism filled with hidden meanings and visuals. They may also function as perceptual doorways into the characters and worlds contained herein.

We recommend caution when viewing said works. We now forbid our internal teams from displaying them around the office.

Don't ask why. —

Amber Bizworth | Head of Publicity at Think Deep Press

RUNNING CHILLS

A Collection of Haunted Horror Tales

STORIES & ARTWORKS BY

RIP GRAVEN

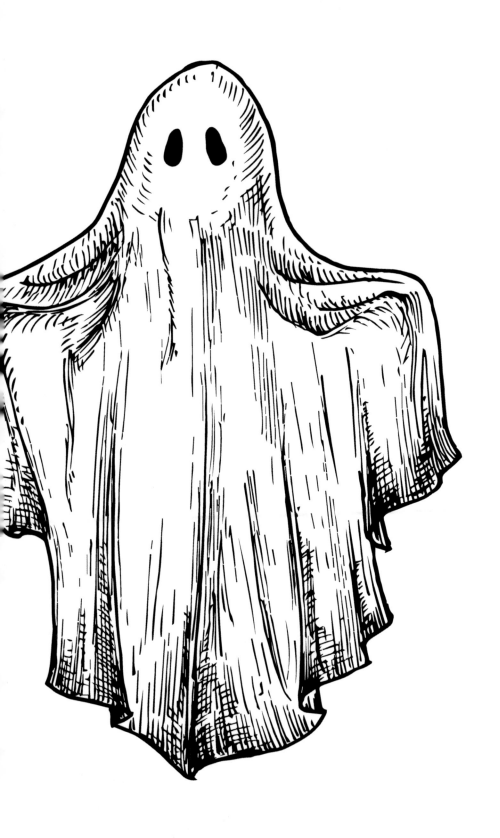

DEAR READER:

I 'd like to welcome you to *Running Chills*. Within these pages you'll find spooks of all varieties—some hiding in plain sight, and others lurking deep in the darkness. Adventures will be had, spells will be cast, horrors will be encountered. Along the way, I'll introduce you to a cast of characters that I'm certain you'll thoroughly enjoy. The included tales span both genre and time periods. Some are novellas, many are short stories, but all can be read during the brief moments of quiet you have among the living.

Running Chills is paired with original abstract surrealist artworks I created for each tale. The artworks contain hidden elements from my stories. For an extended experience, I suggest referencing the playlist included at the end of the book—as every story is also paired with a song of my choosing for further immersion. For those that like to listen to audiobooks, information about the *Running Chills Podcast* can also be found at the end of the book.

I sincerely hope you enjoy my collection of haunting tales. It is my honor to have you read them. Here's to hoping you will never encounter such situations as those contained herein.

YOURS IN SHADOW,

RIP GRAVEN

THE HAUNTINGS OF MIRESTONE

1

Mitchell Branderson hid behind a bush, watching the pair of fellow seniors who had bullied and roughed up his freshman sister earlier in the day. Covertly following the young men to a local park, Mitchell intended to beat some sense into the boys. Rather strong for his age, Mitchell figured he could take them both, as he was well versed in boxing and wrestling through school. Even with all that athletic training, Mitchell didn't plan on having to use his fists to get his point across—today's baseball practice gave him a tool that provided a rather hefty advantage.

Crouching behind the bush as to remain unseen, Mitchell noted these two punks were more interested in drinking liquor and smoking cigarettes than being aware of their surroundings. The sun was setting, and the two were at ease reminiscing about their day—unaware of the impending retribution Mitchell had planned. Mitchell pulled his baseball bat quietly from a duffle bag that lay next to his bicycle—ready to teach these jerks a lesson. As anger swelled in his veins, all he could see in this moment was red.

Touch my sister and I will shatter your hands.

Before Mitchell could announce himself and "adjust" their behavior, something happened that upended the natural world as he understood it. A dark smoke billowed along the ground, rolling across the blades of grass and landscaping toward the pair of upperclassmen. At first, neither of them noticed the low-lying black fog approaching. But as the smoke snaked between them, it rose and took the shape of a woman's silhouette—a pitch black shadow of sorts, despite no person to cast it.

The boys each staggered back at the suddenness of this unbelievable sight. At once, the dark figure reached out and grabbed one of them by the throat, raising him a foot off the ground, instantly snapping his neck. Tossing the body like a rag doll in the grass, the dark figure turned and watched as the other young man ran across the park toward the street. Shaking its head and laughing with a sound that seemed to emanate from all directions, the figure dissolved into a thick black smoke yet again and raced along the ground at an unfathomable speed toward the fleeing youth.

Just as it looked to Mitchell like the other school bully had reached the pavement, the black smoke was at his heel. The smoke formed the shape of a hand and yanked at the student's ankle, causing the fleeing bully to spill into the street.

Mitchell gasped in horror, covering his mouth as he watched these events take place. Unable to comprehend what he was witnessing, Mitchell stayed hidden, frozen behind the bushes in the park.

The remaining bully got to his feet in the middle of the street, doing so just in time to make eye contact with a brand new, cherry red 1955 Chevrolet Bel Air. Despite attempts at braking, the vehicle slid into him head on, sending the young man's body flying.

The black smoke dissipated.

The radio in the Chevy continued to play the tune of "Mr. Sandman", indifferent that the driver had exited and was frantically attempting to wake the now deceased young man. Everyone around the nearby area, including the local ice cream man, came running to see what happened.

Mitchell's presence had gone unnoticed. Finding the courage to stand, he quickly placed the bat back into his bag and hopped on his bike. After riding six blocks away, Mitchell stopped, desperate to catch his breath. A slight breeze blew as he rubbed the sweat from his eyes.

And that's when he noticed a shadow watching him from behind a tree lining the sidewalk. The shadow waved, then laughed in a way that echoed all around him, bathing him in fear, before disappearing once again.

Mitchell pedaled his bicycle away in terror.

Although tragic and mysterious, the town coroner ruled both student deaths an accident. Despite telling his family, the police, the local paper, and even his little sister what he saw that afternoon—nobody believed Mitchell. Word spread through the small town that the poor boy had lost his mind, and that he possibly needed professional help.

2

Kenny was visibly upset. His father had transferred jobs again, causing the family to move to a new town, where they would have to start all over. Again. The previous move had been rough enough, happening right after freshman year in high school—tearing him from his friends and status of being in the "in crowd" at his school. That relocation had put Kenny in a Baltimore cultural context where his west coast clothing styles and way of speaking stood out. It took Kenny a good two years to finally build up enough status with his fellow classmates that senior year was looking promising. Maybe, just maybe, he would be able to get a decent date to the prom and not have to deal with being the "new guy" anymore.

And his dad just screwed all that up.

Figures.

Kenny's father had the gall after two years of rebuilding their social lives to ask for a bank management position in a quiet town so "his family could have a more laid-back lifestyle." The simplemindedness of the idea that the family wanted that—after two years of investing in relationships—just pissed Kenny off all the more.

The most happening hub of activity in a two-hour radius of isolated farms and other even smaller communities, Mirestone was a small rural town located in the heart of the Midwest U.S. Football games at the local high school were something of a religion for the community—embodying the one source of local recreation other than an aging drive-in movie theater. Despite Mirestone's draw for entertaining the surrounding area, jobs were scarce, and many considered the town to be in economic decline. It was in such decline that, despite his father's pay cut, Kenny's family was able to snatch up an abandoned Victorian home (that his mother lovingly referred to as a "McMansion") located in the heart of the town.

Kenny sat in the back of his parent's station wagon with his younger sister Hannah while his mother argued with his father over driving directions. Attempting to drown the sounds of his family out, Kenny turned the volume dial up on his Walkman and blared Tears for Fears through his headset. He impatiently waited for their future home—located in Nowhere, USA, as far as he was concerned—to appear in the distance. Seeing a road sign for Mirestone, Kenny leaned forward and intently looked out the windows.

Their station wagon pulled onto what appeared to be the town's main drag. The entirety of the downtown area was an overly vacant couple of blocks filled with small shops that probably operated more like hobbies than businesses.

Not even an arcade to pass the time.

Kenny shook his head as he took it all in. Just as soon as they happened upon it, the main street ended, and homes began. A short block later and the station wagon took a right before pulling into the driveway leading to their new home.

This house looks like it has seen better days.

Although imposing and rather significant in size, everything about the place seemed dated and in need of work. There were shutters that needed mending, glass windows with cracks, and plenty of paint peeling from the exterior. After exiting the vehicle, Kenny's father took a bow on the porch to great fanfare from his mother and sister. After fumbling with the keys for a moment, his father unlocked the front door while everyone but Kenny rushed inside to check the place out. As the cassette he was listening to came to an end, Kenny leaned against the rear of the station wagon and stared down the street.

Just great, Kenny thought as he pulled the headset from his ears and wrapped the cord around the player for safe keeping. *An old house in a dying town. Just when my life was starting to take shape. My senior year has been officially ruined.*

Kenny's mom returned from inside the house and approached her son from behind, placing a hand on his shoulder.

"Hey sweetie. I know this is hard for you. This isn't what you wanted, and I know that. Think of this as a new adventure. In a year, you will be headed to college anyway, and live anywhere you choose. For now, try to have a brave face, huh? This means a lot to your dad, and your sister is excited—let's not ruin this for them."

Kenny's mother then brushed the hair from Kenny's eyes and put her arm around his shoulders.

"We'll get through this. You'll see."

Kenny shook his head, following his mother into the house. The interior was just as old and in need of work as the exterior. Floorboards creaked, the railing on the staircase was a bit wobbly, and from the state of the kitchen floors, it looked as if there had even been a leak or two prior.

A real fixer-upper.

Various pieces of antique furniture came with the house, all covered in white sheets. Kenny's mom and Hannah began pulling the sheets off everything, treating each object reveal like a present they were unwrapping. Kenny's father watched with amusement, leaning against the kitchen entryway framing. Upon realizing his son had not ventured far into the home and had yet to set his backpack down, he motioned to Kenny.

"Feel free to pick one of the rooms upstairs to call your own. Your mother and I have the master, and Hannah has the small room adjacent to ours, but the other rooms are spacious. Once you pick one out, we'll divvy up the rest for other uses. Go on champ, claim your territory!"

His father smiled sheepishly, tossing a thumb back toward the staircase.

Kenny ascended the staircase and wandered the second floor of the aging Victorian. There were four additional rooms unclaimed on this floor. Each was unique in its own way: a few had decent sized beds, wardrobes, and vanities already. One in particular caught his eye, as it was filled with bookcases and looked to be more of a study. A small window lit the room, but otherwise it was dark and quiet. The previous owners had left various books and small statue figurines on the shelves, and in the center of the room was a huge object obscured by another sheet. Upon closer inspection, Kenny found a grand piano beneath the veil.

Ok, that's awesome. I've always wanted a space to jam out a bit, and I was wondering where I was going to put my guitar and drum set. Hopefully I can find someone in this dust-bowl of a town to play music with.

As Kenny was considering these things, he noticed a slight gap in the framing of one of the bookshelves. After a bit of force, the bookshelf swung open, groaning to reveal an additional staircase.

No way. A secret room?

Kenny's eyes grew large with wonder at this discovery and climbed the stairs to find a door with a skeletal key left in the lock. Giving the key a turn, Kenny heard the mechanism unlock, turned the handle, and gave the door a push.

Light poured with intensity into the dark stairwell. As Kenny's eyes adjusted to the light, Kenny found what appeared to be a large, empty attic, with the walls on both sides filled with windows. From this room, Kenny could see the entire neighborhood, and by opening windows on both sides, a breeze blew through the room. Turning to face the rear wall where he had emerged from, Kenny found a second door. Upon opening that door, Kenny found a dark storage space with many more personal objects left behind: various furniture pieces and trunks. Kenny began looking through the objects, inspecting them for anything of interest.

A small hand grabbed at Kenny from behind in the dark.

Kenny whipped around, tripping on a box, and fell backward with enough force to knock over a vase—shattering it.

The tiny hand that had grasped him in the dark was that of his little sister, Hannah.

"Wow, you scared me, sis!"

Kenny stood up, rubbing his backside.

"That smarted."

Hannah giggled.

Upon hearing the noise, both parents joined them in the attic storage space.

"You ok, sweetie?" his mom asked.

Kenny grinned, glancing back at the broken vase.

"Yeah, the vintage decor, not so much."

Kenny's dad appeared, glancing around the storage space, letting out a whistle to show how impressed he was at the find.

"Well, this sure wasn't in the floor plan or the talking points of the home listing. I knew we were getting a spot for some music, but I had no idea we were getting a super-secret teenage lair."

His dad smiled smugly and winked, shuffling through a few contents of the boxes in the room.

"Son, where do you want to put the fire pole? You know, so you can slide down like a Ghostbuster when we call you for dinner?"

"So, I can claim the whole attic?" Kenny asked, wondering how serious his dad was.

His mom began to protest, but his dad spoke up and patted Kenny on the back.

"Sure thing, son! I did say you could claim your territory and a room upstairs. The attic is as *upstairs* as you can get, I suppose…"

Kenny's mother shot a disapproving glance. She clearly wanted the attic for her painting room due to the natural light and stellar views.

Observing the emotions of the moment, Kenny's dad continued.

"Oh, don't worry darling. Kenny is a teen boy and needs his space. Besides, the music room is attached, and we can sequester all that noise to a self-contained portion of the home now!"

Kenny's mother put her hands on her hips and sighed as she exited the attic, leaving Kenny's father to a cheesy grin while flashing Kenny a thumbs up signal.

Kenny threw his fists up in the air in a sign of silent victory.

3

What Kenny lacked in a social circle during the summer, he more than made up for in having the hangout most teenage dreams were made of. Even Kenny had to admit to himself: there was no way he would have this much personal space back in Baltimore. Kenny set up the old study room to be more his taste with an arrangement of his drum set, guitar, and the grand piano. He left the old books, busts, and statues out as he felt it gave it a cool vibe, but he also added his own touches throughout. The bookshelves behind the drum set were covered with a wall sized poster of an album cover from Journey, various skateboard decks lined the room, and his cassette stereo and Pioneer speakers sat just beneath the small window. A life-size cardboard cutout of Darth Vader took up a position nearest the hallway door.

To the passerby, it looked as if MTV had overtaken the classical nuance of the traditional study.

Up the hidden staircase, Kenny relocated a bed from one of the lower rooms, as well as a couch and a small TV set that he paired with his Nintendo. Kenny filled any available wall space with posters from movies and musical artists he was currently into—even managing to convince his parents to buy him a pinball machine for his birthday—giving the attic a brilliant glow when the lights were turned out. All went exactly as his father had predicted: apart from grabbing something from the kitchen or using the bathroom, Kenny disappeared into his section of their home and left the rest of the family in peace.

Kenny's family had also settled into the aged Victorian rather well. The second-floor rooms were turned into an office, an art studio, and a playroom. Kenny's father went to work right away repairing and replacing elements throughout the home, while his mother made it her mission to repaint the interior. Hannah adjusted well too; she spent most of her time in her playroom imagining beach trips for her assortment of Barbie dolls.

Summer flew by, and soon the school year arrived. Endeavoring to make some friends, Kenny looked for others who seemed like potential allies—going out of his way to do something to help them out—all to win them over. This strategy worked in Kenny's past experiences, and the technique held up well in this moment. Before long, Kenny made a couple of friends in various classes and began to feel more at ease on campus.

Unfortunately, with how classes were scheduled, most of his friends were only available to hang out every other day as their lunch breaks would align. This left Kenny with half a week of enjoyable lunch breaks, and half a week of quiet and isolated ones.

It was during one of these isolated lunch breaks that Kenny happened upon Beth, an attractive girl sitting alone, studying under one of the trees surrounding the school. Beth had curly brown hair and a golden locket around her neck, wearing clothes that felt a little old fashioned, yet tastefully curated.

Kenny worked up the courage to say hello—his nerves nearly getting the best of him. To his surprise, they hit it off marvelously.

Beth had a great sense of humor that matched Kenny's, and the two began spending every other lunch together. Kenny came home and told his parents about Beth, to which his dad gave him a high-five, followed by the typical lecture about being "responsible with the ladies." Kenny would usually nod along, while his mother detracted by spilling the beans on "how responsible" his father had been with her when they were dating.

It was all very humorous and awkward.

Eventually, even Kenny's friends began to ask questions about his love interest, as none of them had met Beth before. Kenny explained what she was like, and his friends cheered him on for the most part, collectively joking and jesting about it—wondering aloud during their lunches together if Kenny had gotten laid yet. Kenny just rolled his eyes and played it cool amidst their joking; the peanut gallery could keep their jokes as far as he was concerned.

Beth was something special.

Kenny was falling for her big time.

4

This was the moment Kenny had been waiting for. *Don't screw it up man, steel your nerves! Time to ask her.* Kenny checked the school bathroom mirror and made sure his hair laid just right.

"Gotta make sure you look the part, huh? She must be special."

An older man in a jumpsuit stood behind Kenny, readying a mop in the bucket beside him. The school janitor looked at Kenny with a knowing smile, as if reflecting on his own youth. Embroidered on a patch over his left breast pocket was the name Mr. Branderson, followed by the school mascot—a cartoonish bull of sorts.

"Yeah man, no pressure, right?" Kenny replied, embarrassed he had been speaking to himself out loud.

The janitor gave Kenny a pat on the back. "You'll do fine. Just be yourself."

Moments later, Kenny found himself sitting with Beth under the tree where they first met. Kenny put his arm around Beth and asked if she would like to be his date to the upcoming dance.

Beth's eyes lit up as she played with the golden locket around her neck. "Really? You want *me* to be your date?" Beth blushed, putting her face in her hands. A quiet settled in on Beth, and it seemed as if she was lost in thought, her gaze penetrating the horizon line with a depth that told Kenny something was on her mind.

"These past few weeks have been something else. Never in a million years would I have thought I would meet someone like you in a small town like this. You are beautiful Beth. I've known I was interested in you from the first moment you laughed. It would be my honor. If that's ok with you, of course."

Kenny then nervously searched Beth for a clue of what was on her mind but was unable to find one.

"Is everything alright? Is it me? Did I say something wrong? If you don't want to go, I'll understand."

Beth turned and met his gaze with tears in her eyes.

"No, no, you're perfect. I've been waiting for what feels like forever for someone just like you. This is just so very…" her voice trailed off as she returned her gaze to the horizon. "…unexpected and lovely."

Without looking at Kenny, Beth took his hand and squeezed it, then kissed it. Beth held Kenny's hand against her cheek and the two sat in silence for another moment.

"My previous relationship ended badly. Many things went unresolved. I never thought I'd get a second chance to find love or feel this way again after all I've been through. I'm sure this is coming off as melodramatic, but that's totally how I felt before meeting you."

Kenny leaned in and kissed Beth.

Beth kissed back and giggled in happiness.

"You need a few lessons on kissing Kenny." Beth teased, pointing an accusatory finger in his direction. "That kiss was far too innocent." Beth then wiped the tears from her eyes and leaned into an embrace by Kenny.

Kenny whispered in Beth's ear.

"I'm available for you to teach me after school."

5

The night of the dance was upon Kenny. Kenny dressed his best, with the addition of a leather jacket over his formal apparel for the evening. Beth had arranged to meet him at the dance, and due to this, Kenny didn't have to go through the charade of having either set of parents take photos or embarrass him with awkward interactions. Kenny grabbed a bite or two of the lasagna his mother had made and then rushed out to meet some friends who were giving him a ride.

And what a ride it was. A convertible Cadillac with the top down: white exterior with gold accents, and a ruby red leather interior—a boat of a car that held more kids than it rightfully should have. This night felt alive to each of them, the evening filled with possibilities. With Billy Ocean's "Caribbean Queen" blaring, the friends shouted into the night air as they cruised the main drag to the school.

The glow of the colorful lights inside the gym cast out of the open doors and onto the pavement walkway leading from the parking lot. While his friends went inside, Kenny decided to wait outside the entrance to the school gym for Beth to arrive. Kenny played it cool, leaning against the building while bobbing his head to Hall & Oates "I Can't Go for That" emanating from the gym's open doors and echoing off the parking lot full of cars.

Beth tapped Kenny on the shoulder from behind and surprised him. Kenny turned to have his heart drop. Beth was stunning in a cute blue dress and heels.

"Wow." Kenny was awestruck.

"Not too shabby, huh? I expected to take your breath away kissing later, but I see I've already peaked. I suppose the night is ruined!"

Beth twirled on her heels before striking a pose.

Kenny just smiled and extended his hand.

Beth took it, grinning from ear to ear, and the two slowly walked into the gym, arm in arm.

6

The night went by as a blur. Kenny and Beth danced away the evening and had the best of times. In fact, they were so taken by each other that they hadn't noticed the snickering and scoffing of those around as they danced. It wasn't until Kenny attempted to introduce Beth to his friends that they began to suspect something was amiss. Despite his best attempts, Kenny's friends all looked at him in an uncomfortable manner as he introduced Beth, and soon after, they ditched him for the night—taking his only ride with them. Beth was comforting and supportive, but Kenny was quite worked up over the ordeal.

"I've never seen my friends act like that. It's really messed up. Screw 'em." Kenny said, taking the small glass of punch Beth handed him.

"It's alright. Maybe something went wrong earlier in their night. I doubt it's worth ruining our date for." With that, Beth kissed Kenny on the cheek. "You know what would cheer you up? More dancing!" Beth smiled and extended Kenny her hand in the same manner he had earlier in the night.

TOTO's "Rosanna" began, and Kenny took Beth's hand and joined the dance floor again. The two danced their hearts out, and as Beth stared deeply into his eyes, Kenny just kept falling more and more in love with her.

Beth is fun. Beth is kind. Beth is gorgeous. And best of all, Beth wants to be with me. I've never had anyone dig me like this.

The colorful lighting created a magical glow on Beth. Kenny was having a blast. Beth giggled as they mimicked each other's stereotypical bad dance moves. Kenny had but given Beth another twirl when their good time at the dance suddenly came to a grinding halt.

Gary and Shelia, along with Brad and Tanya, were the most popular students at Mirestone High. Gary and Brad had approached from behind while Kenny and Beth were dancing—pointing and laughing at them as they danced. Sheila yelled from her and Tanya's position next to the refreshments to Gary, encouraging him to "stop the freak from dancing." Sheila's encouragement was all Gary needed, as he grabbed Kenny by the back of his collar and drug him off the dance floor, much to Kenny's shock.

Kenny spun around to face Gary, breaking the grip he had on him—unfortunately, at the expense of his shirt collar.

"What the hell is your problem?!"

Kenny gave Gary a shove.

Gary snickered, exchanging glances with Brad.

"I have a problem with *weirdos* and *freaks* casting a shadow over our fun tonight."

Brad then lunged forward and punched Kenny in the face, then gut, sending him gasping to the floor. Gary walked up and gave Kenny a swift kick while he was down, all while Sheila cheered as she approached.

The whole situation would have gotten worse had it not been for Tanya.

"Why are you all being such dicks to the new kid? So what if he's weird? I'm not having a good time unless you all stop intimidating the new guy and get me on the dance floor."

Tanya gave her peers a disapproving glance and then pointed out a parent monitor coming their way.

"Thankfully, nobody here has noticed you starting stuff thanks to all the dancing—what WE should be doing RIGHT NOW."

Brad took the hint. He quickly grabbed Kenny and pulled him to his feet, dusting him off.

"Don't tell a soul what happened, or I'll beat the shit out of you and finish the job next time."

With that, Brad grabbed Tanya's hand, following Gary and Sheila back to the dance floor. As Tanya was being dragged in tow by Brad, she turned to Kenny and mouthed an apologetic, "*so sorry.*"

Kenny glanced around, looking for Beth, but she was nowhere to be found. Kenny walked into the gym bathroom, inspecting the damage from the bruising he had just been given.

"That's one hell of a bloody lip you got there. You need help? Just point out who did this, and I'll take care of it with the school administration."

Kenny glanced over at the much more formally dressed Mr. Branderson, the school janitor, now turned dance chaperone.

"Thank you."

Kenny sighed, using multiple paper towels to clot the blood on his lip.

"I think I need to find a way to handle this on my own."

The janitor nodded.

"Sometimes the only way to handle a bully is by taking a swing with your own bat. You owning this situation is respectable. Just don't be afraid to let someone know if you get in over your head."

After saying this, the school janitor adjusted his own bowtie and exited.

Upon returning from the bathroom, Kenny circled the gym one more time, searching for Beth. Unable to locate her, Kenny collected his leather jacket, then used a pay phone to call a taxi home.

She probably ditched me because she thinks I'm a loser who got his ass kicked in front of her.

Kenny climbed out of the taxi in front of his home, wincing in pain from the bruises on his rib cage. Thankfully, his parents had gone to bed, and he quietly ascended the stairs to his room overlooking the neighborhood. Kenny placed his leather jacket over the arm of his sofa, took his shoes off, then threw himself upon his bed, facing up at the glow cast from his pinball machine in the darkened room. Soon, he began to drift to sleep.

Kenny's eyes had barely shut when he heard a light tapping at his window. Kenny sat up, startled to find Beth on the other side. He quickly opened the sliding glass frame, and Beth hopped into his room.

"I'm so, so, sorry for leaving like that."

Beth threw her arms around Kenny and squeezed him, Kenny jerking back in pain.

"Oh my! Those guys really did rough you up. Oh, I'm so sorry."

"How did you find my home or know which window was—"

Beth caressed his side where he had been bruised from Gary's kick and interrupted, "—You've told me multiple times where you live; you must have hit your head really hard tonight. You poor thing."

Kenny sat back down on the bed while Beth paced his room.

"Do you think less of me for getting beat up at the dance?" Kenny asked, reaching over to close the window.

Beth stopped pacing and sat beside Kenny, taking his hands in her own.

"Not at all. I feel it really was my fault, like maybe something is wrong with me. I'm not that popular anymore. Not everyone has eyes for me like you."

"They are fools." Kenny sniped.

"Yes, yes they are."

Kenny rubbed Beth's gentle hands. "I love you."

"And I you. Before those jerks interrupted us, it was the best night of my—well, you know."

Kenny and Beth smiled knowingly at each other and leaned in until their foreheads touched, their eyes closing.

Beth whispered, "Can you just hold me tonight? Can I stay over?"

"Of course."

7

The following morning, Kenny woke to an empty bed and a note.

Kenny-
Had to get an early start and spend time with family this AM.
See you Monday at lunch.
XO
Beth

The weekend flew past, and as it did Kenny's wounds began to heal. Eventually Monday came, and Kenny walked to his school campus. Friday night's aggression hung over his mood like rain clouds, which was fitting as a storm was set to roll in that evening. Just before lunch, Kenny had a chance encounter again with both Gary and Brad in the hallways—the pair running their shoulders into him as they passed.

Kenny balled his fists and considered the idea of giving them a taste of their own medicine. Throwing a few punches could get him kicked out of his classes, so he ultimately thought better of it. Kenny was more interested in seeing Beth moments later than seeing the principal.

The school janitor witnessed Gary and Brad's altercation with Kenny. Mr. Branderson looked on, frowning with concern, leaning on his broom from down the hallway.

Kenny acknowledged him with a thumbs up and patted his chest in a symbolic sign of *I've got this.*

The janitor nodded his head and then gave Kenny a salute of support.

Kenny left the building and found Beth under her usual tree at lunch.

Beth looked up as Kenny approached.

"Well, if it isn't my knight in shining armor!"

Kenny was still quite bruised from the pounding he had been given at the dance and winced as he set his bag down.

"Yeah, more like a knight knocked off his steed as of late."

Beth was amused by this.

"A knight nonetheless."

Changing the subject to their evening together, Beth stood and put her arms around Kenny's neck.

"Thank you again for the other night. I knew you shouldn't be alone after the way the dance ended. And selfishly, I rather enjoyed your heart beating next to me. My getting to rest in your arms."

Kenny nodded and looked into Beth's eyes.

Beth could tell there was more eating at Kenny.

"What's on your mind?"

"Gary and Brad were at it again in the hallways. I'm going to need to put an end to it by confronting them—with violence if necessary. I'd rather it not come to blows, but if that is the only communication that works for them, then so be it."

Beth became visibly upset.

"You know what? No. I've got this one. You took your lumps already. I'll solve it. Today."

Beth crossed her arms, content with her decision and whatever plan to stop the bullying she had in mind.

"Really?"

Kenny was a bit surprised by Beth's resolve, but also notably concerned.

"How are you going to do that?"

Beth smiled with an expression Kenny had not seen before.

"I have my ways."

8

The remaining school day was uneventful for Kenny. Kenny got home just as rain began to pour down and darkness was setting in over Mirestone. His mother was busy preparing dinner and greeted him as he sat his pack down.

"Your father has to work late tonight, so it will just be us for dinner. Did you hear about the coming storm? The news said we are going to have severe weather tonight. The thunder will be pretty loud, maybe even enough to shake these old windows. Kinda fun, don't you think?"

Hannah looked up from playing with her dolls as her mother said this; a worried look upon her tiny face.

Kenny's mother continued. "Dinner is going to be done early, and no matter what, we have plenty of candles and board games if the thunder keeps us up or the power goes out. Your big brother is here to protect you as well!"

Kenny hugged Hannah and exchanged a knowing glance with his mother.

Hannah relaxed a bit, returning to her dolls.

Kenny made the most of assisting his mother with cleaning up after dinner and distracting his younger sister from the storm building outside. He knew this night was going to be restless and enjoyed the family board games as they gave him a reprieve from his homework.

Elsewhere in town that evening, Gary was home alone, putting the finishing touches on a group project that was due tomorrow. Brad was rushing to complete his portion of Gary's project so he could drop it off. And Tanya was biding her time on the phone with Sheila—waiting impatiently for Brad to pick her up, as she wanted to see a movie that night at the local drive-in.

9

S heila could barely hear her friend Tanya on the other end of the phone. Static came through the bright blue handset as she played with the cord coiled from the receiver on her nightstand. Sheila pulled the earpiece away and glared, clearly annoyed at the interruption.

"Tanya, are you still there? If you can hear this, I'll call you back."

Sitting upright, she crossed her bed and slammed the phone down on the receiver. Picking it up again, Sheila attempted to redial, but to no avail. Assuming her parents must have returned home and might have been interfering with the line, Sheila swung her bedroom door open and yelled down the hall.

"Can you guys cut it out? I was in the middle of a call!"

Rolling her eyes, Sheila closed her bedroom door hard enough the Madonna poster she had taped down fluttered off the door. Kneeling to pick the poster up, a dark figure caught her eye in the pink vanity mirror beside her. Turning around at once and finding nothing there, Sheila sighed in relief.

It's just my jacket hanging from the closet door.

After retaping the poster, Sheila grabbed a *Tiger Beat* magazine from her bedside table and began thumbing past heart throbs, wishing aloud the lousy weather would pass. The storm outside was intense and tree branches scraped against her bedroom window while thunder rolled in such a way as to make the floor beneath her bed rumble.

A few pages into the magazine, Sheila began to get the creeping feeling she was not alone. Glancing over the edge of the pages, she caught a shadow move in her attached bathroom. Unnerved, but not desiring to feel foolish, Sheila wrote the shadow off as a trick of the lightning and tree branches from the storm outside.

I'm just getting myself worked up over this storm.

Although she tried to read the next few pages, Sheila's nerves began to get the best of her, and doubt started creeping into her mind about someone else present. Someone else, *there*. The next thunderclap brought her chills and goosebumps. Unable to shake the feeling of being watched, Sheila put the magazine down and searched both her bathroom and closet to make sure she was alone. After nothing further turned up, Sheila checked the window and realized that her parent's car was not in the driveway—that most likely she was still alone in her home.

Seeking the comfort of a friend's familiar voice, Sheila decided to try calling Tanya again. No sooner than Sheila reached towards the handset than the phone rang. The digitized sound of the modern landline was a sharp contrast to the thunder and wind gaining in volume outside. Sheila picked up the receiver and placed it on her cheek.

"Hello? Is that you, Tanya?"

Sheila's voice shook in the moment.

A voice whispered from the other end of the phone.

"Look behind you."

The lights in her home went out as the thunder clapped and the phone line went dead. Sheila spun around to find a shadow-like figure standing in the corner of her room near her bedroom door. Sheila dove across her bed and made a sprint for the attached bathroom. The door suddenly swung shut and Sheila screamed as her dresser moved seemingly on its own to block her path.

The air in the room felt like it was being sucked toward the opposite wall. Furniture throughout the room, even her bed, launched into the air and landed behind the now approaching shadow figure. Sheila realized the only escape route was through her bedroom window.

Go. I need to go now!

Sheila quickly flung the window open, choosing the storm outside over the unknown supernatural intruder approaching. Her feet sank into the muddy grass next to the window as she fled. Sheila made a sprint through her front lawn, catching a glimpse of her parent's vehicle headlamps as they turned down the street toward the home. Yelling and waving her hands in relief as her parent's vehicle approached, Sheila was soaking wet, bracing herself against the trunk of a tree next to the driveway.

It was then she cast a glance back at her home.

There, on the lawn, stood whatever evil had been stalking her.

In a flash of lightning and gust of wind, a heavy branch from the tree above dropped and impaled Sheila. Her parents rushed from the vehicle to their daughter, just as she was taking her final breaths. Sheila watched, gasping for air, as the unnoticed shadow figure on the lawn dissolved into a dark mist.

10

B rad sped down the farm road with the windshield wipers at maximum. Tanya was seated next to him in the bench seat of his older pickup, lamenting about the bad weather.

"It's coming down so hard I can barely see! You sure we'll be ok on the roads?" Tanya asked, seeking reassurance.

"Yeah babe. We'll be fine. I just need to drop this research paper over at Gary's first so he can include it in the group project."

Brad glanced over—noticing how alarmed Tanya was—and motioned to her.

"Come sit over here, we'll be at the movie soon enough."

Tanya slid closer to Brad, and he put his arm around her after shifting gears.

"I was on the phone with Sheila just before you picked me up. The storm must have created a bunch of static on the lines—we were cut off and I could never get her back on the phone."

Tanya stared at the windshield in wonder. *This storm tonight is really something.* Rain beads covered the windows, and as Brad drove into town, the streetlights cast a warm glare upon each individual droplet. Tanya chewed on one of her nails nervously as the thunder rolled.

The lightning flashed and revealed a dark figure in the street ahead.

Brad slowed as he approached.

"Is someone in distress? Do they need help?" asked Tanya.

Brad scoffed.

"Nah, probably just some drunk."

Brad swerved the truck around the figure and punched the accelerator. As he did this, the truck engine died, and they coasted about forty feet from the person standing in the road.

"You must be kidding me. A downpour, the patron saint of skid row, and now *this?*" Brad was visibly irritated. "Not a good start to a night where I'm supposed to get to third base with you during the drive-in movie."

Tanya swatted Brad's hand in protest as he attempted to touch her knee.

Brad scowled.

"Guess I need to check the engine and see what's up."

Brad exited the vehicle and went around front, lifting the hood—much to Tanya's relief.

Sometimes I think Brad is only interested in one thing…

Tanya let this thought trail off.

Tanya's mind drifted for a moment until she remembered the figure they had just sped past. Checking the mirrors but to no avail, Tanya could not locate anyone remaining in the street. "I hope they are alright," Tanya whispered, continuing to search the mirrors.

Tanya was left alone inside the cab. Already nervous as she was about the storm, she began to worry more as each second passed. This engine trouble was only increasing her anxiety levels—the constant flashes of lightning were doing her no favors.

Rain was still pouring down, and Brad was bound to be a soaked mess by the end of this episode. Tanya resigned herself to accepting that a movie was probably not going to happen after all. Tanya was not in the mood for "running the bases" tonight, as Brad so eloquently put it, and she figured the lack of action would put Brad in an even more foul mindset. They were already late—the most likely outcome tonight would be dropping Brad's homework at Gary's, followed by her being dropped off at home after rejecting Brad's advances.

Tanya felt the cab rock a bit. She could hear Brad muttering and fiddling with some elements under the hood. Lightning flashed again and Tanya had about as much of the storm as she could take.

I am down the street from Sheila's house after all; at the very least, I can get a taxi home from Sheila's while Brad gets a tow.

Tanya swung the passenger door open and walked to the front of the truck, the rain pelting her as she crossed the pickup's headlight beams.

Brad was *gone*.

Tanya franticly searched the surrounding area. Calling out for Brad, but never receiving a reply, fear began setting into her mind. Another flash of lightning occurred, and Tanya noticed Brad had somehow closed the hood and returned to the driver's seat amidst the noise of the storm.

Of course, he gets back in the truck and lets me stand out here getting soaked, worrying about him.

Tanya planned to give Brad a piece of her mind about this. Crossing the headlight beams again while smacking the front of the hood, Tanya stormed to the passenger side, climbed inside, and slammed the door.

Then Tanya screamed.

Brad sat lifeless in the driver's seat—the truck's jumper cables wrapped around his neck.

Tanya flung herself out of the truck and bolted down the street towards Sheila's. Crying and out of breath, Tanya screamed for help as she passed her friend's empty driveway. Unaware of the events that had just preceded her arrival not but moments ago, Tanya approached the darkened home. Tanya pounded on the door to Sheila's, but nobody answered. A neighbor rushed outside with great concern, finding Tanya crumpled in a ball, crying in terror, at the foot of the home's front steps.

The neighbor tried to calm Tanya by throwing a jacket over her shoulders—escorting her toward their home. As she walked, Tanya noticed the figure she and Brad had witnessed in the street earlier—now standing under a nearby streetlamp.

All street lighting and power in the neighborhood flickered.

Then the person was gone.

11

Gary turned in the darkness, finding a woman's silhouette behind him. He went for the light switch, but it was of no use, for the storm had knocked the power out.

Lightning flashed in the windows of his home as the silhouette of a woman slowly approached. Her movements felt unnatural, yet terrifyingly smooth. Gary grabbed the nearest object next to him, a chair from the dining table, and swung it wildly in front of him while shouting a warning.

"Stay back, whoever you are! I will fuck you up! Get out of my house!"

The figure was unfazed, continuing her painstakingly slow approach. With a sudden burst of wind, window glass shattered throughout the home. Objects flew left and right with crushing velocity as the wind whipped around the room. The chair was ripped from Gary's grip as if by an unseen force, sending it splintering to pieces against the wall behind the approaching woman shrouded in shadow.

Gary dropped to his knees and screamed, using his arms to shield his face in horror.

Suddenly, all went quiet throughout the home. The storm subsided its howling winds and thunder. The curtains previously blowing horizontally returned their draping toward the floor. The figure paused in the silence of this moment, turning her head as if puzzled.

Gary lowered his arms, confused by the sudden calm as well.

Then the moment passed, and the storm outside resumed its fury. The silhouette crossed the room at an impossible speed and plunged a shard of window glass into Gary's chest.

Lightning flashed throughout the home.

12

The Mirestone Gazette's front page labeled the previous night's events "The Storm of Violence." Front page images of property damage around town nuanced the fact that three teens from their small community had perished the previous night. While on the front-page Gary and Sheila's deaths were explained away as untimely victims of the storm's gusty winds, Brad's death by strangulation was located a few pages deeper in the morning news. Tanya had been brought in for questioning at the police station, and word around town was that she was being treated as the primary suspect due to rumors of a lover's quarrel with Brad.

The entire high school campus was abuzz with gossip and shock at their classmate's demise. Kenny felt slightly guilty that he was happy to not have to run into Brad and Gary in the halls anymore. He watched the clock count down on the classroom wall until he could go to lunch. The day dragged on. Once the bell rang, Kenny made a beeline to his usual group of friends.

"What was going on the other night at the dance guys? None of you acknowledged Beth, and then you ditched me for the night!"

Kenny threw his hands up and looked around the table at his friends, waiting for an explanation.

"Dude, what are you even talking about? Were you taking something and holding out on us by not sharing?" one of his friends replied. "Whatever it was, it must have been good. None of us saw your imaginary girlfriend. What we did see was you dancing around with yourself, acting like a fool."

"Not cool, Kenny. Not even chill." another voice added.

Kenny couldn't believe what he was hearing, and it upset him even more.

"Kenny, you know I love my recreational substances. It's rude not to share!" one of the girls in the group teased.

Kenny's friends all nodded in agreement, taking the moment lightly.

Speaking up as to clarify, Kenny asked again: "So you are all telling me, instead of owning how screwed up that was—ignoring Beth and ditching me—that you would all rather poke fun at me by claiming that she isn't real, and that I'm on drugs?"

"Really, really good drugs." another from the group replied.

"Unbelievable!" Kenny shook his head while turning and walking away.

Another friend mocked him as he walked away.

"Hey, aren't you gonna hook us up? My man! I want TWO imaginary girl-friends, and a high!"

Laughter from the group ensued.

13

"Son, do you have a moment?" The school janitor asked as Kenny exited the school and headed home for the day.

"Sure Mr. Branderson." Kenny replied.

"Please, call me Mitch. We're on a first name basis now that we've gotten to know each other a bit. That Mr. business makes me feel a hundred years old."

Kenny shook the janitor's hand as a symbol of agreement.

"So—*Mitch*—is everything all good?" Kenny asked.

"Well, son, you know those two who were bullying you? The ones that died last night?"

Kenny nodded; his eyebrows raised with interest.

The janitor continued. "The papers say they passed under mysterious circumstances. But I know the truth. SHE killed them." The janitor spoke in a hushed tone, motioning Kenny to come closer. "You need to get out of this town, tonight if possible. You are in grave danger."

Kenny paused, taking this warning in, trying to make sense of it.

The janitor continued, "Whatever dark apparition, demon, ghost or unnatural she is, I haven't a clue—but what I do know is those bullies are not the first at this school to have their lives cut short by this devil. I witnessed her powers myself back when I was a student here, and every couple of years her vengeful spirit returns, looking to harvest the less savory students that take advantage of the vulnerable. Not that I mourn the wicked getting what is coming to them, but you need to be careful and get far from her reach. Especially since she has taken an elevated interest in you compared to the others."

The janitor motioned toward the tree where Kenny and Beth ate lunch every other day.

Kenny looked at the janitor like he had lost his mind, nodding politely, and backing away.

"I've got to get going home, Mitch. I'm not really into ghost stories. But thanks for the heads up. Good talking again."

Kenny then turned and began walking home, bewildered at the advice he had just been given.

"It seems you are, in fact, in a ghost story, my son. I pray you escape it..." the janitor whispered as he watched Kenny disappear around the corner of the school facade.

14

The following day, Kenny made his way to the tree where he and Beth spent their lunch together. Beth sat relaxing, playing with her golden locket as usual while she read.

Beth glanced up from her book, excited to see Kenny.

"Hey babe!"

"Hey."

An awkward pause hung in the air.

"What's wrong, Ken?"

Beth put the book down and stood, her eyes attempting to read Kenny, not unlike the novel in her hands.

"My friends all joke that I imagined you… that I was on drugs, or something, the night of the dance. And then I got the shit kicked out of me because some popular kids at this school thought I was a weirdo as well."

"Popular kids that will no longer bother you again."

Beth smiled while motioning for a high-five.

"A bit too soon, don't you think? They were jerks, but…" his voice trailed off. "Anyway, I keep thinking back to that night. Nobody I've talked to remembers seeing you there with me—it's the oddest thing. And then I remembered: nobody said a negative word to you either, only to me. In fact, we've never hung out with others except for the night of the dance. And even then, once those jerks roughed me up, you were nowhere to be found."

Beth sat down quietly under their tree and leaned back, patiently waiting for Kenny to continue.

"How did you know where I lived the other night anyway? I've never had you over before, and I never told you where I lived. And how would you know which window or room was mine? The more I've thought it over, it doesn't make any sense."

Beth took this moment to tease Kenny a bit.

"Ok, I'll confess… I've been stalking you. I'm your star-crossed lover and you *MUST* be mine!"

Beth giggled in a way that made Kenny feel foolish.

Kenny let out a sigh, gathering himself at the obvious stupidity of it. "Look, I know I'm probably just shook by what happened to those popular punks and it's clouding my thinking, but you must admit from a certain perspective, this is all really weird, right? Why does nobody claim to see you?"

Beth smiled and nervously played with her locket, then brushed her hair with her hand.

Another student from the school approached.

Kenny continued. "I had this idea to prove they are all lying. I'm currently taking a photography class with some major camera geeks. One of them happens to own an instant film camera—the kind that develops a picture right after you've taken it. I thought it was time we took a photo together."

The student approached Kenny, handed him a small photo, nervously glanced at the tree, then walked away.

Kenny stared at the image. A knot rose in his throat, and tears in his eyes as he processed the content of the photograph and its implied meaning. He barely knew how to formulate the words. Kenny became overwhelmed in disbelief.

"You're… *not* really here Beth…"

Kenny handed Beth the photo just taken as they had been talking. Kenny was standing alone under their tree. Beth was not in the image.

Beth laughed. "Well, the cat is out of the bag." Beth tossed the photo into the breeze. "Damn, this was good. I enjoyed feeling so *alive* again."

Kenny's eyes widened as he decoded the undertones of this comment. The hairs on the back of Kenny's head stood up.

Was this what the school janitor was warning about?

"You're probably wanting the backstory, yeah? I was a girl who went to this school. Back then, I met a young man named Stanley, whom I fell head over heels for—he promised me that he would take me to the school dance."

A breeze kicked up and blew leaves past as Kenny took this all in.

"Unfortunately, that promise was cut short by Stanley dying in a tragic accident. I went to the dance alone, heartbroken. I wish that was the end of my sad tale, but unfortunately, it was just the beginning."

Beth stood and began to pace as she recounted the story further. "After Stanley died, another young man had it in his mind that he was going to make me love and marry him. When that didn't come to pass, he decided to murder me for the sake of his twisted fantasy: if he couldn't have me, then nobody could."

Kenny didn't know what to do with all of this new information. Only moments before, he had hoped to prove to everyone Beth was in fact a real person—not that he was being haunted by a ghost. Or currently *talking with one*, for that matter.

"I, however, got even." Beth continued. "I don't understand how or why, but my spirit never left this existence. Along with having to remain here, I found that I have unnatural talents that, when put to use, can bring about my own form of revenge. And so… I haunted the man who took my life until he put a gun barrel to his temple. I then chose to haunt many more, just like him, keeping watch over the students in the decades that followed here."

Kenny's mind began connecting the events of the last few days.

"So, Brad? Did you, uh…" Kenny couldn't finish the question.

Beth smiled in the way she had earlier while telling Kenny she would take care of the bullying.

"Yes. Gary and Sheila too. And many others long before them."

Kenny's blood turned to ice. The bell rang for all students to report to their next class. Kenny glanced toward the students in motion headed back inside.

Beth put her hand on Kenny's arm. "It will be alright. Let's talk some more after school. Meet here again? When you get out?"

Kenny nodded, avoiding eye contact.

Beth watched as Kenny walked away. Just inside the windows of the school, Beth noticed a familiar, if aged face of a boy she once met, now an elderly janitor, looking in her direction.

Beth smiled and waved.

15

Mr. Branderson watched as Kenny walked back inside the school from where the boy spent his lunch under a certain tree. A familiar shadow stood next to the tree and waved at him, causing the janitor to get the chills.

"She casts a shadow over all who cross her path." the janitor warned aloud as he cleaned the glass window before him.

Kenny stopped walking suddenly upon hearing the janitor.

"How did you know?" Kenny asked.

"This isn't the first time she has haunted these halls."

"What should I do now Mitch?"

The janitor stopped cleaning and sighed. "Hell if I know. Would have been better if you had skipped town by now. Does she know you know?"

Kenny nodded, fearful of what this could mean.

"I'll pray for you, my boy."

16

Kenny did not join Beth again under their tree. Once school let out, Kenny made a beeline back home to tell his parents everything.

I don't care if they think I'm crazy, or they lock me up in a mental institute. I just want to be safe. I need to leave town.

Upon entering his home, Kenny realized how poor of a choice his timing was. Under all the stress he had today, Kenny forgot that tonight his parents were at a community fundraiser, and his sister was with her grade school friends at a sleepover. His parents were going to be preoccupied all evening with the event, and he was going to be home all alone. Upon this realization, Kenny turned to head back out the door and find somewhere, *anywhere* else to be.

Beth's voice arose from the top of the main stairwell.

"Oh, come on now, I couldn't have given you that bad of a fright."

Kenny turned, his face pale, realizing he was going to have to confront this moment. He looked up the stairwell at what had been the girl of his dreams, now the girl of his nightmares. Beth was dressed in an outfit that clearly matched the historical period of which she belonged, her hair slightly different, but still wearing her golden locket.

"You stood me up today. That wasn't very nice. We have a lot to talk about." Beth was agitated and looked at Kenny somewhat hurt.

Kenny raised his voice. "You're dead. You kill people. You scare me. Did you ever even love me?"

Beth began descending the stairs towards Kenny. "Those words hurt Ken. You don't mean them. *Of course,* I love you. You are missing a piece of the story."

Beth took off her locket and tossed it to Kenny.

Kenny caught the golden jewelry piece. He turned it over and inspected the inscription upon it.

We'll always be together.

Kenny glanced back at Beth, confusion setting in. He opened the locket to find a small black-and-white image of Beth across from a young man that looked just like him.

"Now you understand. I couldn't believe it myself when I first saw you. Here I was, ready to haunt this new family out of moving into my home, when along comes a young man who looks just like my beloved Stanley. I watched at first, wondering if his spirit had indeed come back for me, but when I realized you were not him… I was tortured by your presence. You carry yourself just like him. You look just like him. You are sweet just like him. So, I revealed myself to you under that tree at the school. You and I fell in love just like he and I did. I began not caring that you were not him. You saw me when nobody else could, and you loved me. You made my soul alive again."

Kenny closed the locket and tossed it back. "But Beth, you are no longer alive. And I am not him. What love can the living have for the dead?"

"Plenty." Beth replied. "You and I can be together forever now, as both the living and the dead. I can possess you, once again having real-world experiences like enjoying a nice dinner or feeling the sunshine on my face again. Our spirits will be lovingly intertwined in such a way that you'll never be alone again Kenny. We'll always be with and have each other. *Forever.*"

As Beth advanced toward Kenny, the front door of the home slammed shut and locked.

Kenny ran toward the rear exit of the home shouting at Beth as he sprinted.

"I want out of this relationship, you're not the girl I fell in love with—you pretended to be something you were not!"

This was all rather comical to Beth.

Beth's form changed to that of a shadow figure. Items flung themselves freely in Kenny's path, slowing his attempt at an exit. Kenny stumbled over various obstacles, making it within a few feet of the back door to the home before a coffee cup from his mother's collection flew up and clocked his forehead, knocking him unconscious.

Beth's shadow form dissolved into a low-lying black fog, encircling Kenny's unconscious body. The black smoke found its way into Kenny's mouth and filled his lungs until there was no trace of the dark mist remaining.

17

Kenny's parents and little sister came home to a tidy house that smelled of cleaning product. Kenny's mother made her way throughout the home, noticing all rooms were neat and tidy; even the bathrooms on the second level had been cleaned. Pulling back the bookcase from the study-turned-rock studio, his mother climbed the staircase to Kenny's bedroom only to find him enjoying an intense game of pinball.

"I didn't realize my son was such the housekeeper! What has gotten into you? Coming home to a perfectly cleaned home was quite the surprise!"

Kenny's mother then noticed a golden locket on his nightstand.

"What's this?" she asked, before picking the locket up and opening it.

Inside was a photo of Beth, as well as a recent photo of Kenny.

"Cute." His mother noted, placing the locket back on the nightstand.

"Gift from my girlfriend," Kenny responded, pulling the plunger, putting another ball into play on the machine. "I think we'll be together a *long* time."

"Oh, that's sweet honey." His mother replied, taking a seat on her son's bed while watching his score increase. "How did you ever get so much cleaning around the house done tonight?"

Kenny smiled with an expression his mother had not seen before.

"I have my ways."

THE TRAIN TO NOWHERE

To Learn
to Live.

There are many interesting and peculiar tales passed down from the western frontiers of America, but few rival that of the legend of Angus "Blood Oath" Holland and his Shadow Horsemen. The exact locations, towns and people involved have become so varied in retellings that it's difficult to pinpoint specific details and authenticate the stories. The legend has earned an air of mystery and garnered those who cast a critical eye toward the believability of the accounts, whilst also gaining enthusiastic followers who swear by the truth of the tale. Historians have altogether avoided the topic, choosing instead to focus on more approachable and verifiable stories from America's rather rambunctious past.

Below is a retelling of events chronicling the rise of Angus Holland's Shadow Horsemen throughout America's western frontier.

Death was but moments away. Famine, disease, and conflict were abundant. In the American west, the law was what one made of it; a bullet was often the decider of ownership rights to land and wealth. If toiling under the societal underpinnings of your family name was not to your tastes or sensitivities—there was but one other profession to consider: the outlaw.

Jack Weatherby suffered no fools. Although his father had been a wealthy real estate baron of sorts, Jack was not taken to wearing pressed clothes and socializing with the Yankee elites as his father did. He longed for adventure and a fight, and upon his father's death, Jack sold all his family's investments. He had no interest in wealth other than using it to fuel his desired lifestyle, that of an outlaw.

Money could buy anything. It could even buy your way out of the noose or prevent lawmen from pursuing you. Jack had plenty of it, setting his sights on robbing a few small-town banks just for the thrill of the action. During his second robbery, Jack shot and killed a Sheriff in the main street, right out in public view. To his shock, the town allowed Jack to take whatever he wanted without a fight. That's when Jack realized there would be no consequences for his actions—assuming his trigger finger was fast enough.

A few towns later, Jack met a dismal collection of men down on their luck, without food or work, drinking away the last of their wages. Jack threw down a satchel of gold before them and offered to handsomely reward each for their allegiance. The men took to joining Jack gleefully, as their lot had never experienced the comfort wealth could bring. Now women, lodging, fine horses, saddles, firearms, and enough food to never hunger again were at their disposal due to following Jack—including copious amounts of drink. When asked where this wealth came from, Jack always pointed to the robberies he had committed—even though this was patently false.

Jack was convincing enough. The men assumed such wealth from robberies would be theirs if they joined him in his outlaw lifestyle. Jack trained his men in the desert to be the fastest six-shooters around, with enough accuracy to claim they could knock the barbed spines off a cactus. The group traveled the frontier from town to town, murdering anyone who stood in their way and rewarding those who assisted them.

Papers in the area began calling their group the "Golden Nine"—as they always robbed from those who could spare a fortune, lavishing that wealth upon the town they were staying in. This took the form of paying townsmen for keeping guard and being lookouts while they drank, or leaving large tips to bar keeps and ladies of the evening. One account claimed the Golden Nine donated an absurd amount to a local hotel needing updates to its weathered facade, just as thanks for a good night's rest. Some residents cheered the bandit's arrival, knowing prosperity would flow into town, even if it was at the expense of their local banker.

Unfortunately, the outlaw lifestyle had its own share of drawbacks; each man in the Golden Nine had warrants out for their arrest. Lawmen from far and wide attempted to apprehend the group, and it was during a rather intense ambush that one of the Golden Nine fell during an exchange of bullets. When Jack and his men regrouped to consider their next move, a sober awareness arose that they were now one man short. Seeking to remedy this, Jack and his bandits eventually recruited a young boy from the next town to train up.

Angus was an orphan who had been taken in by a local parish in an act of grace. The town minister had fed and clothed the boy, teaching him to read from the scriptures as well as maintain the church property. When the Golden Nine, now eight, pulled into his small town, young Angus happened to cross paths with Jack. The rest, as they say, is history. Jack made a sizable contribution to the parish and offered the boy a chance to see the wild west.

Angus took Jack up on the offer. The young boy's fate was now set in motion.

The name Angus translated means "one choice." Indeed, this one choice to join Jack and his men in the Golden Nine changed Angus's fortunes forever, setting him on a path to eventually lead the notorious posse known as "The Shadow Horsemen." The young boy would eventually be come to known as Angus "Blood Oath" Holland.

As the years flew by, Angus grew into an irreplaceable member of the Golden Nine. Jack treated Angus as a prodigy of sorts, giving him the best training in firearms, riding, and the strategic philosophies of excelling as an outlaw. The men in the group had aged and become less capable, while Angus was young and agile comparatively—a strapping young man now in his early twenties, with all Jack's training and expertise to boot.

The Golden Nine wasn't looking so golden in these late days. Their opportunities were getting fewer, and the cuts were getting smaller. Local lawmen were increasing in numbers, while towns that previously cheered for their arrival became supportive of law and order, rather than aiding outlaws for coin. The Golden Nine kept to themselves more now, living in a set of caverns they had discovered in the desert. Other than supply runs and the occasional robbery, the bandits lived on their own terms just outside of the law's reach.

The Golden Nine were restless and frustrated with the lack of action as of late. Lying low began taking a toll on the outlaws. Some men entertained the idea of breaking away and becoming more aggressive with their tactics, while others began considering taking their share of wealth—settling down somewhere far away.

Jack had admitted as much to Angus in private.

Angus, being the most capable of the group besides Jack himself, was often sent to scout out new opportunities for plunder. Truth be told, Angus volunteered to do so, rather than sit around listening to the men quibble on about the "old days" with Jack.

During one of these scouting missions, Angus took note of a rail company that had set up an office of sorts near the main line. The outer wall of the office was painted with verbiage advertising the ability to transport and protect a variety of goods. Clearly, this service opened new opportunities for businesses along the rail lines, but for Angus, this presented something new to exploit on behalf of the Golden Nine.

Angus visited the rail company later that week under the guise of a businessman looking to transport valuable goods. He figured that if anything of high value were to be moved by train, this method of inquiry would make him privy to the details of when and where such goods would be. As it turned out, a guarded shipment full of large crates—filled with precious valuables—was to be on the rails near Red Run Canyon next week. Angus thanked the rail company for this information, excusing himself to discuss the "shipping price" with his "business partners" before agreeing to any contract.

All too easy.

Angus had learned well from Jack.

Valuable information only costs the promise of profit to those who hold such.

Angus rode out to meet the men and inform them of his findings.

Jack was pleased with how easily Angus gained visibility into the movement of expensive goods along the rail line. The men grew in excitement as well, as this was an opportunity to get some action, not to mention considerable profit. The Golden Nine previously robbed banks and stagecoaches, but a *moving train?* A heist of such caliber would put this collection of outlaws back on the map. They might even make the front page of the local papers once again.

Their plan was straightforward enough: two of the men would hide behind rock formations with wagons at the ready to load the large valuable crates. One man would place dynamite on the trestle bridge extending over the canyon and light the fuse. The other six men would ride up as the train rounded Crow's Overlook—a rather tight turn for the rail line—as it headed toward Red Run Canyon. This approach would give minimal visibility to those on the train before the Golden Nine set upon them, as well as force the train to slow enough during the turn for the men to board from horseback.

In a perfect scenario, they would board the train, disconnect the rear boxcars, allow the locomotive to cross over the trestles, then detonate the bridge before anyone was the wiser. With an engine that has no way back across the canyon, the outlaws would have plenty of time to kill those guarding the goods and load anything of value into their wagons before the train was reported missing.

Timing had an enormous impact on the six bound to board the train.

"We'll need to be close enough to the bridge to disconnect the railcars and allow the locomotive to cross without taking note of the load change." Jack advised, pointing to a rough sketch Angus had made of the crossing.

At this, the men became critical of the plan. There were many ways in which things could go wrong.

One voice of dissent could be heard above the discussion.

"Once that bridge is blown, if we engage those brakes too late, we'll find ourselves along for a steep drop into the canyon below. I'm not looking to meet my maker so soon. Pardon the disrespect, but this plan could go to shit at the rattle of a snake."

The majority of the men looked on, somber at this bleak prospect.

Jack exchanged a glance with Angus, then finally spoke.

"You have a valid point. While we need that locomotive to cross the bridge without enough time to understand what we've done, it's to our benefit to engage the brakes early enough to prevent finding ourselves a party to the explosive finale."

The men quieted, eager to hear what Jack was to propose.

"Based on my calculations, we'll need the boxcars disconnected within about sixty seconds of boarding the train at Crow's Overlook."

A chorus of objections arose. Another voice among the men could be heard.

"—the hell. *Sixty seconds?* How are we supposed to cross an entire train from the caboose in under a minute? We've been doing this a long time, but Jack, you may have finally had too much of Jasper's hooch."

Angus grinned.

"Alright men, let Jack finish. We wouldn't be bringing this to you if there wasn't serious coin involved."

Jack pulled his revolver from his holster and fired it into a glass jar full of moonshine. The precious liquid spilled out onto their hideout's dirt floor.

The men gasp.

"Clearly Jasper's bottle of hooch was full, and shame as it was to lose it, I believe my point has been made. Now do I need to empty any other liquor supplies to prove my sobriety, or are we good to move forward with the rest of the plan?" Jack asked, waving his pistol.

This shut the men up.

Jasper was angered a bit, shaking his head at the loss.

"What did the hooch ever do to you?" Jasper whispered.

Jack ignored the comment, continuing his explanation.

"We will not be boarding the train from the rear. We will need to board from about two cars behind the engine."

Silence fell upon the men as they pondered this new information.

"Two cars behind the engine at Crow's Overlook. Sixty seconds and then a decouple. We'll engage the breaks immediately, and the rest should work itself out."

Hopes began to rise as the men found this plan to be of merit.

Jasper raised his hand. "I have one question. Who is the unlucky son-of-a-bitch tasked with the dynamite?"

All the men looked on at Jasper, and no one dared volunteer.

Jack glanced around the room and then smiled at Jasper.

"Looks like we have our volunteer."

———

The big day finally came, and just as predicted, the train came thundering down the rails toward Red Run Canyon. The Golden Nine were ready. Two men remained with the wagons stashed out of sight, while Jasper had the unfortunate assignment of handling the dynamite—lashing all the sticks to the bridge trestles and lighting the fuse.

Angus felt a heaviness in his chest as the pressure from the moment began setting in. The Golden Nine lie in wait as their plunder drew near. The sound of the approaching train filled their ears as canyon walls thundered with what they could *hear*, but not yet *see*.

Jack turned to Angus and gave him a wink, kicking his horse with the spur of his boot. The six rode hard; they only had this one shot at getting onboard the speeding train. As the train rounded Crow's Overlook, Jack was the first to make the jump onboard, then Angus, followed by two more of their men.

Two riders in the rear missed their jumps, and as the train continued on, the distance became too great for them to catch up.

Jack and Angus made quick work of decoupling the engine around the second car. The locomotive pushed onward, unaware that a change in its load had occurred. Jack and his men managed to engage their lead car's brake, and thus the rear portion of train boxcars began a drawn out, extremely loud process of slowing. As the cars ground to a halt and the locomotive continued to cross the trestles that would soon be blown, the four bandits onboard the train boxcars now faced their truest test: eliminating any guards.

Jack gave Angus an order. "Climb topside and cross the train. When you get to the final car, help the two who missed their jump get onboard. Work together and clear the cars of any guards—I'll meet you in the middle of the train and we'll secure the valuable cargo together."

Angus quickly swung himself atop the railcar and dashed across the tops as he approached the rear. Angus had made it more than halfway when an unexpected sight arose from a gap between boxcars.

A lone minister with a white collar and a pistol strapped to his side now stood in his path, holding up a wooden cross as if to repel him.

The fuse failed. Panic beset Jasper, the lone man from the Golden Nine assigned to blow the bridge. A grim reality began to set in: the locomotive noted its missing cargo and had slowed on the other side of the canyon, clearly intent on coming back to claim the missing railcars.

It was up to him to prevent this, and due to the failed fuse, Jasper had a choice to make: abandon his post or give up his life by lighting the fuses at inescapable proximity to the eventual explosion.

The choice was obvious.

Jack opened and cleared the first few train cars with ease. For what was supposed to be a train filled with precious valuables, the contents seemed lackluster—various food items and goods—none of which were worth the trouble of transporting, much less robbing a train for. It wasn't until the fourth or fifth car that Jack realized what trouble they were in.

"The bridge didn't blow!" one of the men shouted frantically after glancing out the side of the now stopped railcars. "That engine is headed back here!"

Jasper had failed them.

Jack shifted his strategy to accommodate; clearing the remaining cars was going to have to wait—they had larger problems. Ordering his men to retreat, they sprinted back to the first car in order to board and capture the locomotive upon its attempt to reconnect.

―――

"Repent! Forgive them, Father, for they know not what they do!" the minister yelled as he held up a wooden cross toward Angus at a distance atop the railcar. A momentary pause hung in the air.

Then the priest made a move for his holstered gun.

Sweat stung Angus's eyes as he drew first. This moment felt as if in slow motion; memories of a kind parish minister taking him in filled his mind as he faced this similarly clothed foe. Angus knew his bullet would hit its mark before the priest could draw on him. He also sincerely regretted that he had to pull the trigger on a holy man.

The minister dropped easily enough.

Angus approached, taking the scene in. Sure enough, the two men who had missed their jump rode up on the final railcar and began boarding. Beneath him lie the minister, a bullet hole through his temple—as well as the cross he had been holding up.

"What belief led you on such a fool's errand? Giving your life—all to protect the wealth of others?" Angus asked the corpse, as if waiting for an answer.

His question was interrupted by the metal railcar roof beneath him, shuddering as the locomotive attempted to recouple the train cars—dramatically shifting them after impact one by one in a ripple effect, throwing Angus on his backside atop the current car.

―――

Jack and his men waited until the locomotive secured a connection once again to the rear cars. Just as the engineer double checked the connections and chains, Jack kicked his car door open and fired multiple shots into the engineer's chest. The three men moved with significant speed, clearing the two cars ahead of them as well as the engine with ease. At this point, it was better to protect the locomotive, so Jack assigned the men accompanying him to hold it and repel any attacks if they came.

Just as this was happening, Jasper rode up and joined Jack.

Jack gave Jasper a stern look.

"You and I will have some words later."

Jasper nodded along in an apologetic fashion.

"For now, make it up to the men by clearing these cars and aiding us in securing the goods."

With that, Jack tipped his hat to the two assigned to defend the engine and motioned with his pistol to Jasper and toward the rear cars.

***

A ngus got back on his feet. He could hear shots being fired from the rear car. Deploying the element of surprise, Angus dropped in the opening between the boxcar nearest him, silently making his way through the remaining car interiors so as to flank the guards firing upon his men. There were four priests with a mix of long and short guns taking up a position behind a few of the large crates. By the time the ministers realized Angus was behind them, it was too late.

Angus quickly dispatched the lot of them.

The mission wasn't without its first loss: the holy men had shot and killed one of the two members of the Golden Nine who had boarded from the rear. The other was wounded in the shoulder, but otherwise fine. Angus and his wounded man searched the remaining cars until they encountered Jack and Jasper.

Unexpectedly, there were no additional guards on board the train throughout their search of the railcars. This was enough for Jack to recall his men from protecting the locomotive while signaling to the wagons to pull alongside the stopped train.

It was time to load the valuables they came for.

After searching the train, the only large crates sealed with valuables seemed to come from the rear section of the boxcars where the priests had been keeping watch. The Golden Nine, now eight again, failed to understand why these crates warranted ministers with long guns and not the typical lawmen guarding their contents.

"Whatever the cargo, clearly it has value." Angus surmised aloud.

"Worst case, we have stumbled upon priceless relics or something of the sort." Jack remarked. "We'll sell whatever we find and take the proceeds that way if need be."

The men were downcast about this prospect, while also upset over losing one of their own, but none had time to dwell on these things or to inspect the crates before loading them up. With the sun setting in a few hours, they needed to be gone before anyone else came along. All agreed that the best way to hide their sloppy handiwork would be to rewire the dynamite fuses, blow the bridge, and then run the train into the canyon.

Jack and the men rode back with the wagons, leaving Jasper and Angus behind. Jasper detonated the bridge as Angus supervised, making sure the job was finished this time. Once the bridge was finally blown, they got the train up to speed and then ditched it. As Angus and Jasper watched the train disappear into the canyon gorge below, the two men said a prayer for their fallen brother, whose remains would be forever entombed in the wreckage below.

The sun set as the two rode back without speaking.

———

It was nightfall before they arrived back at their hideout in the caverns of the desert. None of their group's usual laughter or quarreling could be heard. Other than the flickering flames of the interior cavern campfires, not a sound emanated from the familiar walls of stone.

This didn't sit right with Angus, who knew something must be afoot.

"Did they take the loot and run out on us?" Jasper whispered, anger weighing on his brow.

Angus put a finger to his lips and motioned to his revolver. The two of them drew slowly as they approached the inside of their home in silence.

What they found next could only be described as a bloodbath.

Once inside the caverns, Angus and Jasper found a blood-soaked floor, all their men dead and bloodied, Jack included. Multiple crates were opened, revealing the contents that the priests had guarded on the train: gold, art, various treasures from European nations, as well as multiple black coffins.

The coffins were *open* and *empty*.

Angus whispered in disbelief, "What the hell happened here? We need to leave, *now*."

Angus had no sooner muttered these words aloud when a shadow dropped from the cave ceiling upon Jasper and feasted upon his flesh. Screams for help from Jasper ensued as Angus unloaded his entire revolver into the figure. Realizing his ammunition had no effect, Angus sprinted toward the cave exit. What seemed like a gust of air hit him in the chest. The being, whatever devil it was, dragged him backward as it flew through the air. Despite the creature's might, Angus broke its grip and once again advanced toward an escape. This time, multiple shadows stood at the cave exit, blocking his path.

The truth was sobering now: there was no escape from whatever had besieged him.

In one last desperate plea, Angus cried, "What is it you want?"

A figure stepped forward and raised its hand to stop the approach of the others. A calm voice arose in response.

"To learn to live. In the American west." the figure replied.

Sharp fangs plunged into Angus's neck from behind. His blood pooled on the cavern floors just as his brethren of the Golden Nine had. When all hope seemed lost, the figure that had answered Angus cut his wrist and allowed his own blood to pour down onto the lips of Angus.

A ngus Holland was then and there, born anew. No longer an outlaw toiling under the sun, Angus took this gift and became one with the night. His new peers taught him all they knew about their own history and ways, and in return Angus taught them how to dress, talk, use firearms and ride. The west was full of outlaws wanted dead or alive, and the law was all too happy to be rid of a few villains with inconspicuous bite marks on their necks. The rewards paid well, the company was lively, and the adventures were plentiful.

Their posse became known as Angus "Blood Oath" Holland and the Shadow Horsemen. Rumors swirled that no outlaw, no matter how formidable, was out of reach from the law while Angus and his men rode at night.

Legends about their activities and pursuits could span multiple volumes. Some claim they were so effective that the U.S. government commissioned them to protect the President and form the first iteration of the Secret Service. Others claim the U.S. sent them to the front lines during both World Wars. Still others claim to see riders, in the dark of the night, wandering the deserts near Red Run Canyon to this very day—seeking something other than water to quench their thirst.

THE WOMAN
WITHIN THE DARKNESS

It's just stress.

*I*t can be said that New York City has the ability to swallow you whole. *You are both someone, and no one, among a sea of faces while walking the city's famed streets. So often, the simple kindness and humanity afforded elsewhere can be lost among crowds of indifferent people, listening to their own forms of entertainment, all headed toward something of more importance to their day than you or I.*

So it is, with our tale of the woman within the darkness.

Brianna's discomfort with the underground transit systems was palpable. The dark tunnels of the subway system gave Brianna a sense of dread each time she made the descent to her usual platform. Unfortunately, Brianna had a daily routine that included traveling from the Vernon-Jackson line in Long Island City to her place of work in downtown Manhattan. Trying not to gag from the smell of what most would describe as putrid air during the commute (namely a humid mix of mold and urine), Brianna would often contemplate what lurked deep within the tunnel's infinite shade of black.

At a minimum, Brianna understood there were rats. She also hypothesized there may be homeless people, ghosts, or other oddities witnessed by maintenance crews deep in the subway tunnels—or so Brianna vividly alleged to her therapist each week. Seeing those small lights deep in the tunnel's darkness indicated to her a train was fast approaching, and that her time underground would soon be over (for the moment, anyway). Those tiny headlights against the dark always brought Brianna a sigh of relief—allowing her chest to finally relax from the unease of being beneath the city.

To say that Brianna had anxiety while commuting would be an understatement. While onboard the 7 line leaving Vernon-Jackson, Brianna would pop her wireless earbuds in, turn on the latest podcast, and attempt for the six-minute ride into Grand Central Station to not make eye contact with other passengers. Brianna's noise canceling headphones aided in keeping her imagination and dread from running wild during her commute through the darkened underground veins of New York City.

Today was no different. Brianna stood with her back pressed against the rear of a packed train car. She avoided eye contact as usual while listening to her podcasts by staring out into the pitch black of the passing tunnel through her train car window. The subway car rocked back and forth while in motion, and Brianna steadied herself by grabbing the rail just above her head. About halfway through the journey, Brianna perceived a woman glaring at her from *outside* the subway train glass. A pale complexion, dark hair, a ragged and dirty white sweater, paired with sinister stern eyes.

This sight turned Brianna's blood cold.

Rubbing her eyes thoroughly, Brianna scolded herself for having another anxiety induced episode.

Most segments of subway tunnels barely have enough room for passing trains, much less room for a woman to be standing outside passing train cars!

Brianna pondered what could be triggering her.

Could it be the rooftop happy hour late last night? Maybe I should take it a little easier on a weeknight and get more rest?

Brianna, satisfied with her reasoning, turned her attention back to the window.

As Brianna glanced out the window of her subway car again, the woman reappeared outside the train, close to the glass. The ghastly face directed an intimidating glare that pierced into her very soul. Chills went up Brianna's spine as the woman disappeared in a flash of light—her train entering the well-lit platform of Grand Central Station. Brianna quickly turned to the other passengers and asked if any had witnessed the woman in the window.

Passengers gave Brianna puzzled looks due to their own headphones and music drowning out her questions. This devastated efforts to verify what she had just witnessed. By the time Brianna could begin explaining what she saw to those around her, the doors to the 7 line opened. With odd and disapproving glances, the passengers quickly scuttled off the train to board the nearby escalator, no doubt headed to other trains and locations all over NYC.

As Brianna eventually departed the subway system and headed upward to street level, she couldn't shake the feeling that she had just experienced something truly terrifying. Either she was completely losing her mind, or she just saw something physically impossible during her morning commute. Both options seemed like too much drama to embrace, so Brianna skipped mentioning this event to her coworkers as well as during her therapist appointment after work. Another day, another commute went by. Then another week. By the time a month had gone by, Brianna had faulted too many cocktails and not enough sleep as to why she had an experience of seeing a ghostlike woman in the subway tunnels.

It was on the sixth week to the day, however, that the rationalization of her experience unraveled entirely. Brianna once again stood on the platform at Vernon-Jackson, waiting for her subway train. Once again, the putrid air from beneath the city filled her lungs. Once again, Brianna stared down into the depths of shadow in the subway tunnel, searching for those tiny oncoming headlights of an approaching train.

It was in the darkness that she spotted again the ghastly figure of the woman she previously saw while riding the subway.

Brianna's chest tightened.

The woman was walking towards her along the rail tracks at an eerie, sauntering pace. The same unnerving stare was upon the woman's face. As this stern personality from the shadows drew close, the woman outstretched her hand toward Brianna and pointed an index finger as if to claim or single her out.

Briana felt the hairs on her neck raise and her heart pound. Everything in her mind told her to run. Brianna lost her composure and attempted to bolt away from the platform.

It was just at this moment that those small lights appeared, indicating the approach of an oncoming train. Passengers moved in, pushed together on the platform in anticipation of the train, and blocked her escape from the edge of the platform. Brianna ran along the edge until she was completely boxed in by other passengers, all in a hurry for their own morning commute. When

Brianna turned back around, glancing at the tracks in terror—the woman was *gone*—and only the rush of the train past the platform remained.

The passengers nearby Brianna paid no attention to her as they waited to board.

Too many headphones. Too many devices.

Did any of them see the woman in the tunnel?

Brianna's reaction to what she had witnessed, as well as her emotional state afterward, went unnoticed by fellow passengers on the platform who were all too ready to board the next subway car. Shaken and afraid, Brianna squeezed through the crowds at Vernon-Jackson station towards the exit stairwell, opting to take the ferry to Manhattan that day.

Brianna's fears and anxieties due to these incidents drove her to avoid the subway altogether and finally admit to her therapist what was going on. As you can imagine, the therapist prescribed medication for her anxiety, chalked the experiences up to stress in the "Big Apple", and continued to offer sound counsel for Brianna's workplace and social life.

A year went by without further incident.

The next year's winter was extremely cold. Ice formed in the East River, and the ferry route Brianna took was closed due to weather on a particularly snowy day, as were some roads due to snarled traffic. Brianna had a deadline and an important presentation to make at the office, and as such, she couldn't afford to be late. As much as she dreaded it—these closures forced Brianna to use the subway to get to work.

Brianna walked down the stairs to the 7 line at Vernon-Jackson, and a familiar sour odor entered her nose. The platform was before her, crowded with passengers waiting for the next train, most staring down at their phones while waiting, all eventually glancing down the tunnel into the darkness. As Brianna stood near the rear of the crowded subway platform, she at once noticed the horrifyingly familiar woman she had previously witnessed in the train car window and walking along the subway tracks. This time, however, the woman was *on the platform*, and her wraith-like hand was placed upon a young man's shoulder who was waiting to board the next train.

The woman turned her grim gaze and made eye contact.

Brianna's heart felt as if it stopped.

The woman smiled with a twisted grin and then pushed the young man forward off the platform onto the tracks below. To everyone's horror, a split-second later the train came blowing through the station, throwing its brakes.

Brianna screamed.

It was too late.

The young man had been pulverized by the oncoming train. While all passengers on the platform were in shock, Brianna kept her eyes on the ghastly specter of the woman. During the hustle of passengers moving around the platform in the aftermath, the woman turned and took steps forward toward Brianna, pointing at her once again, as if to claim her. The woman smiled with a joy rooted in pure evil, raised the point of her index finger to her lips as if to indicate *silence* to Brianna's terrified tears and shouting, and then turned and disappeared into the shifting of the crowd's movement.

Police arrived on the scene and took statements. Both security footage and eyewitness testimony showed the young man to have jumped, with no woman present behind him as Brianna described in her statement. Official reports declared the incident a suicide.

Brianna could not bring herself to accept that explanation.

After many further therapy sessions following these events, Brianna was diagnosed by her therapist with an acute case of social anxiety, depression, and schizophrenia. Medication was prescribed, and Brianna seemed to her friends and coworkers to be doing much better after the switch to her new treatment. During the following six months, Brianna was said to have invested time in hanging out with friends and coworkers at rooftop restaurants, visiting her extended family back in Virginia, and even going on a date or two with a new guy at the office.

Life was looking up for Brianna if you asked any friends that knew her well.

Unfortunately, all that came to an end when Brianna chose to dive off the bow of the East River ferry she was using for her daily commute to Manhattan.

Reports and security footage indicated her death as a suicide.

There was just one tourist photo taken on the upper deck of the ferry moments before Brianna's death. It showed a woman in a ragged, dirty white sweater with her hand upon Brianna's shoulder.

Neither the police, passengers, nor any of Brianna's coworkers or friends could ever identify the woman or her relation to Brianna.

GROWL

YOUR ATTENTION, PLEASE.

I t's often curious to us what level of superstition possesses you when confront-ing the supernatural, as if somehow your being silent, or your lack of movement, will fool those of us who so clearly are breaking into your here and now.

That such forces could take on the magnitude of effort involved in revealing our-selves on your plane of existence, yet somehow be fooled by your mortal efforts at proverbially playing dead! Did you really think staying silent and not moving would help? That somehow, we would be unable to perceive your eyes darting around the room or hear your altered breathing state? After all the work we've done in the effort of revealing ourselves on your terms, in your context, that we would not detect achieving our goal—your attention?

The truth of these matters is this: your tactics of stalling in the dark while frozen in fear are only delaying the inevitable. Likewise, the turning on of lights makes no difference to your situation, or our intent. Neither do your televisions, phone calls, or silent prayers.

It's far past time for your kind to embrace reality. Whatever shadow now stands at the foot of your bed clearly sought you out. This spirit has come too far to be denied their moment. Consider yourselves our captive audience—for better or for worse.

―――

A nthony wasn't alone. His bedroom was eerily silent. Anthony's eyes darted back and forth across what he could see of his bedroom in the dark. Irrational levels of fear filled his mind. Anthony dared not make a move toward his phone or the lamp beside him. Trying his best to remain silent and still, Anthony did his best to reassure himself of all the informa-tion from his psychology courses relating to perceptions of the supernatural.

My mind is playing tricks on me late at night after this crazy day.

Anthony shifted in his bed to his side and closed his eyes, resolute in not letting his imagination get the best of him.

At this, his bathroom door slammed shut.

Flinging himself upright, turning on the lamp next to his bed, Anthony examined the room.

All familiar.

Nothing out of the ordinary.

Anthony grabbed the handgun he kept in a safe below his bed, his fingers trembling. If this was a home intruder, he felt it would equal the odds. If not... Anthony didn't desire to finish the thought. He checked the bathroom adjacent to his bedroom thoroughly.

Nothing.

He then did a sweep of the rest of his small suburban home.

Every door was secure. Same with the windows. Even his security system was still armed and had not triggered. Anthony set the gun down on his coffee table and glared through the blinds at the neighbor's home. All was quiet on his street, as it should be.

A phone began vibrating from his nightstand on the other end of the house. Anthony rushed into his bedroom, hoping he would not lose the caller. Glancing at the screen, he was relieved to see it was Zachary reaching out.

"Hey Zach."

"Hello love. Did I wake you?"

"I was having trouble sleeping too."

"I was lying here sleepless, thinking about how spooked you were earlier during the seance. Holly really appreciated your support today. She's just trying to get closure on her brother's passing."

Anthony didn't really want to admit what he just experienced, and in some odd way, this call was grounding his mind. *Not that the events earlier in my day were too far off from the activity in this house tonight.*

"I feel bad for how Holly has taken her brother's death, but I think, in retrospect, a seance is too far for my comfort zone. I'm just not a fan. I tried to go along with an open mind, but clearly my nerves got the best of me. I think I'll pass on future crystal ball opportunities."

Zachary assured he respected and understood how Anthony was feeling.

"How about a date tomorrow to make up for it? Just you and me—maybe we can watch that movie. You know, the one you wanted to see, the new musical with what's-his-name?"

Anthony sighed with relief.

"You're the best."

"I'm sorry for pressuring you to go today. Get some rest. We'll all get through losing Eric soon enough. We all need time to process I guess."

Zachary ended the call with the promise of sweet dreams, then sent a few heart emojis via text for emphasis.

Anthony returned the phone to his nightstand. As he went around his home one last time, checking everything was secure, Anthony reflected on his earlier experience at the seance.

He sincerely believed the event to be a money-making scam by the medium. Anthony was offended when the medium chose to embody the conversational style of Eric, Holly's brother, during the "communication" part of the performance. Anthony knew Eric's goofy mannerisms and way of speaking. It was simply uncanny how well the medium imitated Eric's supposed "voice from beyond." Surely the medium had studied videos online of Eric prior to their arrival time. Anthony was certain they got bonus believability points from Holly while performing that bit, as tasteless as he found it.

Both Zachary and Holly had assumed Anthony was freaked out by the moment of interaction from beyond the grave, but this was not what upset him.

What alarmed Anthony was the reflection, in a mirror directly behind the medium, of an otherworldly beast putting its claw *upon his shoulder*.

Anthony could almost feel the weight of a presence just behind him, and the moment was enough for him to jump from the table and exclaim "I'm sorry, that's enough—I can't do this!" and then swiftly exit, waiting outside for them to finish up. Fearful of looking foolish, Anthony kept the details of this experience from Zachary and Holly.

Upon reflection, Anthony realized what nasty tricks the mind could play.

Here I am, mentally exhausted, trying to support my boyfriend and Holly in their time of emotional need, seeing figments of my imagination, losing sleep, and then running around my perfectly normal suburban home with a loaded gun in the middle of the night. I need a vacation, or at minimum some rest.

After securing his home and turning the lights out, Anthony remembered leaving his gun on the coffee table in the living room. He returned to the living room and collected his gun, making sure to secure it in the safe under the bed. Wrapping himself in his bedsheets, Anthony dozed off to sleep almost immediately.

A loud crash and the sound of heavy footsteps filled Anthony's home.

Anthony flew out of bed, quickly retrieving his gun from the safe. Pointing the barrel down his dark hallway toward where the sounds originated from, Anthony clung to the walls while searching for any trace of movement. Rounding the corner to the living room, he quickly noticed his possessions in complete disarray.

The coffee table was flipped. The TV smashed. His leather sofa was ripped. Anthony found the alarm disabled—its pad pulled from the wall and left dangling, as if for added effect. Not wanting to face whatever caused this, he sprinted back down the hall to his bedroom, locking the door behind him. Anthony trained his gun on the door—grabbing his phone in an attempt to dial for help. Anthony cursed in disbelief, as his phone had no service. He fumbled with the lamp closest to him, quickly coming to the conclusion the power was disrupted as well.

Heavy footsteps paced in front of his bedroom door.

"Leave or I'll shoot!" Anthony shouted.

There was a slight air pressure change in the room. Only silence remained.

Clink. Roll. Clink. Roll. Clink. Roll.

This small sound shattered the silence. Anthony glanced to the floor just in front of his doorway, now connecting the dots between the sound he was hearing and the source. From under the door came rolling what appeared to be shiny bronze tablets.

Bullets.

Clink. Roll. Clink. Roll. Clink. Roll.

To his horror, Anthony flipped his gun over to find the magazine was missing. He quickly checked the chamber to find that it, too, had been emptied.

His weapon was utterly useless.

Anthony moaned out loud, realizing the collection of bullets on the floor was a sign that his bluff had been called. A slight breeze from an unknown origin entered the room and ended just as quickly as it had occurred. A shadow took form in the far corner of Anthony's bedroom. The shape was familiar—that of the monstrosity previously seen placing its claws upon him in the seance mirror.

Anthony's mind reeled backward.

It followed me home, he cried to himself in disbelief.

The moment immediately following this revelation held the deepest absence of sound a person can experience. The shadow remained motionless and still for what seemed like an eternity while Anthony remained paralyzed in fear.

And then, from the corner of his bedroom, came a *growl*.

WHEN THE FIRE GOES OUT

...ONE LAST TIME.

W alt stoked the flames of his small fireplace, lost in a sea of his thoughts. As he sat in his small wooden armchair and reflected, light from the flames danced and flickered around his small cabin. Outside, the winter months had set into motion the icy frigidness that enveloped Walt's cabin with snow several feet high, and it seemed at the moment a blizzard of ice and snow was bearing down on his tiny shelter. With nothing but a small hearth to provide light and heat in the vast darkness of these wintery woods, Walt wrapped himself in his warmest clothing and blankets while keeping watch over the fire in order to survive the brutal cold.

Walt gazed as the flames moved back and forth across the logs he had stacked upon the fire. He pondered how it came to be that he was here, so isolated and alone. The nearest town was a mile away, and the storm had clearly made the roads impassable. Walt had plenty of supplies, as he had planned for quite a different winter. His wife, Beverly, and his bloodhound, Roscoe, were to have joined him here, by this very fire.

Fate, as you would have it, had differing plans.

Being in their elderly years, Walt and Beverly had lived a decent life together. Walt found success in the logging industry, and Beverly's father had been a

well-known butcher in their hometown. They didn't come from extravagant means, but they did well for theirs. Walt and Beverly built a beautiful home on the coast of the Hudson, as well as this secluded cabin a few hours inland. The cabin was used for going on holiday as a family; they spent most of their time at their primary Hudson residence. Together, Walt and Beverly enjoyed quite the social life and were well known and beloved within their local community.

Beverly gave Walt both a son, George, and a daughter, Wendy.

Wendy died tragically at a young age due to a problem with her lungs. George, however, grew to be a wonderful young man, filled with a generous spirit. Their boy was well-built—so athletic, in fact, that he competed in various local sports, much to the adoration and cheering of his hometown. George was also an excellent student; many spoke highly of his prospects to become a lawyer or even hold a political office later in life. Beverly felt George was the pride and joy of her world—the accomplishment of all her years as a mother. Walt enthusiastically agreed that their son had achieved a greatness beyond the sum of their abilities to raise such a noble and kind young man.

It was an unfair twist that George's young and aspiring life was cut short by the knife of a lesser man. After joining his friends down at the local pub one evening, George heard a woman's screams for help down a set of alleyways while walking home. A desperate and destitute man was attempting to rob a young, defenseless woman under the cover of night. George, always the noble and valiant of heart, wouldn't let her cry go unanswered—and in so doing, laid down his life to protect hers.

The church bells rang out that evening as news spread of a young man stabbed in an alleyway because of a heroic attempt to defend a woman in need. Walt rushed through the streets of his hometown upon hearing the news, and eventually found the bloody body of his son as the town doctor looked on and relayed the news that it was too late. Walt held George in his arms for quite some time and wept bitterly. When Walt finally returned home with the news, Beverly collapsed on their kitchen floor and was unable to be revived until the following morning due to shock.

Beverly and Walt were crushed. All their hard work in this life was seen as having been for naught; nothing felt of any value following George's murder. Bread had lost its nourishment, meat had lost its flavor, and drink had lost its sparkle. Possessions were slowly sold off to settle outstanding debts, and Walt and his wife began to recluse from society. With only Roscoe the family hound and themselves for company in their elder age, the years passed by, and they were forgotten by their neighbors, friends, and community.

Upon reflection of their life together, and as a last-ditch effort for happiness, Walt and Beverly decided to sell their home, move into their old cabin, and permanently leave their hometown—never to return again. The fond memories of their children laughing and playing in the small stream by the family cabin seized on their hearts, and they chose to make better of it by spending their declining years in the solitude of nature and their memories.

But it wasn't to always be.

After a short, delightful remainder of the summer that year, fall set in and Beverly caught fever. The speed at which the fever took her shook Walt to the core. In a matter of days, he lost the love of his life.

In but a few more, he was to lose Roscoe as well.

While out gathering wood, Roscoe was set upon by wild wolves who fatally injured the poor hound. Walt spent the days prior to the onset of winter grieving the loss of his wife, while slowly watching the life slip from his loyal companion Roscoe. When Roscoe, after a few days of agony and refusing food, stirred no more—Walt knew in his heart the bitter truth: he was, in this moment, all alone in the world.

And so now, Walt sat in solitude, seated in front of the flames as he reflected on these things. The fire from his cabin hearth popped once and then hissed as Walt poked at it from his sitting chair. Embers floated from the source of the sound to the area just in front of his feet and slowly faded away. The wind bore down on his tiny cabin with all the fury winter could muster. A lone tear formed in the corner of Walt's eye as he tried to remember the sound of his Beverly's laughter.

It was at this moment there came a heavy rapping at the door. As Walt stood to face the cabin entrance in disbelief, a shadowy figure moved near the window and held up a lantern.

This is highly unusual. Walt thought to himself. *How is it any person would dare this treacherous storm, all the way out here, alone in the woods?*

For a moment, Walt considered turning away this stranger of the night, but mercy got the better of his judgement: surely if turned away, this poor soul faced certain death in the blizzard.

Walt opened the cabin door to reveal a man covered in dark robes, face hidden by his hood. There was no bag or mode of transportation to be seen—the only other features of note were a pair of frail-looking, frozen hands, clasped to the lantern that previously shone in Walt's cabin window.

"Sir, would you consider bestowing the blessing of shelter upon me as I've traveled a great distance? This storm seems intent on freezing me to the bone! My only request is the warmth of your fire and your hospitality for the evening." the stranger pleaded through a raspy throat.

Walt, seeing the intense nature of the storm, and he himself desiring very much to close the cabin door and return to the warm fire, ushered the distant traveler inside. Pulling an old rocking chair close to his hearth, Walt grabbed an extra blanket from a chest at the foot of his bedside, and quickly wrapped the stranger in the warm wool, seating him by the fire. Without hesitation, Walt hurriedly put together the makings of a soup in order to cook it over the flames and offer it to this unexpected guest. The traveler looked on from the rocking chair in silence and wonder as Walt did these things without so much as a word—without even showing the slightest amount of inconvenience.

When Walt finally joined the stranger by taking a seat at the fire, Walt looked on as he stirred the cooking meal, and then mentioned softly, "I'm certain you've had quite the evening in all this. You must be exhausted, friend."

"Indeed, my soul is rather spent. I am humbly in your debt, as you have so kindly taken me into your home on this frigid eve." the traveler replied. After glancing from one end of the cabin to the other, he rose a query. "May I ask, are you alone on this dreadful night? I see the touches of a woman around this small cabin, toys that clearly brought joy to younger hands, as well as a bed for a four-legged companion, yet I only find you on such a stormy eve?"

"I'm afraid you find me at my hour of solitude." Walt replied, while continuing to stir the warming liquid in the kettle. "My beloved bride, Beverly, passed but a few weeks ago with the onset of an aggressive fever. My loyal pet, a bloodhound, was attacked by a pack of wild animals not too long after. My children have long slept in their graves for some time now. I find myself alone and left to my grief these past winter days. Had it not been for your sudden figure in my window, I doubt I would have seen another soul this winter."

The stranger nodded intently, placing an icy hand upon Walt's knee. "Though I may not be as lively as the family you loved, I hope to keep you company tonight all the same. You've been so kind to me granting shelter—it's the least I could do. A stranger I might be, but as two are gathered, a fellowship may grow between our spirits."

Walt was deeply moved by this gesture and these words. Indeed, the solitude had been insufferable all these dark winter days.

Walt nodded to the traveler, and seeing that the soup was fully cooked, offered it to him. The traveler took the hot bowl and held it in his hands for many moments before setting the bowl down on the small table beside him. "It feels like ages since my hands have had the blessing of warmth from a lovingly prepared meal, or the hospitality of a fire. This is a moment to be cherished, as I'm sure it will not come again."

The traveler traced his boney finger over the edge of the rocking chair's armrest as Walt considered these words.

"I'm sure you'll find warm lodging and good company once you make it into town." Walt surmised out loud. "What exactly brings you this way, on such a night as this?"

The quiet crackling of the fire passed between the two for some time. Outside, the snowstorm seemed to ease up, and in its place remained an icy, dark stillness.

"I've come all this way to deliver a message to you, good sir." the traveler responded quietly as he rocked, gazing at the small fire. "Believe it or not, transporting this message is of the utmost importance, and come storms or what may, I am sworn by oath to make sure you receive it."

Walt sat back, his wooden chair squeaking under the shifting of his weight, at this revelation.

"I'm thankful for your efforts and determination to travel at such great risk to yourself to bring me a word here, in these isolated woods!"

Walt rubbed the back of his neck while looking around his unassuming cabin, and then intently looked at the hooded stranger, hoping the fire would provide enough illumination as to give Walt a glimmer of detail in the face of the person sitting across from him.

"What news have you for someone as humble as myself?"

Another moment of silence passed by for what seemed an eternity. The hooded traveler leaned forward in the old rocking chair, and in a calm but assured voice, finally spoke.

"Your life has come to an end, my most gracious host. I have been sent as an emissary to collect your soul and guide you from this point forward. Have no fear, for nothing will harm you and there are *great joys* to behold in the hereafter."

The robed stranger then touched the edge of the dinner bowl that had been handed to him.

"You have lived a blessed life—and while not always easy, there were clearly moments of pure love and happiness. A life filled with such beauty requires the dignified honor of companionship for this next leg of your journey. Your soul is *pure good* sir—there is no fault those of us onlooking can find in your life. You consistently have given of yourself to others—even tonight to a stranger of the dark, you provided the warmest of cloth and meals. You've shared your shelter, your flame, and even your grief. Your soul deserves no less than the best companionship and ease of transition death can offer. And so it is—that I have volunteered to be the messenger and guide to bring you to your beloved family. They are ready to receive you now."

Walt had a knot in his throat, both anger and tears filled his eyes. Walt was not one for superstitions, and the idea of the supernatural paying him a visit seemed unlikely.

Maybe this stranger had come to rob him blind with no witnesses and leave him for dead?

Walt pondered these things, frozen in his chair, all the while never shifting his gaze from the traveler. The moment was so heavy with unknown possibilities, and Walt's mind raced to catch up. Walt could not form a response due to a mixture of fear and disbelief.

Sensing the distress before him, the traveler looked again into the flames from the fireplace and spoke softly.

"I assure you, I mean you no harm and that these things are true." Shifting slightly to one side of the rocking chair, he continued, "I know you are a good man, Walter. I have watched you throughout your life and I can personally attest to it. It's why, when given the chance, I volunteered for this assignment."

The traveler's hand slowly reached up and lowered the hood of his cloak. There, before Walt, sat what appeared to be the slightly decayed, spitting image of his *son*, George. His face was pale and thin, with flesh missing in portions revealing the bone of his cheek—but there was no mistaking the face of Walt's long-lost son.

"My *son*—" Walt gasped, clenching his eyes as tears began streaming down his cheeks.

"Indeed, father."

George rose and walked to put a withered hand upon Walt's now heaving shoulders. George comforted his father while this moment sank in.

"I have come to guide you to my mother and sister, so that your journey shall not be alone, and so that we may once again enjoy each other's presence."

Walt, trembling in shock, began to accept the reality before him.

"I have a request, son. Can we have a time of fellowship here in this cabin— *one last time*, before I follow your lead?"

"So it shall be granted to you, father." George replied, "Place as much wood on the flame as you desire, and we shall make merry one last time in this cabin—the temple of our memories. Our time here will conclude when the fire goes out."

And so, Walt gathered the largest of his dry logs and loaded them into the cabin's humble fireplace. Standing before the hearth of the cabin he had built, Walt glanced around at the memories that filled his family's wooden retreat. Walt and George reflected on good times, laughed about old love interests, spoke of how the world had changed, and even played a few matches of chess, just as they used to when George was but a small boy.

"I remember whittling you these very chess pieces over a summer we spent here when you were but a boy."

George picked up a few of the chess pieces, smiling as he felt each piece with his skeletal thin-skinned hands.

"I never believed I would get the opportunity to visit this place again."

George sighed as he reflected on his prior life.

"You were an amazing father and a good man."

Walt once again embraced his son, tears welling in his eyes.

"No, son, you became a better man than I could have ever hoped to be."

As the night turned to morning, Walt and George stood at the window and watched the sun rise from their family cabin, one last time. George had his arm wrapped around his father's shoulders as the sun brilliantly made the horizon glisten, as if the mountains around them were made of crystal. As they stood at the cabin window, a slight draft blew in from under the cabin door, and neither of them turned to notice the final dying ember of their fire fade out.

***

It wouldn't be until months later that locals would happen upon Walt's cabin the next spring. When a hiker finally stumbled upon the cabin, they found Walter's body sitting in his wooden chair near the hearth of the cabin. A kettle was hanging in the fireplace where once a meal was cooked. There was a rocking chair placed across from Walt with a wool blanket laid neatly over its arm, a bowl was set to the side as if Walt had been entertaining during the winter, and a wooden carved chess set was found seated on a small table nearby. The local papers hypothesized Walt must have passed away in the cold of winter, perfectly preserved until his discovery later that spring.

There was but one other resident in that area of the woods during the winter, who when asked if they had seen or heard anything, reported spotting two men in cloaks with a lantern walking deeper into the forest the morning just after a bout of bad weather. When the resident asked the travelers if they needed any assistance, the robed men simply explained they were finally headed home after a long time apart from their loved ones.

FREE OVERNIGHT DELIVERY

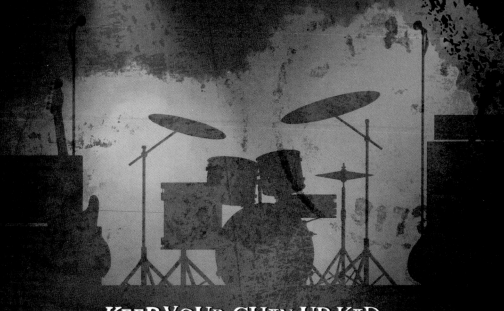

KEEP YOUR CHIN UP KID.

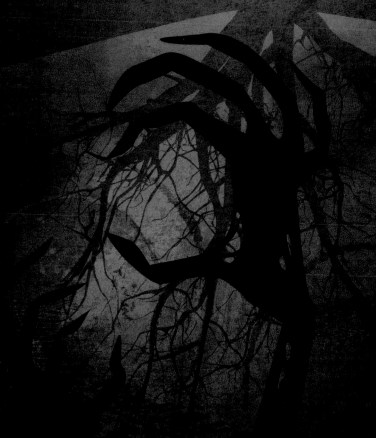

Known as a prodigy musician among his high school peers, Drew was filled with anticipation for the opportunity to achieve his dreams. To write and perform music of his own in front of friends and family, much less his new girlfriend, was a goal realized. Drew stood backstage at the Dry Harpoon, watching the audience. The crowd cheered the opening band of the night as they took their positions onstage for the performance.

The journey up to this moment played back like an old movie in his mind. Drew started playing bass guitar in 6th grade after a failed stint at the trumpet in his school's year one orchestra ensemble. His failure was so great at mastering the instrument that a teacher approached Drew's parents after a miserable winter performance and scolded them for enrolling him in the class.

With a glance toward Drew's heartbroken mother, then at the music teacher walking away in disgust, Drew's father told him he would purchase any instrument Drew wanted to pursue outright.

"Never let others decide what you can become. Follow your heart, son."

Drew remembered his father's support in such a soul-crushing moment. His dad reassured him that if he continued his music studies in private, Drew could easily prove this teacher wrong. Drew could and *would* become as musically talented as he desired.

This led to the purchase of a now well loved, broken in, beginner bass guitar. Drew took to the bass with an extreme focus—it was said among the music teachers at his high school he could play at the level of musicians twice his age. So much time and effort had been put into his playing of the guitar that even at the age of sixteen, Drew was constantly invited to join in on gigs as a guest bassist when a local band's usual guitarist needed to miss a show due to schedule conflicts.

Drew loved these opportunities. Because of his talent, Drew got to jam with many friends and peers that were a little older than him, namely seniors in his high school. The fact that he was often the youngest (and shortest) musician to play with these groups only cemented the idea in Drew's mind that his talents were meant for something really big one day.

Despite being dropped off by his mom, Drew would grab his beginner bass (now worn from constant use), step out onto the stage with his older peers, plug into an expensive amplifier (borrowed of course from the regular guitarist), brush his hair from in front of his eyes, and hit the first sweet note that began a performance. Being awesome at playing music was Drew's drug of choice.

Drew's reflection on these things was interrupted by the opening band of the night launching into the first chorus of a song the crowd knew well. Drew glanced back, wondering how soon the rest of his band would arrive at the venue.

To say he was nervous would be an understatement. Excitement, hope, the pride of achievement, and his reputation were all tied up in the performance he was about to give.

Drew's parents had promised to be in the crowd, as did his new girlfriend.

No pressure tonight at all… Drew thought to himself.

Just then, Jake and Conor arrived through the back door of the venue. They both nodded in acknowledgement as they sat some of their gear down. Drew stood backstage, not long after joined by the pair, peering at the current group onstage receiving thunderous applause and a warm welcome.

W hat previously held Drew back was his gear—or lack thereof. How could any bassist be taken seriously without a high-quality guitar or amplifier?

To rectify this, Drew had spent the better part of the last month searching used goods for sale through an app he had recently downloaded to his smartphone. He surmised that if he could find decent enough equipment on this app, that he might afford it with the money he had saved from his entry-level job at a restaurant in town. Drew recognized he was very lucky—not only did his parents support him in his passion for developing his musical career, but they also entrusted him with a significant amount of freedom—from getting his own job to the lack of a curfew.

"You're a responsible young man now, with your own job, getting ready for college and all, my dear. If you want to spend your hard-earned money on this, then I think that's wonderful…" his mother had reassured upon hearing his plan. "…just remember—you'll need a car soon, so keep some cash set aside for that too."

Time went by, and one afternoon, the impossible happened. An incredible amplifier appeared via a listing in his for-sale app.

"Like new. Used a few times. Got an even better setup." read the description.

Drew could not believe his eyes. The price was considerably low, much lower than most of the crappy, barely functioning, older guitar amps out there in the classifieds. Something felt a bit off about this steal-of-a-deal.

Could it be too good to be true? Or maybe some sort of scam?

Drew pondered these questions as he reached out.

Drew sent a direct message to the seller. "Is this amp for real? Does it work properly? Are there any issues?"

"No issues!" the seller replied. "I just happened upon another opportunity to snatch up a better amp. I thought this amp would make someone happy and I want it to go to the right home, thus the attractive price."

Drew thought about this for about 30 seconds until his joy overwhelmed him. In an excited string of messages, Drew typed back, "Ok great! I'd love to buy it. When would I expect to receive it?"

"I offer free overnight delivery for the right buyer." the seller typed. "And you are the right buyer!"

And with that, the purchase was made through the app.

The following morning, Drew awoke to his parents getting ready for work. Remembering he had his amplifier being delivered today, Drew ran past his mother making breakfast, forgetting he was still in his boxers—causing a small giggle to erupt from his sister.

"Drewy has stinky butt underwear." his sister teased, exchanging a naughty yet innocent glance with her mother.

Drew rolled his eyes while laughing to himself as he opened the front door. Low and behold, there stood a package half the height of Drew, containing the expensive amplifier of his dreams. It took a ton of dragging and shoving for Drew to pull the box inside, but as the door closed, Drew was diving headfirst into the package, soon revealing his newly acquired prize possession.

"Wow hun, that looks expensive!" Drew's mother commented, somewhat shocked at the feat her son had just pulled off in acquiring such an investment. "How did you afford this?"

Drew explained how he found the item and had purchased it via his phone. His mother seemed satisfied with his explanation, albeit somewhat shocked at the apparent low value some other seller ascribed such a piece of hardware. Drew quickly got ready for the day and threw his book bag, guitar, and new amp into his mother's van.

School was unusually somber that day. Apparently, a student at a rival school had gone missing. This young man was last seen after toilet papering a cheerleader's home while driving wildly on the road at midnight in his bright blue vintage pickup truck that sported a white stripe down the side. Police were searching for any students who were out that night. In an announcement over the loudspeakers, the officers on campus made it known that they were interviewing any students that could come forward with information.

That evening, Drew got together with a few new guys from different schools to practice for an upcoming show. The group's usual bass player had just moved a few towns over. The group had extended the opportunity to Drew to fill in based on his musical reputation. Drew wheeled out his brand-new amp. The other musicians looked impressed at his new setup.

The group was composed of the lead singer, Jake, a skinny guy who was soft-spoken but had a sweeping voice and an amazing knack for writing lyrics, Conor, a keytar wielding punk rocker of Irish descent that was attempting to bring back the flat top, and Brandon, a tough-as-nails kid who could own any challenging drummer in a battle of the bands.

Drew took to Jake and Conor quickly, but the jury was still out in his mind about Brandon. Brandon was known to be a huge bully at his high school. All most kids needed to know about Brandon was that he had tattooed on his right wrist "Fuck the Police" and that Brandon either used his fists for smashing faces or drumheads. Drew wondered in advance if Brandon was going to be an issue for him. After giving it a bit of thought, Drew assumed that if he excelled at playing his bass, he would never be on the smashing side of Brandon's fists. Drew humorously thought to himself, *It's not every day a band has a drummer AND their own bouncer.*

Their first practice went amazingly well for Drew not having played with them before. Brandon seemed quiet and reserved, but Jake and Conor were thrilled.

"We want you to join the band, permanently." Jake beamed, with Conor nodding and smiling in acknowledgement. "We have a huge spot to fill, and if you are consistently this good over the next month, we'll play a show at the Dry Harpoon together and make the announcement live on stage. Hell, you should write a song and we can work on it during these practices as a fresh addition to our set list for that show!"

Drew was star-struck at this offer.

"That sounds awesome! I'd totally love to."

The band packed their gear after that and Drew rushed home in his mom's minivan to tell his parents the news. When he got home, the lights in the house were off. After unloading his things from the van, Drew made his way along the hallways, flipping light switches on as he went. In the kitchen, he found a note left by his mom that read:

"Hey Hun! Dad and I are at your sister's art and crafts night. Pizza is in the fridge. Love ya!"

That's right, Drew thought to himself. *My sister had her class show-and-tell tonight. Guess I'm free to play video games on the large TV!*

As Drew plopped down on the living room sofa, he noticed a message alert in his for-sale app. The seller of his new amplifier had asked how it was sounding and if all was ok with the delivery.

"It's fantastic!" Drew replied. "Not a scratch, and it sounds like a dream. I played it tonight with some new people, and they invited me to join their band! I'm going to write a song and we'll perform it live at a show soon."

"So glad to hear that my amp went to the right person." responded the seller. "Drew, you wouldn't happen to be looking for a newer high-end bass guitar to replace yours, would you?"

Drew had to think for a moment. His existing guitar was sufficient, well loved, and sentimental... but he could not deny that a higher quality bass would bring his musical quality and appearance to another level. Drew calculated that he had blown most of his extra income on the amp purchase—the remaining amount of cash he had needed to go toward a vehicle.

"I'm sorry, I don't think I would have enough money—I've got to save for my own ride you know! I need a car."

Drew watched the messaging area in his for-sale app indicate the seller typing. When the seller's message finally came through, Drew was presented with another offer that seemed impossible.

"What if I could sell you both a better bass guitar and a starter vehicle for what you have saved up? As I've said before, I tend to snatch up new things all the time and I'm constantly upgrading. I want to make sure my items go to the right people, who will uniquely care for and appreciate them. You, Drew, seem to me to be the right kind of person to appreciate these. I'll send photos and create a special listing for you to review. If you would like to purchase, they are yours, with free overnight delivery as usual."

A few moments later, a link appeared from the seller, showing another listing. As Drew clicked the link, he was greeted with images of a fabulous profession-al-grade bass guitar and an old red pickup. Although not necessarily his color or style, the vehicle looked like it could get him from point A to B, had room for him to throw his gear into, and the price of buying both the guitar and a vehicle was just too amazing to turn down.

"I will take them both!" Drew responded as he paid through the app.

With that, the seller replied, "Enjoy!"

Drew let his phone flop down to the floor and stared at the ceiling.

This must be the best day of my life. An Amp. A Band. A New Guitar. And a ride of my own—all in one day!

As Drew reclined on the sofa thinking about what all these turns of events would mean, he uncharacteristically fell asleep in the living room. When his family came home, they quietly went to bed for the night and let him sleep on the sofa undisturbed.

In the morning, Drew awoke to his sister poking him.

"There is something for yoouuuuu…"

His sister giggled and then ran away to her room.

Drew rose from the couch, picking up his phone and rubbing his eyes while glancing at his watch.

I must have been super tired.

As he made his way into the kitchen, his mother and father were looking on in bewilderment at the old red pickup on the curb. It took some explaining, but Drew told his parents that he had found an amazing deal on the older vehicle yesterday and used his hard-earned money from his job to buy it. His mother's eyes got misty when she said something about "my baby is growing up" but other than that and a high five from dad, who commented "you should study for the stock exchange at this rate" the new vehicle went over well.

Drew was relieved when he found his new bass guitar hidden behind the seat of the truck, because at least he didn't have to show this off to his parents and explain it as well. Drew sent off a thank-you message to the seller that morning and then, after getting a quick shower, headed to school.

At lunch that day, Drew noticed another message in his inbox. The seller had written back, "Glad you like them! You owe me a concert now. Where can I see you play that new bass guitar?"

After passing the info for the upcoming show onto the seller, Drew once again thanked him for the opportunity to buy these items at such a steal of a price.

Drew's friends loved his new ride, his new band mates gave him props for getting a new bass, and through the course of a month, he wrote and practiced his new song with Jake, Conor, and Brandon for their upcoming show. In a matter of three weeks, the new guitar and amp brought Drew's musical ambitions and goals into reach, and his new ride even landed him a new girlfriend who was super interested in going to Drew's shows and riding around with him after school. Drew was elated by all that was happening around him.

You could say that Drew had finally come into his own.

B randon appeared backstage at the Dry Harpoon after the first band finished opening the show, and soon they all began bringing his equipment through the back door of the venue. Brandon looked like he was in a bad mood tonight and walked past Drew multiple times without even so much as a hello.

"What's that about?" Drew asked, with a puzzled glance toward Conor.

As Conor began to speak, Jake interrupted.

"Drew, we need to chat about something. I-I... I don't know how to say this, but you won't be playing tonight. It's not you. It's us. As much as Conor and I have enjoyed playing with you, Brandon has never really warmed up to you. That was fine and all when we didn't have any other options, but our original bassist is back in town permanently—his parents are getting a divorce. It's an awful thing for him, and he really needs our support right now. Brandon and he are very close, and Brandon was adamant that we bring him back. He threatened to walk out on the show tonight if we didn't make this call... we're so sorry, bro."

Drew stood there, backstage at the Dry Harpoon, stunned in silence. His previous band mates hustled around him with their gear, not too long after being joined by their former bassist. They were setting up on stage in such a hurry that they didn't even acknowledge Drew as he remained standing in place backstage where Jake had broken the news moments earlier. Drew's mind was flooded with panic and embarrassment. He knew that a few feet away, his new girlfriend would watch as he was just publicly sidelined from the band he had told his entire school and social circle about. Not to mention the disappointment his parents were about to experience.

Drew wished he could crawl into a shell and hide somewhere, anywhere other than this moment, in this place.

Brandon hurried down the steps from the stage and grabbed a water bottle from backstage.

"Beat it dude. There's no room for crying fans of the band behind the scenes."

Brandon then scoffed and headed up to the stage for a sound check.

Drew collected himself in anger, gathered his things, and exited the venue. After loading his gear into his truck, Drew returned to the backstage door but was stopped by security for "not being part of the band." Humiliated and angry, Drew walked around to the front entrance. His band had already started playing, and to add insult to injury, Drew had to now cough up the cash for entry just so he could collect his parents and soon-to-be *ex*-girlfriend. As Drew's hand was stamped for entry, his band was finishing up their first song of the night.

His parents and girlfriend looked obviously confused as Drew appeared in the pit and pulled them from the show. Drew's girlfriend was silent and awkward. His father looked at the pavement as they walked back to their vehicle. Drew's mom could be heard reassuring him with something to the effect of "Oh hun, I'm so sorry."

At this point, Drew was completely numb.

And then the cherry to top the night off. As he opened the door to his older red pickup for his girlfriend (knowing that he was going to drop off this poor girl who found herself dating a *failed* musician) Drew caught the sound of the song he wrote. A song HE wrote. Being played by HIS band, without HIM.

Drew was so upset he punched the side of his pickup.

"I'd be careful with that beauty."

An older man walking in the parking lot offered the warning. His eyes met with Drew's, whose eyes at this point were misty with emotion and pain. The older gentleman spoke softly and motioned to Drew's tears.

"I'm sure you are going through a lot tonight, but you seem to me to be the right kind of person. One who will always come out on top, no matter what life throws at you. Keep your chin up kid."

The older gentleman spit what Drew could only imagine being tobacco and walked away towards a convenience store down the street.

That night was awful. But the next day was worse. Gossip spread like wildfire, and Drew felt his confidence escape him. As assumed, his new girlfriend thought it would be best to "be friends for now" while other musicians around the school reassured him that he would find "the right crew" to play with at some point. After a day full of saving face and pretending to be alright, Drew collapsed in his bedroom after being sure to turn some music up and lock his bedroom door. He wasn't one to show his emotions often, but he felt burned. So very, very burned.

A buzzing started in Drew's pocket. Drew pulled out his phone to discover he had a new message in his for-sale app from the seller.

"How did last night go? Sorry I couldn't make it."

Drew opened up and confided in the seller what had happened. It was cathartic, to just speak his feelings and explain how wronged he was last night.

"Sorry for emotionally dropping all this on you." Drew wrote as he finished explaining the events that took place the night prior.

The seller wrote back a note of encouragement.

"Keep your chin up. You'll be alright in time." After another moment, the seller added, "Hey I have something else that I think you are the right kind of person to appreciate. You could say I snatched up some musical equipment recently that I believe you will enjoy. This one's on me kid. Free overnight delivery as usual."

"Thanks so much, you are too kind." Drew replied. "I'm pretty lucky to have found your profile."

"Don't mention it." the seller responded.

The following morning, Drew awoke to his mother opening the door to his bedroom, handing him a box addressed to him. After thanking his mother and closing the door, Drew opened the package.

A horrific stench hit his nostrils as he opened the box.

Enclosed in packing peanuts were *two severed hands holding drumsticks.*

As Drew dropped the package to the floor, blood splattered and stained his bedroom carpet. It was *then* Drew noticed Brandon's familiar tattoo on the bloody wrist of the right hand.

———

Police responded to Drew's home to the sound of a 911 call involving Drew's mother crying in terror. After collecting evidence, taking statements, and getting access to search Drew's phone, the police ran the vehicle identification number of his old red pickup truck parked on the curb.

As it turned out, the current plates were expert-crafted forgeries. Upon further research, the police found a body and paint shop claiming to have serviced Drew's truck a month earlier with two specific requests—the first, to remove a racing stripe, and the second, to change the vehicle's color from bright blue to a deep red.

Drew quickly learned that some sales are too good to be true, and some prices are too costly for being too low. The student who had gone missing from another school was the prior owner of Drew's truck. In addition, all members of Drew's previous band had gone missing.

Police were quoted in the news to be actively pursuing all leads in the community to solve "this horrendous crime against our children and our city." The authorities added patrols to Drew's high school and felt it was best to keep him in classes until they had more questions.

As Drew went to his first class, one of his fellow classmates was excited to show him a used instrument they had just purchased—an all too familiar keytar that Conor had once played.

"W-w-where did you get that!?!?" asked Drew.

Drew's peer enthusiastically replied, "I found it online at an amazing price! I even got free overnight delivery!"

THE ANTIQUE WINGBACK

Kelly needed a change in decor. A change in scenery. A mini vacation. A road trip. Something. *Anything.* 2020 had been the worst year of her life.

From Kelly's vantage point, she was clearly overworked. The pandemic had hit her employer hard and left Kelly burned out and stressed. She had gone from regular office hours and a budding social life—to working 12-plus hour days from a computer screen in the middle of her condo with barely any outside contact. It seemed her social calendar was over for the foreseeable future as well—at least until the medical community could come up with some sort of treatment or cure for Covid-19.

Downtown Portland previously held a quirky charm, but now with everything that was happening in the city, Kelly wasn't so certain Portland was for her. She felt trapped in an uncertain future. Her condo, once cute and exciting years ago, began to feel suffocating—nothing had changed about its overall design since she originally moved in. Kelly daydreamed of possible changes around her condo that could lift her spirits while this pandemic raged on. Kelly desired a refresh of her surroundings—one part furniture and decor upgrade— and one part new paint.

Kelly's condo wasn't the only thing that needed a refresh. Her mind spiraled thinking of some possible way to escape for a weekend. She needed fresh air and to get out, if for nothing more than her own mental health. After a bit of planning, she landed on the concept of a road trip along the Oregon coast, with some added shopping to boot.

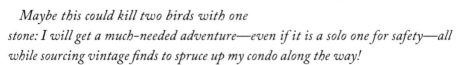

Maybe this could kill two birds with one stone: I will get a much-needed adventure—even if it is a solo one for safety—all while sourcing vintage finds to spruce up my condo along the way!

Kelly arranged to swap vehicles and borrow a small, covered pickup truck from a friend. After booking a hotel room for an overnight stay on the coast, she set her mind to packing. With hand sanitizer, disinfectant spray, her own bedding in a hamper, and a box of masks—Kelly was ready for a socially distanced weekend coastal adventure. The most awkward road trip experience, to be certain, but at least she would get a change of surroundings while following the wisdom of the medical community and remaining *safe.*

———

The man-made structures of the city slowly turned to open freeways, and open freeways soon turned into misty forests. As Kelly drove toward the coast, she continued to reflect on all that had happened this year.

I would have preferred a zombie apocalypse to this pandemic. At least then, the desk jobs and video calls would be over, and I could be interacting in-person with a band of survivors—more afraid of being bitten by a corpse than of the air my friends breathe.

Kelly noted this was a rather dark thought and quickly dismissed it. Clearly, the circumstances of the year had taken a toll on her overall mood.

In truth, 2020 had transformed Kelly's life from a haven of financial security and in-person relationships to a virtual sea tossed by the storm of the pandemic: layoffs were a constant threat at her workplace, and all her relationships ended up becoming video calls—calls where everyone assured each other things were ok in their lives—when clearly everything was not, *not even close.*

The neighborhood Kelly lived in that once had the charm of local shops and dives to eat in became hollow affairs. While many were thankfully able to remain open, the businesses all became transactional and eschewed the relational culture and activity they were originally characteristic of due to social distancing. Even Kelly's condo became a prison of sorts—transforming from a cute place of rest and relaxation into walls that confined her as she dreamed of her previous life before all this.

Kelly took a deep breath as she thought about the situation. She needed change, or at least some small variety in her schedule. This new way of living was *tough.*

As the forest road wound before her under patches of mist, Kelly came to the epiphany that this newly manufactured "digital life" during the pandemic had been replacing the real one she was losing.

If I'm forced into isolation, it should have been a beach house somewhere, filled with nothing but books to read, not a small condo with a billion glass screens demanding more of my effort—despite the world burning.

The world had indeed been burning. Or at least Kelly's small portion of it. Early this fall, a fire had consumed everything in its path, just 12 miles south of where Kelly lived in downtown Portland. The smoke was so dense that the sky had turned orange, and it truly felt like the end of the world had come—with smoke and ash being so thick, Kelly couldn't even see the end of her street from the condo's bay window.

2020 was really something.

While the nightly news was busy throwing out flashy stories exaggerating unrest in Portland streets, a disease was sweeping through and killing the masses, and the earth was literally on fire around her city—one could easily understand a growing desire for counting horsemen and preparing for the end. If this all sounds overwhelming, that's because it indeed was. In contrast to these thoughts and reflections, the trees passing Kelly by on her drive were cathartic. The further from civilization she drove—the more Kelly began to feel like herself again.

As time passed, Kelly finally found herself driving along the coast, from small town to small town. Kelly had prepared a list of antique and vintage furniture shops to visit, all in the quest to freshen up her living—now also working—space. Each shop had something unique and worth collecting: a small painting of a lake reminding Kelly of her childhood vacations, a cute Mid-Century bar set, a retro lamp, a small sculpture, and an intricate hand-crafted coffee table.

There was one item Kelly was searching for more than any other: a vintage recliner with a stool to complete her reading nook in the condo's bay window—hopefully giving her a much-needed relaxation space at home.

Despite visiting a handful of shops on her list throughout the afternoon, a viable antique recliner evaded Kelly's search.

Concluding the first day of her journey without finding what she was hoping for, Kelly settled down into her own bedding, placed over the hotel mattress. She began reading a novel that she couldn't create the mental space to enjoy at home. Exhaustion and rest finally came to her before she finished a chapter, and for the first time in a long while, Kelly slept deeply and peacefully.

Kelly awoke the following morning much later than she had anticipated, yet she was completely fine with this. She refused to push herself or even set an alarm, as she wanted to naturally gather the rest on this trip that her condo and job did not afford her. After a small breakfast, Kelly loaded into her borrowed pickup truck and hit the coastal freeway again. Large pines extended out over the cliffs skirting the Pacific Ocean, and huge stone boulders jutted up out of the water along the drizzly morning drive. After another small beach town had disappeared in her rear view, Kelly noticed a sign indicating an antique shop full of one-of-a-kind finds. This location wasn't on Kelly's list of stops to visit but, living in the moment and ready for the unexpected, Kelly pulled off the main road and slowly pulled into the parking allocated at the front of the shop.

The facade of the antique store was made to look like the stern of an old sailing vessel. Nautical ornamentation and clutter taking the forms of old life preservers and ship helm wheels were abundant. Across the stern facade, in old time letters, *The Crow's Nest* was written. The storefront lettering was built out of incandescent bulbs and shaped metal, reminding Kelly more of a carnival boardwalk than the seafaring theme she supposed the shop was going for. Flickering flame lamps hung by the sides of the wooden double door entrance, which was slightly obscured by a large sculpture of a mermaid in the walkway.

I'm not sure if this shop is going to have anything close to what I'm looking for, but it's quirky and this is an adventure after all. Why not?

Kelly donned her mask, gave the heavy door a pull, and entered the store.

There is a unique smell of old, musty sweetness that usually greets antique store visitors, and this shop was no different. Kelly took note of the dim lighting, but other than the over-the-top nautical themes throughout the store's decor, there was nothing out of the ordinary.

Pirate jewelry display? Check. Lighthouse dining furniture set? Check. Assorted beach items for the obvious coastal tourist? Check.

A parrot cackled, "Ahoy Matey" from his perch behind the cash register.

Ok, now that's funny.

"Well, hello there, little friend." Kelly spoke to the bird as she approached.

"He's kind of a one-trick pony," replied a small, withered, elderly woman with dark glassy eyes, smiling from her stool behind the counter.

Kelly was taken aback for a short moment, as she had not perceived this woman among the various objects surrounding the parrot and the register.

The old woman adjusted her mask covering and then continued.

"Petey here only knows the one phrase. But it works perfectly in all cases: whether you are coming or going, he always gets your attention."

The woman laughed to herself, the laugh becoming a cough near the end. Her old bushy eyebrows shot up, mindful of the hyper-aware nature of a public cough these days.

"His greeting works well for shoplifters, too. I've seen grown men crap themselves, thinking they were alone in the store. Petey keeps an eye on all the shiny objects we have, don't you, sweetie?"

The bird then bobbed his head as the woman took a small cracker and fed it to him. After the snack, he hopped onto the counter and trotted over to Kelly while cackling, "Ahoy, ahoy-ahoy, matey!"

Kelly smiled beneath her mask at this odd introduction.

"What brings you in today?" the aged woman asked, her deep, dark glassy eyes locked on Kelly.

Kelly glanced around the shop while she explained her quest.

"I'm just taking a much-needed break from my reality. I drove out from Portland, and although I'm picking up tiny finds here and there, what I'm really looking for is a recliner. I have this little spot at home where I want to create a reading nook, and all I'm missing is a good chair and stool."

Before Kelly had finished speaking, the elderly woman walked with a surprisingly youthful speed to a barn-style door and began pulling it open. The door creaked and moaned as it rolled on the track it rested on. Dusting her hands off, the woman clapped twice, and to Kelly's amazement, a furniture showroom of sorts was revealed by the added lighting. Exquisite pieces of furniture were displayed throughout, all in unique styles and with a quality that seemed unmatched by the dusty shops Kelly had previously visited.

"Wow."

Kelly was in awe of this hidden gem. The old woman clasp her hands with excitement, and then went back to the front desk. Kelly walked alone along the antiques, running her hands over the various curves of each furniture piece, wondering what lie around each corner of the room. Eventually, Kelly happened upon a wingback antique chair that perfectly fit what she was looking for. The chair even included a matching footstool, and Kelly was quite fond of it. Finding the price to be more than reasonable, Kelly pulled off the price tag for the item and returned to the front counter.

"So, you found what you were looking for, I suppose!" the old woman teased, taking the tag. The woman began to type into a register that looked as if it, itself, was an antique. "That chair and stool were a special find, one of a kind, I say. It came in just the other day! Must have been meant for you."

"Really?" Kelly replied. "How often do you get furniture like this?"

A loud thump that sounded like a baseball falling on the floor came from the back of the shop. The old woman paused and then glanced back with a scowl, scanning the room but finding nothing out of the ordinary. After a nod of disapproval and then an awkward glance at Petey, who seemed unfazed, the woman returned to jotting down a sales receipt for Kelly.

"All the time. Some poor soul is always having to entrust us with their beloved items. Estate liquidations and such. I see it as a form of stewardship. You know, these antiques have a life of their own—their story continues beyond their first owners."

"Indeed, it's quite an honor to own such a beautiful piece." Kelly responded, signing the sales slip and placing her credit card back in her purse.

Kelly loaded the chair, stool, and cushions into the truck. As she was doing this, she could hear Petey calling to her, *"Ahoy! Ahoy!"* from the now open door where the elderly shopkeeper stood watching. After Kelly closed the truck bed and camper shell, the woman waved to her and shouted, "Take care, my dear!"

Kelly closed the door of her borrowed truck, now filled with all she had been seeking. She cast off the mask she was wearing, then turned the ignition and drove away.

That shop was such a find!

Kelly couldn't wait to get back home and redecorate. This short adventure had been exactly what she needed, but the pandemic fatigue was starting to get to her in a new way: she longed for the mask-free comforts of home again. Also new to Kelly: being exhausted of too much activity?

Weird how I'm suddenly back to wanting to be cozy at home after this little trip.

It seemed to Kelly that in 48 hours she had done more outside her condo than the last few months combined.

K elly would take any ounce of connection to others these days—she made quick work of posting to social media the documented progress of her picturesque reading nook to the likes and comments of her friends. Kelly spent the next two weeks re-arranging her condo, adding in the new furniture and decor elements, and finally getting around to painting that turquoise accent wall she wanted in the living room to make her home a bit more vibrant.

She staged her new lamp in her bay window, repurposed an old side table of hers and then added the antique wingback chair. The spot was perfect for reading and reflecting, all while watching her neighbors walk the streets below.

Kelly sat in her new chair and read a book while the sun was warm through the glass. The sun eventually set on the horizon. Relaxed and perfectly content with herself, she fell fast asleep.

The sound of something hitting the wall across from the reading nook awakened Kelly.

Coming to with such a start, Kelly tried to figure out what had just happened. Everything in her head felt groggy, and it took a moment to realize where she was. The bay window was dark, only the streetlights and traffic were illuminated below.

Must have fallen asleep, she thought to herself.

As Kelly stood up from her chair, her head throbbed with a small headache. The reading lamp next to her was the only source of light on in her condo, and visually searching for the noise that had woken her, Kelly found the book she had been reading on the floor, over 10 feet away. The book had been tossed with such force that it left a small scar in the new turquoise paint job that Kelly had given the accent wall.

That stinks.

Kelly yawned.

Now I need to touch this up tomorrow. Bummer.

Kelly placed the book back on the seat of her wingback chair and turned the lamp off.

It wasn't until Kelly had moved slowly to the kitchen where she got a glass of water that the *how* of her book being thrown at the wall from the reading nook crossed her mind.

Was I thrashing in my sleep? Having a bad dream so deep, I grabbed my book and tossed it? That's so wild…

Kelly couldn't make heads or tails of it. She decided to call it for the night and turn in, hoping her headache would subside. Kelly took a melatonin pill and an ibuprofen, then laid down in bed—throwing the comforter over her head. Within seconds, she was fast asleep.

The next morning, Kelly was seated at her kitchen counter on a barstool with her laptop open and a cup of coffee in hand. Kelly had positioned the condo living room as well as her reading nook behind her for scenery. In "pandemic office culture" you were clearly judged by your space, or at least your ability to augment your working area in a fashionable way, and Kelly knew this well.

Most settled for a poster or some basic artwork on the wall behind them, some chose bookshelves in their spacious home office, but the less fortunate among her coworkers settled with children's playrooms and the constant need to mute their microphones. Kelly had more than once gotten compliments on her new decor. She held a small amount of pride and blushed when others pointed out how nice her place was—if she couldn't have friends over, the least she could do was make her condo a beautiful place as well as a reflection of her design tastes.

Logging into her video conference, the laptop screen looked like a modern version of Hollywood squares.

In this corner, we have my boss the loveable Ms. Sam Blique, over to the right we have my reliable contributors Jack and Mary, that tile over there has the company clown and all-around productivity vacuum Dan, and over here we have Edith—the one person three ranks below everyone else that loves to assert themselves—taking up most meetings with questions that should have been discussed with her manager prior to our video call. All accounted for, are we ready for this overly long meeting?

Kelly hid her smirk at this thought behind her coffee cup as she took a quick sip before things started rolling.

…and my boss was just assailed on screen by her needy golden retriever—no distractions working from home—am I right!?

The meeting went about as one would expect. Reports were discussed, projections were laid out, and it soon came time for Kelly to present to everyone. As Kelly started speaking, Dan began laughing uncontrollably and interrupted her.

"—Who the heck is that!?"

Kelly stopped speaking for a moment, completely puzzled. After pausing a moment, thinking Dan had just forgotten to mute himself, Kelly continued, "—as I was saying, if we compare last year's projections to this year's—"

Dan interrupted again. "—Kelly, who IS that? I just can't focus with that going on."

At this point, a knot started rising in Kelly's throat. Turning to look behind her seat and not finding anything out of the ordinary, Kelly returned her focus to the laptop screen, now full of her coworkers' shocked expressions and stares.

"I-I'm sorry," Kelly responded. "I'm not quite sure what you mean. What are you seeing?"

At this point, Kelly's boss spoke up, nodding with understanding.

"Hey Kelly, so sorry to jump in here, but I can confirm what may be distracting the team. Do you have your grandfather staying with you or something? There was an elderly gentleman walking behind you, and uhhh—unfortunately, he was not in the proper attire for a workplace meeting. Maybe we can reschedule this—and you can check to see if he's doing alright?"

Audible laughs from the team ensued.

Kelly became visibly uncomfortable. Looking to save face in the moment (as well as feeling the need to search her apartment), Kelly quickly replied.

"Yeah, let's reschedule this for a bit later. So sorry to disrupt the meeting!"

She immediately logged off and closed her notebook. Kelly searched the condo from room to room, finding nothing. After a visual sweep of each of the closets, Kelly assumed someone must have played a prank on her. She knew there was an augmented reality feature built into her video call software that could change backgrounds. Kelly also remembered reading a news story recently about hackers using video call software, exposing callers to porn and other things in their video streams.

Maybe someone hacked my meeting video?

Either way, Kelly knew she needed to act quickly to salvage her reputation at work. Kelly logged back into her computer and opened a private message panel with Jack and Mary.

"Hey guys, so sorry to do this, and I know this is going to be an awkward conversation, but what exactly did you guys see on the video call? I do not, I repeat, DO NOT have a relative staying with me. Nobody was here in my condo with me at the time, and after the call, I searched my entire home and found nothing. I'm completely thrown for a loop due to this, as clearly even our boss saw something in the feed, but I don't know what to make of it. I was wondering if it was somehow a hack or something. Should I report this to HR? I probably need to cover myself."

A notification appeared in Kelly's chat window to indicate the typing of a reply. Kelly sat, anxious, awaiting her coworker's response. She stood up after a moment and began pacing her living room, thinking about how to have a conversation with her boss about this morning's meeting. As Kelly paced, her knee caught her book and knocked it from the coffee table to the floor.

Odd, she thought. *I remember putting this on my recliner last night.*

A bell sound came from Kelly's computer, notifying her that a reply from one of her coworkers had been sent. Kelly walked back over to the screen. Mary had replied.

"Super spooky. I clearly saw an elderly guy in his birthday suit come strolling by behind you. So, you are saying nobody was there? I'd be freaked out right now if I were you. I don't think hacking has come so far as to insert old men into your home walking around. It looked real to me! I'm also chatting with Jack, and I think Dan sent him a couple of screen captures while it was going down. Dan was, of course, joking about it privately over email. He is such an ass. Give Jack a moment. He says he'll send them to you."

Kelly typed back, "Thanks, appreciate the help—sorry our work didn't get shown in a positive light today."

A moment later, Mary responded. "No problem. Our work was shown in a bright light today. That old guy needs a tan! Just kidding, but really, I hope you are doing ok."

Kelly sent back two emojis, one for laughing and the other for cringing. Right about this moment, Jack's images came through. Sure enough, in the sequence of images, a naked old man could be seen scowling and unhappy, standing next to the reading nook. The next image showed him picking something up, followed by another image of him setting something down on the coffee table, before strolling past Kelly's left shoulder and then out of frame.

Upon zooming in a bit closer, Kelly realized that the item in question being moved was her book from last night. A small chill went down Kelly's spine.

I knew I wasn't crazy, the book was moved!

Kelly's mind began connecting the dots between the events of this morning and last night.

What if, just what if… I didn't toss my book in my sleep last night? What if it had been thrown by someone… else?

This thought made Kelly's skin crawl. She attempted to talk herself out of this headspace.

You are playing mind games with yourself. Stop the fantasy. There must be some normal reason for all this. And the images—most likely a hacker of sorts trying some new video trick!

After agonizing a bit, going back and forth on her perspectives, Kelly finally decided the best path forward would be the cautious one: she would call her boss and involve HR in order to make it known something was amiss in the video feed. She would chalk it up to a software glitch, and since she had some personal time saved up—she could request a week off for mental health. Kelly made a few calls. Her boss was totally supportive, thankfully, albeit quite concerned about their corporate web security tools.

Good luck to the IT department, Kelly mused.

———

K elly decided to use the time off to set some things right in her condo. She was new to the whole "maybe my home is haunted" mentality, and thus searched online for advice. After reading a few blogs on the subject, a spiritual cleansing of her home seemed as good an option as any.

I have a friend who once hired a medium to do something like this in her loft apartment. Maybe she could reach out on my behalf?

Kelly was only considering this as a peace of mind measure—just in case the ghost of "Mr. Nude" was indeed a new resident of her building.

Kelly scheduled a date for the medium to come by at their first availability. As she waited patiently for the cleansing, Kelly left lights on across the condo and hung out in her bedroom watching TV, distracting herself from thoughts of what had previously occurred. All was quiet, and as the days went by, Kelly began to doubt anything other than a digital video prank had happened.

When the medium finally arrived one afternoon for a tour of her home, Kelly was glad to be moving on.

Finally, this mess will be over. I'll have peace of mind, and my home back.

The medium, a smooth talking 6-foot man with a southern accent—presenting a little more Baptist pastor than seance in Kelly's opinion. He made a bit of a deal with being required to mask up in her home, but Kelly insisted that if he was going to spiritually cleanse her condo, the least he could do was avoid contaminating her home with coronavirus. The medium finally caved and slid a mask on. The man walked into Kelly's condo, and after setting his bag down on the kitchen countertop, walked over to the reading nook and stared out the window.

It was raining outside and overall, rather drab. The medium looked back at Kelly, then crossed his arms and sighed, returning his gaze to the window.

"I don't like it." the medium whispered.

Before Kelly could react to this statement, the man walked over to his bag, picked up some sage and lit it, waving it around her condo while muttering something she couldn't really make out. Rather than interrupt and ask for a play-by-play, Kelly decided to leave this situation to the "expert" and allow him to do what he came to do.

Ten minutes went by. Then another ten. At about a half hour, the medium finally began packing up, albeit slightly perturbed.

"Is everything alright?" Kelly asked.

"All good, spirits are gone, your home is clean." He then smiled with his eyes in a way that didn't give Kelly a ton of confidence that this whole spiritual "home cleansing shindig" was *not* some sort of scam. "Now about my payment..." the medium queried.

After settling with him on a price that was way more than she believed he deserved—about the cost of hiring a real cleaning lady for the week—Kelly wished the gentleman well and closed the door behind him. Following up by opening the windows and spraying a bit of disinfectant around her home, Kelly began placing scented candles throughout the condo and lighting them. Once everything began to smell like her home again, Kelly closed the windows and turned on her fireplace. The condo quickly warmed and smelled wonderful.

Kelly began preparing dinner for herself not long after: sliced steak over a garlic kale salad. This was her favorite dish, and she decided to treat herself to a glass of Malbec while enjoying it, basking in the glow of the fireplace and TV. After the TV was turned off and the dishes were done, Kelly queued up a relaxing playlist on her wireless speaker. As Billie Eilish's "I Love You" played softly, Kelly reclined into her wingback chair and began to read again.

Since she had no work this week, Kelly's schedule had slipped into a cycle of staying up late and sleeping in. The evening went on, and eventually Kelly's playlist ended.

Another chapter and then I'll head to bed, Kelly thought.

All was quiet until Kelly noticed a low, strange pattern of breathing coming from behind her.

Kelly turned, knowing someone standing behind her chair was an impossibility, as her chair backed up against the glass of her bay window. Moving to her knees in the wingback recliner, Kelly stared out the window the chair was situated against.

Nobody outside. And how could they be? I'm a few stories up in the building.

Kelly had no sooner had these thoughts when the lamp beside her, as well as all lighting in the condo, flickered with the sound of a static charge and then went out completely.

Facing the glass of her bay window, light reflected from her fireplace and created a flickering impression of the room behind her. As Kelly glanced back into the living room, fear began to grip her. She turned once more toward the window reflection, and as she did, the shadow of a man came running through. Turning swiftly in her seat, Kelly came face to face with—nothing.

Nobody was there.

Kelly sat frozen, terrified, with no sounds other than the fireplace and the trembling of her own breath. After a moment or two had passed, Kelly began to sit forward in the chair, and as she did so—the book she had been reading was flung from beside her into the fireplace.

Kelly screamed and began crying in terror.

Another completely still moment. Not a sound, not even from the neighboring condo units or the street below. Kelly sat frozen in shock and fear, attempting to gather the will to flee her home, but she lacked the courage to move through a room that contained a malicious entity unseen. Seconds later, her footstool was pulled with supernatural force across the room, and a deep, booming voice yelled, "*MINE.*"

Kelly screamed again, but this time, she lunged for her cell phone before attempting a getaway. The phone moved on its own and flew across the room, hitting other furniture pieces before falling to the floor. Kelly ran for the phone, but as she approached, she saw the screen was completely shattered—so instead she bolted out the door of her condo.

Running out of her doorway while shaking with tears, the last thing Kelly saw of her home was the fire go out, with the silhouette of a man standing in her reading nook at the bay window, next to the wingback chair.

The shadow let out a rage fueled, raspy scream.

"*NOW GO!*"

Kelly bolted down the hallway and into the staircase, sobbing as she ran down all flights until she finally burst out of her building and sprinted two blocks over to a friend's apartment.

———

Unbelievable as all this was to Kelly and those she told, it was clear she was deeply impacted. Thankfully, Kelly's friend allowed her to stay in their home while everything was sorted out. A couple of friends went over to her condo to collect a few of Kelly's belongings, and unsurprisingly, they found nothing unusual—other than Kelly's phone busted on the floor and some ash from a book in her fireplace. The building management was also consulted, as well as residents directly around Kelly's condo, but nobody reported having a power outage or hearing Kelly's screams that night.

After gathering some personal items for Kelly, the friends arranged a company to come in and run an estate sale on her possessions, to liquidate everything in the condo and put it on the market for sale.

The estate sale did rather well, and the condo sold quickly in the overheated housing market. With the money Kelly gained from the sales, she moved back to her hometown—closer to her parents, taking a new job to work for a company she felt more appreciated at.

As the years following these events passed, Kelly became a volunteer counselor, assisting those who were dealing with past traumatic spiritual experiences. Though many in her regular life doubted her tale about the haunting, she found comfort in providing psychological and emotional support to those who experienced events similar to her own.

S arah was thrilled to be out and about after being closed up so much this year due to the pandemic. Her boyfriend Marcus was pumped too, because they both had received vaccines that gave them the confidence to go out more.

Their last estate sale stop had landed Marcus a vintage Sega for under fifty bucks. Marcus was recounting his childhood memories of the games they would play together, and the pair were in overall great spirits during the drive to the next stop. As they both climbed the stairs to the condo where the next sale was taking place, Marcus asked if there was anything Sarah had in mind to find today.

"I'm looking for a cute vintage chair to add to our apartment that you can play video games in," she replied, putting her hand in the back pocket of Marcus' blue jeans. She then looked to Marcus and winked, trying to flirt a little.

Being out and about felt fantastic after being isolated for so long.

2020 made me appreciate the little things, like the value of getting out and spending time with people that matter.

Sarah cherished this thought and how lovely today was.

The pair walked into the estate sale and were immediately taken with an antique wingback chair and stool positioned by the condo's bay window. Marcus negotiated an unbelievable deal, and together they carried the chair and stool out to their vehicle.

It was meant to be, Sarah thought, as she and Marcus drove away.

Marcus reached for, and then squeezed, Sarah's hand.

Sarah smiled back at Marcus.

Both were unaware of the reflection in the rearview mirror: a nude, elderly man—clearly annoyed in their backseat.

"THIEVES!" the old man shouted.

Marcus and Sarah stopped the vehicle suddenly, turning their heads to find nothing but their estate sale purchases in the cargo area.

ON DEALING WITH INTRUDERS

INSIGHTS FROM THE TEAM AT

HAUNTER'S MONTHLY

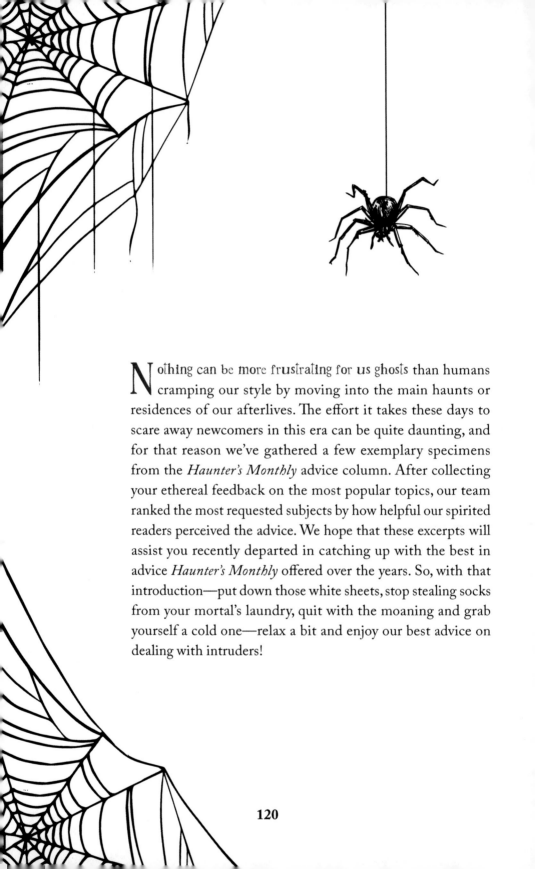

Nothing can be more frustrating for us ghosts than humans cramping our style by moving into the main haunts or residences of our afterlives. The effort it takes these days to scare away newcomers in this era can be quite daunting, and for that reason we've gathered a few exemplary specimens from the *Haunter's Monthly* advice column. After collecting your ethereal feedback on the most popular topics, our team ranked the most requested subjects by how helpful our spirited readers perceived the advice. We hope that these excerpts will assist you recently departed in catching up with the best in advice *Haunter's Monthly* offered over the years. So, with that introduction—put down those white sheets, stop stealing socks from your mortal's laundry, quit with the moaning and grab yourself a cold one—relax a bit and enjoy our best advice on dealing with intruders!

On Dealing with Intruders

Dear Ghastly Gossip,

Recently, a family with children moved into my place, and I wonder: should I make them leave, or should I seek out a new location to reside since I value the quiet? As the recent housing crisis has ensured fewer and fewer homes are left unoccupied, it's clear to me that my options for solitary peace seem limited to abandoned cabins, storm-damaged theme parks, and dusty caverns. What would you do?

Yearning to Rest in Peace,

Beverly Bone

Ms. Bone,

Indeed, the housing crisis has put a horrific squeeze on the residential market. We suggest considering if solitary peace is something you need, or if you can continue to perish without it. Forcing humans to flee your home, while initially enjoyable, can backfire spectacularly. Take a lesson from a poor chap named Greggory who previously wrote in: his theatrics ended up causing the owners to remodel the home and operate a haunted bed-and-breakfast out of the ordeal. Or take Whitney's experience: her mortals decided to demolish the old home and build a new one from scratch!

There is an art to a proper send off if you attempt to scare humans away, and usually the act involves research on your part: Is the home to remain in the family estate for years to come? Will the house be sold? Who may end up moving in next if they leave? These answers may frighten even the cleverest of spooks, so make sure to plan properly before attempting such an undertaking. It may be wisest to learn to cohabit with the family—besides, children can make entertaining playmates! Who knows, you may end up with a young friend if you stick around.

Seeking out another location is rather risky, and we advise against this unless you have been specifically invited to another soul's haunt. Due to market conditions, the likelihood of you scooping up an uninhabited, cobweb infested residence is slim to none. If you do find such a place, odds are you'll find yourself boarding with grim roommates as removed from the living as you are. Remember, annoying mortals only stick around a few years, but an annoying immortal roommate can drag your peace much further than six feet under.

Take care to not make such a decision in haste; we recommend weighing your options and opportunities.

Best of luck with the grave market conditions,

GG

On Dealing with Intruders

Dear Ghastly Gossip,

My new mortal tenants seem to be obsessed with their smartphones. How do I get their attention? The prior residents at least acknowledged my presence; now I'm just left feeling invisible. What's a ghoul to do with this technology obsessed generation?

Neglected and ignored,

Shelby Mush

Ms. Mush,

You will indeed have your hands full (or at least they will) with this situation. The current generation loves social networking and keeping up with the latest during their finite time existing; they seem much more absorbed in their own happiness and how they are perceived than prior generations. This leads to complexities that the long deceased feel too out-of-touch to approach, but fear not: we have a few useful tips on how to remain relevant, despite the never-ending glow from phones upon their faces in the dark.

The best way to understand their technological habits is to liken their activities with those of our vampiric friends. With the invention of smart devices and social media, humans have begun to trade their glorious days in the sun for dim lit, nighttime pursuits of content to feast upon. Whereas the vampire has teeth, humans feast with their eyes upon stories, events, and opinions fed to them through their custom information portals and friend networks. Think of the information an average human consumes like the blood our vampiric brethren require for sustenance; without the constant feeding, they would make quite the nuisance. In the same way, this generation is attached to their devices—not so differently than a curse upon its intended subject.

Once you understand this attachment, you'll be much better equipped at generating ideas to become noticed. Recently a reader wrote in telling us their favorite thing to do was stand imposingly behind their mortals for all selfies taken, in hopes that the image captured might just give their presence away—possibly even generating social media content and gossip around who could be haunting them. Others have written in taking a more direct route, whether by constantly hiding charging cables to disable the offending devices, or even by knocking the phones about in the night while the humans slept, so that a shattered screen may grant a reprieve from their constant use.

Our personal favorite tactic would be writing random texts to various contacts in their phones while they are unconscious. While not directly acknowledging you, the act makes for great entertainment, and you can keep the gag going for quite some time, possibly even scaring off a significant other so that you only must share the space with one mortal. Broken domestic relationships are also a fantastic way to blow off steam, as you can toss the separating party's belongings around the home and allow the partner to take the blame "as a crime of passion."

Other ideas include flipping the breakers to their residential unit's power, making yourself heard in the background of their phone calls, writing on their shower mirrors, and if all else fails, try the door slamming method. Essentially, you'll need to become more of interest to your subject than their "glowing infotainment portal of glass." We understand that takes a lot of work, but it's the best advice we can give to gain and retain this generation's attention spans.

One final question you must ask yourself: do you really need the attention? Many spirits of yesteryear happily resided alongside these preoccupied tenants and only raise a fuss if the town minister comes over for Sunday lunch. If you can manage, try becoming a helper to your mortal roommates, such as moving their vehicle keys to a place they have already searched so they are more likely to find them. Or join them when they watch a scary movie in order to set the proper mood in the home. The living may not know you are there, but they will be thankful for your help, nonetheless!

Wishing you the best in your haunts,

GG

Dear Ghastly Gossip,

My problem is somewhat unique. What does a spirit do when they are constantly being pulled into highly annoying conversations? My mortals have recently acquired a Ouija Board, and they keep pestering me. I'm often summoned for conversations of the silliest nature. **Lov**e interests. Dead family members. Future predictions—as if I could travel through time or something! The list goes on and on.

I was more than happy to reside in the attic quietly. Now the family staying in my home wants my input at their beck and call. Frankly, I feel it's rude! I fear I'll never have down time like I used to. What can be done?

Looking for wisdom from beyond,

Kathleen Chatters

Ms. Chatters,

Being social in the afterlife really does take a great deal of effort, and the bone you desire to pick with the living in your home is understandable: nobody likes to be disturbed for the entertainment of others, especially in the wee hours of the night. While it is natural to jump to conclusions and assume the worst, we advise a more measured approach: assume them foolish and oblivious to the discomfort they are causing you. This will go a long way in bringing about a desirable outcome. The last thing you want is a priest waving some sage around your beloved home due to starting the relationship off hostile—and we've seen this happen to others in your predicament when they lose patience and good faith.

The best method for solving these disturbances to your peace is to communicate clearly. Have you possessed at least one of the individuals whom summoned you? Did you politely ask to be left alone in peace as you rest? Also, are their questions genuine in nature? Since you brought up questions about a deceased family member in your letter, we assume that has played a role in why the living may have made contact. One possible solution would be to impersonate their dearly departed as to bring comfort and closure to their minds. Many a Ouija Board have gathered dust because mortals move on with their lives after finding comfort that their loved ones are at peace in the afterlife.

Whatever the situation has previously been, you must do your due diligence and discover their motives for desiring to commune with you. Remember, you were once alive and had many questions too. Have empathy, and work to resolve their issues if possible.

In the event that you discern that you are being toyed with, all bets are off. You have nothing to lose at this point, so we would advise giving it all the gusto you have: really put in the effort to show them who has the upper hand in this situation. If your relationship is indeed this poor, our suggestion is to seek one of two best outcomes: you either scare them so much that they abandon playing with the board, or you cause such a fright that they see moving as a better option than staying in the home and trying to cleanse it of you. You'll have a very short window to accomplish these things, and it's best if you cut the mortals in question off from their phones, internet, devices, and anyone who desires to interact. It's also best you avoid any possession at this juncture, as that will move the living from a defensive posture to an offensive one in order to reclaim their own.

Through your actions, make it hard for them to get any rest—either drive them out with a crescendo of activity, or make the point of haunting their pants off the second they touch the Ouija Board (driving home the dangers of bothering you). Boundaries need to be set, and as we all know, sometimes a bully needs a good punch in the nose to leave you be. Obviously, no sane entity among the living or dead would go looking for a fight. However, be of courage if a fight comes your way; a ghost already has all they need to win such a dispute, they just need to break the living down psychologically enough to get their way.

We believe you'll find these tips will put things back to normal. Be it through helping your mortals with their issues or setting boundaries with them through your activity in the home, clear communication is key.

We wish you a quick return to resting in the peace of your attic.

GG

On Dealing with Intruders

Dear Ghastly Gossip,

I have mortal children now living in my home! I've made multiple attempts to befriend them, scare them, or frankly, just be noticed by them. No matter what I attempt, the children seem obsessed with their video games! What's an imaginary friend to do?

Exhausted by the 8-Bit horror,

R. E. Spawn

Mr. Spawn,

We have no doubt that video game obsessed children present a new set of challenges for poltergeists everywhere. The days of turning on and off television sets while drawing them in with abstract sounds and static seem to have gone by the wayside, along with the older technology. While some video games require a stationary entertainment system, much of the market has shifted to portable gaming devices—thus ensuring young mortals are distracted throughout the home, instead of containing those distractions within the traditional restraints of living rooms or bedrooms. With these new circumstances in mind, we have a few tips that will bring the children back to teatime, or at least asking their parents for a night light.

Timing and isolation are now the name of the game, so to speak. You'll want to do things around your haunt like hide batteries, chargers, cables, and the like. The less power sources for portable gaming, the better. Delaying the children from playing with their handhelds (due to a lack of power) is of utmost importance. For entertainment center connected gaming systems, make sure to create interference with the home wireless network, or at the very least unplug it. As lots of gaming devices these days are connected through the internet, a lack of connection could easily lead the children to put their controllers down and begin using their imaginations again.

Once you've created opportunities where they will be less distracted and isolated, then it's back to the basics! You can befriend the children as their "imaginary friend" or simply spook them when the moment is right by moving their toys, sending them running for their parent's bedroom. A neat modern trick for the lonely spirit is to possess the voice of the home smart assistant and communicate with the children that way. Their parents will assume the device just has a programed response, and you'll have free rein to talk in an approachable format with any young mortals present.

One additional idea to try if the gaming addiction continues: possess the controllers. Children cannot stand when their movement in a game is stifled or incorrect actions are input; it robs them of their joy during the experience. The many reports in the gaming industry of "joystick drift" and faulty gaming hardware are easily chalked up to our readers who were fed up with the lack of attention they were getting around the home.

We hope these ideas will assist you in gaining and retaining the attention of your lively children. Now the rest is up to you.

GG

Dear Ghastly Gossip,

The young couple that moved into my haunt is an odd lot. Upon move-in, they began remodeling the home, which at first, I was irritated about. I began smashing brand new windows as they were installed, possessing power tools on the jobsite, you know—the typical stuff. The living blamed all my hard work on the sketchy neighborhood and a rise in break-ins. It was maddening to get them to see what was really going on, and I was highly discouraged. During construction on my home, the drafts were causing the wind to howl louder than I could moan, so in the end, I eventually caved and let them finish the remodel. Then, instead of "flipping" my haunt, the young couple decided to stay.

I accepted this as the perfect opportunity to spook them as they were the only residents in my home (no kids thankfully!) and as they could easily be isolated due to each other working late, etc. To my displeasure, both young adults enjoy falling asleep to the TV being left on. It really takes the fright out of my night, as they chalk anything I do up to whatever is on their television. What should I do to break through the noise?

Dead tears streaming,

Justin Pieces

Mr. Pieces,

In this era of never-ending television content on demand, it's not surprising you are having this issue. Many a mortal have chosen to bask in the glow of their TV sets over the years, setting their minds at ease through both illuminating their rooms at night while also filling their spaces with what they call "white noise"—simply explained as background noise so they can drown out other sounds in their homes and neighborhoods.

For a spirit to overcome this obstacle, they'll need to take physical form and make an unmistakable impression. We recommend standing at the end of the living's bed and speaking audibly. Waking a person up to an unknown figure imposing upon them is sure to stir quite the terror and allowing your voice to be heard will drive the experience home. Your mortal's friends and family will claim they just had a bad dream, all the while you'll put the sleeper on edge, and thereafter they will take notice of your activity throughout the home. Claiming credit for your hard work sometimes takes bold moves such as these, but fear not, the living will eventually come to an awareness of your presence. Once this has been achieved, what you do with their attention is up to you!

Best of luck with rising above the distractions,

GG

Dear Ghastly Gossip,

After years of cohabiting with a mortal family in my home, I'm ready for some freedom. I've put in the years, and had hoped that as their children went away to college, I could haunt the basement and exist peacefully in quiet darkness.

Unfortunately, the family's youngest son, a 33-year-old man, remains living in the basement—watching anime and filling the space with collectable action figures. His rent-free lifestyle of freeloading off his parents really angers my spirit.

I understand the living can fall on hard times and reside with relatives, but this just feels wrong. Without a job, the son wanders the halls as if he indeed was among the deceased, moaning on about what there is to eat in the home. While the aging parents are away at work or social clubs, the son is inviting his adult friends over to play board games centered around dungeons while ranting about science fiction.

It's all rather unbearable. Please give me some guidance on how to give a mooch the spook.

An apparition just wishin',

Izzy Gone

Mr. Gone,

Adults are living with their mortal parents longer than expected in this generation, to be sure. While the living may be content to let things lie, those of us in the hereafter may not have the same level of patience. While we would normally advise utilizing social isolation and chaos to remove mortals from a residence, for the mooch, these tactics are simply ineffective. The mooch is comfortable in his social isolation, and as their life already resembles unstructured chaos, tossing things around their dwelling will make no noticeable difference to their already messy quality of life. Instead, we suggest a more subtle approach.

First, realize that the mortal mooch is tied directly to comfort, a lack of expectations, the availability of food, the spending of financial gain on pleasure only, and simply has no desire for the future other than to exist. With this understanding, you can more accurately target the pressure points in the mortal mooch's life that will bring about a change of proverbial "couch surfing locale."

Being that your mooch most likely entertains themselves at all hours of the night, it's important to force their hand, keeping them deprived of comfort or sleep during the traditional waking hours. Removing the mooch's comfort by making just enough noise to keep them awake at all hours of the daylight will go a long way to priming them for what you have in store next: possessing their usually indifferent mother in order to berate and badger them on topics such as where they spend their time, money, and if they will ever get a life of their own.

A great tip is using the time you possess the mother to ask for rent! By using the mother in your haunt technique, you'll remove their assumed safety of never being held to account for their situation. As the discomfort grows, so will the mooch's desire for change.

Next, go after the food sources in the home. Open fridge doors, snack bags, and beverages so that food spoils quickly. Hide the snacks you find in unexpected locations throughout the home. Follow these actions up with knocking over expensive items in the mooch's collection and damaging them. What you are going for is less of an impression to the mooch that they are haunted and more of an impression that their life, and its comforts, can't survive the current residential environment.

Odds are, the mooch will vacate their parent's basement within weeks if you keep these activities up. In the event they do not (and their life really is such a disaster that they are unmotivated by all the above) we have another idea: simply possess the mooch, *permanently*.

Since the mortal mooch has already given up their life among the living anyway, the fact that their existence would be forfeit is of no real loss *to them*. On the other hand—*you* would get a new opportunity to permanently walk among the living again! Who knows, maybe you can clean up their act, gaining praise from all about how you magically turned "your life" around. You'll know the secret to that change—but keep it to yourself and enjoy your second life. You'll have earned it!

To new beginnings.

GG

BUMBLE THE CLOWN

L eeroy was down on his luck. A retired rodeo clown, Leeroy knew what it was to take a hit or two in his prime. But the financial blows that kept coming were beginning to weigh so heavily on his meager livelihood that Leeroy wished he could have just been knocked around by a bull instead.

Financial ruin has so much in common with a bull, Leeroy thought to himself.

They both throw people without notice and can wound you fatally.

It's not that Leeroy hadn't made an effort to set himself up for success once he retired. To the contrary, he had done what many would consider the right things: he invested his savings, purchased a small mobile home that he could afford on a fixed income, and had even made efforts to come out of retirement from time to time as a for-hire birthday clown.

Unfortunately, the one thing Leeroy had not planned on was a lawsuit.

During his career, Leeroy was known to guests and fans alike as a loveable comic genius in between rodeo riders, but it was during the events his real job took priority: protecting fallen riders from the dangers of a bull angry enough to kill. Leeroy's brightly colored rodeo clown outfit concealed the truth of his role–distracting a bull once its rider was in serious danger, giving the rider just enough time to escape unharmed. A month before Leeroy was set to retire, one such event went horribly wrong. The bull ignored the efforts of Leeroy to draw attention and instead gored a rider in a near-fatal accident.

As horrifying as something like this happening under your watch could be, the real horrors waited until Leeroy had finally left his rodeo clown career. The injured rider, seeking financial compensation for many months in the hospital and his lost potential earnings, decided to sue the venue holding the rodeo, the managing company providing oversight, as well as Leeroy himself about a month after Leeroy had retired. Normally, in cases such as these, employees would be covered by insurance policies, but there was one major problem: Leeroy's employer had allowed their insurance policy to lapse before the accident.

Leeroy's employer, when faced with the lawsuit (adding to financial troubles of their own), decided to file for bankruptcy, leaving Leeroy with no real options other than to hire his own lawyers to defend himself. This put the responsibility and financial burden on Leeroy to attempt a lawsuit against his employer for the lack of insurance coverage—a grim, costly prospect against an entity that had already gone out of business.

These lawsuits drained Leeroy of his once cushioned savings and investments. Leeroy now had to choose which bills to pay in order to get through each month, and he knew it was only a matter of time before he lost his mobile home—the last remaining ounce of wealth Leeroy had to his name.

To stabilize himself, Leeroy attempted to leave retirement and gain employment as a rodeo clown again in other areas of the country, but word had spread about the lawsuits and the accident. Although nobody would tell Leeroy to his face, they all believed hiring him at this point would be more potential trouble than it was worth, given what had happened. Outside of attempting to be reemployed at the rodeo, Leeroy would entertain at birthday parties for children—trying to make a few dollars here and there.

It was at one of these birthday parties that Leeroy finally broke emotionally due to the financial stress he was under.

The party was set for a 5:30pm arrival of "Bumble the Clown." There were to be at least twelve children attending based on Mrs. Jacobson's estimate. Balloons and face paint would be on the menu, followed by a birthday cake and a few magic tricks that would wow children but annoy any teenage siblings present.

I've got this, Leeroy encouraged himself, as he loaded his car.

The drive wasn't far. 10 minutes later, Leeroy found himself at the door of your typical three-bedroom suburban home—complete with a minivan in the driveway, a drab beige paint job of a home that looked exactly like all the rest on the block, and a "*Live. Laugh. Love.*" doormat on which Leeroy now nervously stood. As soon as Leeroy pressed the doorbell, he could hear kids running about the house screaming and playing tag, or some variation of a pillow fight. The children all seemed to yell at each other, "the clown is here"—as this was breaking news to all in the home.

The door swung open, and a teenage girl of about seventeen stood uncomfortably in the doorway.

"Come on in, sir, er…. *Bumble*," she spoke as she rolled her eyes, equal parts creeped out at Leeroy's appearance, and completely exhausted of the overly energetic children behind her. "Mom, the clown is here…" she yelled while swiftly closing the door behind Leeroy as he stepped inside.

"Heather, please have him see me in the kitchen, and quickly!"

Mrs. Jacobson was everything you would imagine a strung out, superficial person trying to play the perfect mom on the internet would be. Mrs. Jacobson supposedly ran some sort of online mommy blog that had garnered enough attention to land her spots on the local TV stations as a guest, providing parenting advice and do-it-yourself activity tips. To many in the community, she represented "parenting done right." In real life, away from the internet and cameras, she was an overwhelmed and irritably impatient person.

Ironically, her real name was Karen.

Mrs. Jacobson glared at Leeroy as he headed down the hall toward the kitchen.

As Leeroy walked to meet her, he glanced over toward the other room. The room contained seemingly out-of-control children.

"I can't believe you didn't come earlier to start entertaining at 5:30 exactly! How long will this take to get going?"

Leeroy chuckled to himself at how sometimes the universe provides the best punchlines by chance. *Her name really is Karen. How fitting.*

"Bumble the Clown, ready to bring the laughs to a rumble, and your frown to a tumble!" Leeroy cheeringly quipped, extending Mrs. Jacobson his hand.

Mrs. Jacobson scoffed and ignored the gesture, opting instead to yell at the children to quiet down.

The party went about as you would expect. The balloons were received well, minus a few teen friends of Heather's comparing balloon swords to deflated penises. The face painting was popular enough, except for Leeroy's lack of talent in painting the perfect unicorn—thus causing a very young attendee to cry enough to be taken home early. The birthday cake wasn't made with the correct buttercream icing per Mrs. Jacobson, and eventually the cake ended up being in a food fight between the children. The magic tricks contained the children's attention spans for a whole seven minutes until the hoard were off to the backyard to play. The teens cracked snide jokes about Bumble as they came and went about with their refreshments, and the tired parents basked in the glory of preoccupied children while they caught a moment together without them.

Mrs. Jacobson was scrubbing one of her dining chairs furiously, trying in vain to remove the sticky post-food-fight residue from her dining set. Leeroy began packing up his props, preparing for the awkward exchange that would follow, as he had yet to be paid. Once fully packed, Leeroy cautiously approached Mrs. Jacobson, as she was clearly irritated.

"It was a pleasure to entertain your guests on this special birthday for your son. I hope I helped create some wonderful memories for your family, and I would like to thank you for the opportunity."

As Leeroy spoke, Mrs. Jacobson never glanced in his direction or made an effort to acknowledge him.

"I'm about to head home. Do you happen to have my fee for today?" Leeroy asked in a quieter tone.

Mrs. Jacobson scowled.

"Your fee? You are lucky to get any business at all! By my count, you were late to the party, not as funny as we expected, less than talented when it comes to balloon animals or face paint, and you couldn't bother to assist with preventing the children from throwing their food around. Hell, you couldn't even keep their attention doing magic for more than ten minutes! You are pathetic. I heard the story of how you couldn't even keep bulls entertained—I assumed at the very least you could manage some children! You can't even do that, can you? I plan on not only telling others in the community about this experience, but I'll make sure you are never booked for another children's event in this town—you have my word."

At that, Mrs. Jacobson tossed a check at Leeroy and loudly demanded he leave her home in front of all the guests. As Leeroy exited the Jacobson home, shocked and confused, he heard the woman apologizing for the worst birthday entertainment ever, while others in the home laughed.

Embarrassed. Exhausted. Broken. Leeroy put his bags into his trunk and then slumped down into his older mid-sized sedan, defeated and filled with hopelessness. All he had done was attempt to share joy with children while making just enough to get by, and as thanks the universe saw fit to punish him with a public humiliation by the most influential mommy blogger in the community. A lone tear welled up in Leeroy's right eye, and as he wiped it away, the tear created a streak in his face paint.

Leeroy looked down at the check Mrs. Jacobson had written him. The amount was nearly half what they had agreed upon. In the notes area of the check, Mrs. Jacobson wrote, "You were half as useful as I thought." Leeroy laid his head back against the headrest of his seat and glanced back at the Jacobson home through his window.

What am I going to do so I can make it another month?

The wind gusted at that moment enough to cause a small card tucked underneath his wiper blade to waver in the wind, a detail Leeroy had not noticed until now. With a few quick movements, he opened the door, snatched the card, and closed the door again. Upon further inspection, the card read:

QUIT CLOWNING AROUND
Professional Jester Placement Services—from
Merry Andrews to common fools, we help put a smile
on your career opportunities!

What an odd business card. Is this a prank?

Leeroy wondered if this was the work of one of the teenagers who attended the Jacobson birthday party.

No respect at all.

Leeroy tore the card in half, then proceeded to drive away.

⸻

That night, Leeroy had troubled dreams. Crushing debt, the rodeo accident, teenagers laughing—all combined with a Machiavellian speech about talent from one Mrs. Jacobson. Leeroy woke with a jolt in a pool of his own sweat. The air was stuffy and hot. It appeared that his small air conditioning unit had finally bitten the dust.

Figures, Leeroy thought to himself. *There is no way I can afford to replace it.*

Leeroy moved to the living room, turned on a fan, and sat in his recliner watching the morning news. Around 9am a phone call came in, shattering the solitude of the morning with the low rumble of vibrations from where his phone rested on the coffee table.

"Hello?" Leeroy answered. "Who is this?"

"Hi, my name is Darcine with Professional Jester Placement Services. I'm looking to speak with Leeroy, is now a good time?"

"Speaking. Uh, sure, how did you get my number?" asked Leeroy.

"Oh, we've had our eyes on your career as Bumble the Clown for some time now! We know of the tragic incident at the rodeo, and while that's been a major loss for the rodeo, we see it as an opportunity to recruit fantastic talent that might be undervalued, such as yourself. You can do so much better than being an average clown for hire. We have a potential set of contracting opportunities coming up and feel you would be perfect. And, of course, we pay handsomely! Our clients always pay us well for top-tier performers. Are you interested?"

"I... I don't know what to say."

Leeroy was nearly speechless due to being so flattered.

"I didn't know my career had been so well known, or that someone of my talents would be in demand enough for a recruitment call."

"Oh yes, we can use all the help we can get!" Darcine replied. "We're juggling lots of entertaining opportunities—*pun intended*—and we can't keep enough positions filled due to demand. Today is your lucky day!"

Leeroy was impressed.

"Ok. I'm in. What would the next step look like?"

The two spoke at length of details and arranged an interview. The interview would provide a chance to meet other clowns in their employment, taking the form of an in-person opportunity to showcase Leeroy's skills during a paid event. This initial gig would act as a trial employment, and if all went satisfactory, there would be a bonus fee structure and a permanent scheduling of events Leeroy would be able to work indefinitely going forward.

At last, Leeroy thought, *some stable income and a future beyond the rodeo!*

The days leading up to the trial and interview flew past for Leeroy. Pulling out all the stops (not to mention blowing his budget)—Leeroy invested in a premium set of face paint supplies, as well as an upgraded pair of cowboy boots for Bumble's clown outfit. Arriving ten minutes early, Leeroy parked next to what appeared to be an abandoned warehouse in the old industrial district of the city.

GPS says this must be it. I hope this is for real and isn't some gimmick.

Leeroy glanced around nervously, noting trash blowing through the parking lot, not unlike apocalyptic tumbleweeds. Stepping out of his car, Leeroy caught a glimpse of what used to call this warehouse home back in its heyday: the words "DELFIRE OPTICS MANUFACTURING" were rotting away from the side of the brick and metal exterior, paired with a previously colorful—now drab—caricature of a smiling magician holding a box.

"Well, hello there friend!" arose a booming voice from directly behind Leeroy.

Leeroy jumped a bit as he turned around, clearly startled by the unexpected proximity of the voice. Before him was a clown dressed in Victorian era clothing, complete with coat tails, a top hat and a cane.

"The names Vance, Vance the Victorian!" the clown announced, and stuck out his hand for a greeting shake. "And you must be Bumble the Rodeo Clown?"

"Yours truly."

Leeroy met Vance's hand for the greeting. Immediately—a shock went up Leeroy's arm, painful enough for him to accidentally curse out loud.

Vance howled with laughter.

"It's not every day you meet a humble Bumble!"

Vance grinned and then displayed the buzzer hidden in his right hand as the source of the shocking exchange.

"Forgive my juvenile introduction; shall we be off to meet with the others?"

Leeroy nodded, a bit shaken by the prank, but otherwise intact.

As the pair walked around the far side of the building exterior, they came across a newer van with some modifications that had been themed as a clown car. Vance pointed as two more clowns joined them at the vehicle.

"May I introduce Merry the Mentalist and Sledgehammer Sam."

Merry's clown outfit seemed to be themed around a crazy lab doctor, while Sam's was more of a sledgehammer-meets-mime affair. The parties exchanged pleasantries and then began to load themselves into the van.

Leeroy turned back toward his vehicle.

"Oh, I need to grab my props for the event!"

"You won't need them!" Vance replied rather hastily.

"We need to get going right now or we'll miss our moment! You'll not be doing your normal routine tonight; this event requires a group performance!"

Leeroy turned, his posture reflecting his confusion.

"Should I have prepared anything? Did I miss some communication on the plan for tonight?"

Merry broke in, clearly ready to get on the road.

"Improvisation. This is a test of your abilities tonight. Consider adaptation and flexibility to be part of the gig."

Sam and Vance enthusiastically nodded in agreement.

Once all four clowns were seated in the vehicle, they were on their way. It was starting to get dark, and Leeroy wondered what type of event he would be performing at. He spent much of the drive reassuring himself that he was ready for whatever comic genius would be required of him for entertainment purposes.

Vance leaned toward Bumble and in a low voice began explaining what the night entailed: A client had hired the team to surprise a few guests with an inspiring message. The night would include a surprise entrance to a gathering, and then performing some sleight of hand magic for entertainment. Finally, they would be required to deliver the client's well wishes and capture the guest's reactions for social media.

Leeroy mulled over these details.

It all seems straightforward enough, although a bit hokey for the typical corporate get-together. Entertaining adults is a bit difficult, especially when they don't expect you. But pay is pay, I guess. I'm not complaining.

"You know how to do a quick card trick, don't you?" Vance asked Bumble.

"Absolutely." Leeroy responded.

Vance continued, handing Leeroy a custom deck of cards.

"We need you to take this deck, and whatever happens, we need the volunteer to draw the queen of hearts. They should sign the card or something like that to add the full trick effect. Have them put it back in the deck, do your thing, and make sure they get it back."

"Will do. Pretty easy trick."

"That's what I want to hear from our newest talent, Bumble!"

Vance then looked out the windows.

"We're almost at the location. Now, here is where things get a little fun: the guests will be leaving dinner and walking through a shopping district, totally unsuspecting. The volunteer for the magic trick needs to be a specific young woman—you'll recognize her because she'll be wearing a blue dress with a butterfly necklace, and she'll be near the main fountain. This individual is the whole reason for the celebration today, and our client really wants to make sure her day is extra special. You'll walk up, offer up the magic trick posing as a street performer, and then come back to our van. We have our own similar roles to play as entertainers, and then once the surprise is over, we'll pack up and call it a night. Super short and simple, and the client will really be delighted."

"That's it?" Leeroy asked in disbelief.

"Yep-a-roo," joked Vance in a western John Wayne accent. "Now go rope yourself the young lady we are to entertain!"

And with that, Leeroy began walking from the parking garage where the clown car was parked and headed to the outdoor strip mall where he could find the guests he was tasked with entertaining. The night was warm. Lights were strung between the various shops, illuminating the walkways and happy passersby. Couples on dates, teenagers out having a good time and catching a movie, a night out for friends shopping together. Leeroy noted that although it was warm and humid this evening, there was a sweet smell in the air.

What an odd gig on such a wonderful evening.

As Leeroy continued toward the main fountain, he would wave at various groups strolling by with children that made positive eye contact.

Making people happy is why I became a clown.

This evening's walk among the shoppers while in costume as Bumble was reigniting his passion and love for why he chose the profession in the first place.

The fountain wasn't too far from the parking garage and was located in the center of the shopping district. Various restaurants surrounded it, with multiple shopping corridors extending from the main fountain area, not unlike the spokes of a wheel. Stone angels sat atop the fountain, attempting to empty their stoneware of water contents into the pool below—a task that seemed to never reach its conclusion. Multiple groups stood around the fountain, some taking photos, others basking in the fun of the evening.

Leeroy searched the crowds in the area until he spotted a young woman wearing a blue dress. She was accompanied by two young men, one wearing a varsity jacket and the other a pair of sunglasses, despite the dark hour, combined with a fashionable denim jacket. Leeroy put himself into character for the upcoming introduction. As he approached, Leeroy assessed that this crowd would be more of the teenage range.

"May I ask what the special occasion today is?" Bumble asked in a clearly over-the-top southern accent.

The three individuals turned to see the odd figure of Bumble the rodeo clown, colorful boots and all.

"Oh my God!" the young man in the varsity jacket cackled toward the young woman in the blue dress. "Did your mom hire the awful clown from your little brother's party to ruin our date to the formal!?"

"*Shit*, you're not joking, it's the same guy! But he has flashier boots now!" the sunglass wearing teen added, smirking.

Leeroy was speechless for a moment, realizing that the young girl in the blue dress wearing a butterfly necklace was, in fact, Mrs. Jacobson's teen daughter, Heather.

How could this be?

Leeroy started to panic.

Have I been set up, or pranked myself?

"Is that you, Bumble? Did my mom put you up to this?" Heather asked in an equally irritated and astonished tone.

Realizing that he was more than likely being watched and could miss his employment opportunity if he messed this interaction up, Leeroy played along.

"I'm unsure of who wanted to make this day so special for you! Rather than concern ourselves with that, my job is to delight you with a little magic trick this evening! Would you kindly draw a card? Any card!"

With a flick of his wrist, Leeroy produced the special deck of cards that Vance had provided him. Ensuring that the card Heather drew was the queen of hearts, Bumble allowed her to take the card and show it to her companions without revealing the card to him (although he already knew what she held). "Please sign your name or write something identifiable on the card," Bumble instructed, extending a small pen with a sunflower on the end of it.

Heather looked at both her friends, and then giggled as she wrote something privately on the card. She showed the writing to both the young men, each laughing and shoving each other as they were shown the card. Heather then placed the card facedown back into the deck, confident that what was coming would be well worth the wait.

"Alright, let's find that card!" Leeroy hollered, gaining a bit of an audience as others from the fountain came walking up to see what all the fuss was about.

Leeroy then executed a couple of trademark Bumble card shuffles—even the one where he made part of the deck pop up from one hand into the other before a shower of cards were intermixed and then cut by his left hand. Bumble was known in earlier days for his smooth sleight of hand, and he poured his years of polish into this moment.

"Ok, is this your card?" Leeroy asked, flipping over the top card to reveal a six of clubs.

"Not even close." Heather scoffed, beginning to grow tired of the moment, ready to move on with her evening.

Bumble the clown then executed another shuffle and then another card reveal—with the same result.

"That doesn't seem right."

Bumble then clasped the deck in both hands and shook it rigorously.

Approaching the denim and sunglass teen, Bumble announced, "I give up. Can you please find the card?"

"Sure thing, cowboy."

Heather's all-too-cool companion searched the deck backwards and forwards, but to no avail.

"It's not in here," the young man griped, showcasing a spread of the cards to both Heather and her date.

"This trick *blows*." Heather's date in the varsity jacket replied.

Bumble motioned toward the young athlete's pants pocket.

"Check your wallet! Maybe you'll find what we're looking for there?"

Reluctant at first, the crowd had gathered in such a way that there was immense pressure on the young man to play along. In addition to cheers from the crowd, even Heather's interest at this point had peaked. Not wanting to seem like a chicken, the young man quickly produced his wallet and opened it. Unbelievably, seated between the cash he planned to use for tips as their night unfolded, was a solitary playing card. Pulling it from his wallet, and to the amazement of the crowd—as well as Heather—he covertly showed it to her, and she immediately confirmed that the card was indeed her card.

The crowd roared with applause and excitement at the moment, all three companions in disbelief.

"Now reveal the card to the audience so they can indeed see you signed the card." Bumble instructed.

Heather crossed her arms and changed her posture, leaning back on one heal as she raised her right arm and held the card up, the card back facing everyone. She rotated the card to reveal its face, and sure enough, it was the queen of hearts.

Unfortunately for Leeroy, this joyful moment was cut short, as both he and everyone in the audience could hear Heather read aloud what she wrote on the card. In big letters diagonally across the card Heather had written:

BUMBLE THE CLOWN FUMBLES WITH CHILDREN

The audience roared with laughter. Parents quickly ushered their kids away from the gathered crowd—desiring their children not to catch on to what was being inferred. Teens documented this moment with their phones on social media. Many snickered and kept their distance from Leeroy as the moment began to pass.

"Fantastic parting gift." Heather said, as she tucked the playing card into her clutch. "Excellent entertainment value as well."

She smirked, turning to follow the two young men now walking away.

Leeroy was devastated. Humiliated. Everything in him felt like he was sinking like a stone.

I could just drown right now in this fountain. That would end it.

Leeroy began making his way back to the parking garage, consumed by his thoughts. Unsure of how he was going to explain tonight's events to his new employer, Leeroy began resigning himself to what would undoubtedly be his fate: a lack of passing this initial trial and the continued financial burdens that would ensue. As Leeroy lifted his head, he realized that he had made it all the way back to the garage. He took the immediate set of stairs to the right and ended up on the second floor of the parking structure where the van was parked. Nobody was around in the parking structure. Thankfully, the van had been left unlocked, so Leeroy opened the door, seated himself in the vehicle, and then closed the door.

Leeroy checked his phone to see if any further communication had come from the team for the night. Just at that moment, Leeroy heard familiar laughs echo through the garage. As Leeroy looked up from his phone, he watched as Heather and her two companions walked toward their parked truck and unlocked it, disabling the vehicle's alarm. None of the teens had noticed the clown themed van, or Bumble, sitting in the front of the vehicle, just feet away.

As Heather's date opened up the driver's side door to his truck, the door was slammed shut by Merry—who was staring at him with a hollow gaze. Merry had his other hand in one of his lab coat pockets and quickly rushed forward— pulling a knife from his pocket and plunging it repetitively into the soft exterior of the jock's varsity jacket. The young man made a disturbing sucking noise as his lungs were clearly punctured and as blood began soaking the jacket he so idolized. As the athlete fell to the ground, eyes filled with terror, gasping his last breaths—Heather screamed and fell to her knees. Her sunglass sporting friend grabbed Heather by the shoulder and pulled her back, trying to collect her for an attempted sprint to safety.

Merry smiled, holding the bloody knife up, and with a flaming flash, the knife became a red rose—one which was tossed at Heather's feet. Leeroy, in a state of shock and panic himself, jumped out of the van.

"Get out of here—RUN!" Leeroy shouted.

The remaining two teens were terrified by the appearance of Bumble the Clown, and momentarily forgot about Merry behind them as they faced Bumble in front of the clown car. It was at this moment that Merry produced a Yo-Yo and did a small cradle trick before whipping the toy around the remaining young man's neck.

Heather looked up and screamed as she realized her friend was in the suffocating grip of a killer clown. Heather turned to bolt away just as Leeroy charged in to help. Heather used her clutch as a whip and hit Leeroy squarely in the groin—wrongly perceiving him as a threat.

Leeroy fell to the ground quickly while crying out loud, "I'm trying to help!"

Heather bolted down the row of cars, screaming all the way. She had made it almost to the stairs when a cane popped out from behind a vehicle and tripped her—causing her to hit her head on the pavement.

"The entertainment is not over yet, young lady!" Vance announced gleefully as he arose from his hiding spot, his cane in one hand, a phone recording in the other. Vance quickly moved between Heather and the stairs, creating a blockade of her exit strategy.

Heather rose slightly disoriented from the fall, blood dripping from her forehead. As her eyes darted around the garage looking for an escape, she spotted the elevator to her left and began a dash toward it.

"Ah, good, a bit of sport!"

Vance laughed, as he continued recording with one hand while tossing his cane with the other. Vance used his one free hand to pull an old-fashioned revolver from his Victorian coat, and waved it wildly towards Heather, then began firing.

Leeroy had barely gathered himself and stood up during all of this, when Merry approached him, holding a gun withdrawn from his other pocket.

"Great job improvising Bumble! Her friend would have been a tad more difficult had you not distracted him!"

Merry glanced at the chaos evolving with Vance and Heather and told Bumble to stay put, motioning with his pistol for emphasis.

"Don't want the new recruit making a rookie mistake, you need a little more training first."

Leeroy glanced back at Heather and Vance, unable to help and in a state of shock at what was unfolding before him.

Vance fired his revolver multiple times all around Heather, as if he was intentionally trying to miss her with his bullets. Heather reached the elevator crying, mashing the button endlessly, hoping for safety.

"And *what* is behind door number one?" Vance joyfully announced, dropping his revolver and grabbing his top hat while dancing toward Heather's location.

When the parking garage elevator doors opened, Heather wasn't sure which she recognized first: the mime, or the silver glint of an axe the clown swung down through the opening doors at her. As horror filled Heather's eyes, Sam's axe landed directly into her chest cavity with the disturbing sound of a *thwap* while Vance and Merry shouted with applause. Heather sank to the concrete pavement, an axe embedded in her chest. As she lay bleeding out and dying, her last memory was that of the mime's shoes, and an old piece of gum from weeks before, most likely discarded and stepped on until it became a permanent fixture of the parking garage floor.

Leeroy let out a soft cry. A broken man, in all but decency. This moment he knew must be his last. There was no way he would live to tell this tale. These clowns would surely kill him and frame him to blame for the carnage of this night. Even if he did survive this night of evil laughter, no police officer in their right mind would seek to uncover his innocence.

His life, career, and world at this point were forfeit.

Merry smiled and waited quietly as Vance and Sam made their way to join them.

"Why so glum?" Vance sarcastically questioned, as he pointed the still-filming smartphone in Bumble's direction.

"The clown of the hour, Bumble! Only the best in entertainment for our clients!"

"Why?" Leeroy asked. "Why *me*? Why *them*? Why *this*?"

"He doesn't get it. Please spell it out for him." Merry sighed, rubbing his painted forehead.

"Oh alright." Vance quipped, stopping the recording on his phone and pocketing the device. "Our client hired us for their entertainment. We all performed exactly as expected..."

Vance then paused to raise an eyebrow.

"...some even better than expected. Our client wanted to make it clear the clown profession should be respected, and that anyone publicly attacking our line of work must face the most serious of consequences. The loss of Mrs. Jacobson's daughter drives that point home pretty clearly, now wouldn't you say?"

"You are all monsters!" Leeroy shouted, tears welling up in his eyes.

"Indeed." Vance replied, "We are monsters, magicians, maniacs, and jokers—all true and valid perspectives. While some clowns delight, some clowns fright! But either way... we always entertain. Nobody ever walks away from us without experiencing the highest art-form performance, the act of a fool."

While Vance was orating his perspective on the profession of clowning, Leeroy was planning his escape.

Too many guns and weapons present. Can't overpower them. Can't outrun them here. Best opportunity would be to take my chances jumping over the edge of the parking garage. I'll take my odds landing in public view, as these murderers will want to get away from the scene of the crime. A life in prison is still a life, and maybe I can help get these homicidal fools locked away once I'm in custody and can tell all I know. To the edge of the garage. Now!

Leeroy ran from the very startled three clown companions, clearly caught off guard that Bumble would attempt an escape after the killer talents displayed moments earlier. Merry raised his handgun at Leeroy as he ran, but Vance put his hand over Merry's raised aim, telling him to *cool it*.

Vance shouted at Leeroy, "Bumble, where exactly do you think you can go that we can't reach you? You passed the interview; your financial troubles are over!"

Leeroy made it to the ledge and threw all his weight into hopping over the side.

L eeroy was witnessed in security footage landing on the pavement just outside the parking garage as a driver rounded the corner and accidentally hit him. The driver noted in the police report that he was shocked to find a random clown diving into the road from above.

Other than footage of Leeroy's jump, no evidence of foul play, security footage from the garage, or witnesses could shed light on the events of that night. The three teens were never found, and despite a community campaign to find them, it was as if they had just disappeared. Police even had the teen's truck searched for prints, but to no avail. The authorities eagerly awaited a discussion with Leeroy as to the events of that evening, but as the days passed, Leeroy remained in a coma, and his health continued to deteriorate.

It was about a month after the events of that violent night when Leeroy passed away. Nurses found nothing out of the ordinary about Leeroy's passing, save one playing card tucked into his bedsheets. It was a joker card.

The day after Leeroy passed, Mrs. Jacobson received a suspicious envelope. In the envelope was a bloody butterfly necklace, a queen of hearts playing card, and a photo of Heather's clearly deceased face wearing the red nose of a clown.

THE SPELL

UNNATURAL. COUNTERFEIT.

LOVE.

"**A**re you sure you want me to cast this?" Sandra asked, unsure if Kimberly understood all that would follow. "This spell is potent, the kind I cannot reverse once it goes into effect."

Kimberly nodded, eager to begin.

"And you have a possession of his to bind this spell to?"

Kimberly quickly produced Jeff's ring: a custom mix of titanium, wood, and stone that he purchased as a souvenir on his family trip to Oahu last year.

Sandra took the ring and placed it upon the altar, along with a photograph of Jeff.

Kimberly had recently taken the photo with her favorite retro camera the week before. Initially, the snapshot made her laugh, but now...

The photo made Kimberly sad—her heart sinking while looking at Jeff's all-too-perfect smile.

The room was shuttered in darkness with candles lit all around. The flickering of the dim lighting reflected off Jeff's ring and photo. Sandra cast the spell, waving her hands about with her eyes closed—seemingly using all her mental and spiritual might to channel some unseen power upon the object placed before her. The process was quite involved, taking nearly ten minutes to complete; eventually her work came to an end and Sandra's eyes met Kimberly's watchful gaze.

"The spell is cast. Give Jeff the ring and wait for him to put it back on. Once he has placed it on his hand, the spell will begin working. Due to the spell's power of attachment, he will instinctively avoid taking it off. However, upon removing the ring from his person and presence, Jeff will slowly return to his former self."

The Spell

Sandra glanced through the various pages of research and incantations she had used for the spell. Casting a worried glance at Kimberly, she raised a note of caution and warning.

"Think this decision over carefully. You can keep the ring for as long as you like before pursuing this, and honestly, you could just bury the ring in the event you do not need it. Natural love is so much deeper and purer than the unnatural counterfeit I have conjured here."

Kimberly snatched the photo and ring, quickly paying Sandra for her services. As she left the darkened home, the New Orleans bright sunlight beat down upon her. For all the dim lighting and cold air conditioning inside Sandra's witch-for-hire residence, it was the opposite experience outside on this hot and humid day in July. It was not long into the walk back to her car before Kimberly removed her cardigan and donned designer sunglasses; the brightness and heat emitting from the pavement was almost unbearable.

Unlocking her small commuter vehicle, Kimberly tossed her purse and cardigan into the passenger seat before closing the driver-side door and turning the ignition. Hot air blasted from the automobile vents as she fiddled with the climate controls, turning them as cold as possible while waiting for sweet, sweet, air-conditioned relief.

Waiting for the air to cool in the vehicle's cabin, Kimberly took out Jeff's ring and inspected it. The band looked as it had before Sandra put her powers to work: a titanium loop that held a wooden inlay with a pattern simulating the ocean horizon and a small stone representing the sun. A one-of-a-kind piece—Jeff was never seen without it, that is, until now.

Jeff had left the ring on Kimberly's counter by accident after helping her fix a leak that had threatened to ruin the small apartment where she resided. The likely reason he managed to forget it was the argument that followed the repair—he chose then to reveal he was breaking up their budding relationship of three months, all because his ex called him crying and wanted him back.

The freaking nerve of it!

Kimberly fumed, tossing the ring and photo back into her purse.

What makes Jeff think she won't just cheat on him again, for the billionth time? Meanwhile leaving ME, after a perfectly great three months?

With cooler air now circulating her vehicle, Kimberly made the trip back to her apartment. After making herself a spread of cheeses and veggies, Kimberly cracked a bottle of Sauvignon Blanc open. She texted Jeff, reminding him that she had a few of his belongings. He made arrangements to collect them, provided she would give him the opportunity to explain himself further. Kimberly accommodated this request.

It couldn't hurt, given my activities with Sandra earlier today.

About an hour later, Jeff graced the front door of her small apartment. After talking things over, it appeared Jeff had come to his senses. He had decided to permanently break things off with his ex, as Kimberly was far better for him, or so he explained. Kimberly expressed how hurt she was that Jeff could have even considered returning to his ex, but eventually, seeing as Jeff seemed genuinely apologetic, Kimberly agreed to continue seeing him and the two spent the evening together drinking and watching old classic movies.

In the weeks that followed, Kimberly sighed a bit of relief over not having to use the ring Sandra had enchanted. She hid the ring deep in her closet, and never made mention of it to Jeff as the days went by. She assumed Sandra was right: true love was indeed a much better alternative than something manufactured through a spell.

The weeks turned to months, and the months a year. Kimberly and Jeff went to a delicious seafood restaurant in the French Quarter to celebrate a year of dating each other, and Jeff surprised Kimberly with an impromptu trip to Europe. All seemed as it should be. It wasn't until a friend sent a set of incriminating images to Kimberly that their relationship came into question again.

Kimberly cried for two days straight. The pictures were of Jeff and his ex out at a bar dancing; it just so happened Kimberly's friend was at the very same location and had caught them together. Had it not been for this chance encounter, she would have never known Jeff had been covertly seeing his ex on the side.

Kimberly decided then and there that she was going to dump Jeff.

That is, until she remembered the existence of his old ring.

Why should this woman get to win and destroy us? Kimberly rationalized.

What do I have to lose? Jeff will pay for his betrayal by being forced to remain loyal to me, and his ex will have to deal with the pain of being permanently shut out of his life. It's a win-win in my book.

And so, the following day, she presented him with his lost ring. Jeff, unaware of that she knew anything of his cheating, was all too excited to get the ring back and quickly placed it on his finger. Kimberly carefully observed Jeff for any noticeable difference, but nothing apparent changed in either his mood or behavior. Pondering if Sandra the witch had scammed her, Kimberly broke the news of what evidence she had discovered to Jeff. Swiping through photos— she began the process of breaking up with him, scolding and swearing as she fumed over this betrayal.

Jeff fell to his knees, weeping and begging for her forgiveness. He immediately called his ex, explaining how deeply in love with Kimberly he was, and how she meant nothing to him compared to Kimberly. Clearly in shock, Jeff's ex broke into tears, shouting about how he had lied to her about leaving Kimberly. She wished Kimberly luck with this pathetic man and she hung up on him.

Satisfied with herself, Kimberly offered Jeff the door and told him she would be in touch if she decided he was worth her time. Jeff left, broken and in a state of depression and despair that she had never witnessed before.

Well done, Kim! she congratulated to herself.

The following day, roses appeared en masse on her doorstep. Kimberly noted how well the spell must be working, as Jeff called and left voicemails multiple times throughout the day. That night, she decided to call him back, and made plans to go out to dinner the following evening.

At dinner, Jeff asked Kimberly to move out of her apartment and move in with him. As she considered this request, Jeff got down on one knee and presented an engagement ring, asking for her hand in marriage. Swept with emotion and reflecting on the prior year of happiness, Kimberly said *yes*. She threw caution to the wind as the spell would guarantee Jeff's faithfulness, and despite concern from her friend who had caught Jeff cheating, Kimberly began planning for the wedding.

Jeff wanted the wedding to take place as soon as possible, so the date was set ninety days out and the overall guest list was kept small. After considering multiple venues, they decided upon a small beachside chapel on Oahu, and sent invites. The wedding day came quickly, and most in attendance perceived the couple happy and deeply in love.

With the wedding behind them, Kimberly settled into Jeff's house comfortably, busying herself outside of work with painting accent walls and swapping out furniture to her taste. Before long, Jeff's home began to look like *their* home, and Kimberly was pleased. Jeff's ex stopped by once teary eyed, begging for him to reconsider their relationship, but Kimberly had the pleasure of watching Jeff tell his ex to get off their property.

The spell had worked wonders, and Kimberly was all too happy to revel in her accomplishment.

The optimism Kimberly initially had began to fade over time, however. What started off as picture-perfect transformed into a nightmare day by day. First, it was Jeff's requests that she take more time off work and spend more time at home. Then it was Jeff's desire to have kids and for Kimberly to get pregnant as soon as possible. Jeff pressured her for sex constantly, and to Kimberly, it felt as if his thirst for her attention was unquenchable. After arguments with him where she refused to stop birth control, he would storm out of their bedroom, only to run back into the room moments later, claiming how attracted to her and in love with her he was.

Jeff's focus on her beauty was overwhelming. Soon he pressured Kimberly on what she should wear, how she should style her hair, and even what jewelry to wear for the day. Next, Jeff micromanaged her schedule: who she could spend time with, where she went, and for how long. Along with this came financial pressures about how much they saved together, what they would invest in for their future, and how little Kimberly was allowed to spend out shopping.

Before long, Jeff began controlling everything about Kimberly's life—from where she spent her time to what she did with it. Their relationship had become *obsessive* on Jeff's part at best, *abusive* at worst. The toxicity angered Kimberly greatly, especially when they argued about these things and Jeff would claim it was all "out of love" and that "she showed him how much she loved him by how she submitted to his leadership and decision-making."

Whenever Kimberly rejected Jeff's preference, Jeff made it known by escalating to the physical: slamming doors, threats, and trying to intimidate her with his presence.

The irony of these moments was that the spell held fast and powerful; the instant Jeff would take such abusive actions, he would immediately apologize and profess his undying love for her.

Kimberly eventually sought out advice from Sandra, the witch, as things kept getting worse.

Sandra looked on, knowingly disappointed at the situation, and reminded Kimberly, "I warned you, unnatural love manufactured by a spell is impure and shallow. I cannot reverse this spell even if I wanted to; your best bet would be to get the ring from Jeff and make certain that he can never find it again."

Kimberly let Sandra's words resonate as she considered her next move.

By the next day, Kimberly had a plan.

Jeff sat upon the warm coastal sand of the Gulf, smiling in the setting sun after a day of fun on the beach. Kimberly had convinced him to have a little outing so they could make some good memories, and Jeff was more than eager to call out of work and enjoy the day off.

Taking his hand in her own, Kimberly caressed Jeff's hand and asked him to close his eyes. He raised an eyebrow, questioning her for a moment, but she persisted, promising something good was on the way. Jeff closed his eyes, and Kimberly quickly slid the ring from his finger. She stood up and quickly sprinted into the crashing waves, tossing it into the ocean.

Jeff was horrified, shrieking as he ran from their spot in the sand, at once diving into the surf to search for the ring. After a few minutes, he came back, visibly upset, unable to recover his prized possession. Kimberly put her arm around Jeff and told him she loved him. She apologized for the "prank gone terribly wrong"—lying to him about never intending to let the ring slip out of her hand—and claimed that it was an accident. Kimberly asked for his forgiveness, telling him that she "learned her lesson," and promised to buy Jeff a new ring on their next trip to the Hawaiian Islands.

Depressed and defeated, Jeff nodded and gave her a hug, telling her he forgave her, but that he was still disappointed and upset at the loss.

Kimberly watched as Jeff drove home, noticing him relax considerably compared to how he had been acting under the spell. With the enchantment broken, there was nothing forcing Jeff's obsession-fueled love to remain, and although she worried what that might do to his desire to remain married to her, the alternative was much more valuable: Kimberly would soon have her life and freedom back.

As the weeks passed from the loss of the enchanted ring, Jeff returned to his former self, quickly becoming the person he was when they had only been dating. The more Kimberly thought about it, the more she preferred this version of the man she had fallen for. The risk to Kimberly of losing Jeff to infidelity paled in comparison to the controlling toxicity of what the spell had done to him as a person. That ring had such a negative impact on her life through his spellbound abuse—Jeff always controlling her and acting out aggressively in the name of "love"—that Kimberly was at peace with the possibility of heartbreak on the horizon.

A year went by and eventually Kimberly became aware of an affair that Jeff had begun with one of his new coworkers. After she calmly confronted him on it, the two decided it felt best to divorce and go their own ways. Kimberly accepted this result; maybe now she could finally move on from the mistake of casting a love spell over a man who was not worthy of her heart in the first place.

The Spell

A few more years went by, and Kimberly married a new, better man—one that genuinely loved and valued her. She became a better woman herself by not using spells to keep such a man around. The pair decided to have a child on Kimberly's terms, all without setting aside her career goals or personal preferences.

Her life had taken an incredibly positive turn.

One night, after tucking her daughter into bed upstairs and kissing her on the forehead, Kimberly heard her home doorbell ring.

Odd that someone would be coming by so late in the evening, she thought to herself.

Calling down, Kimberly asked her husband who it was. She became hyper aware and concerned when her husband did not respond. Kimberly walked down the stairs to find her husband unconscious on the floor—a pool of blood growing from under his head—and the front door of her home wide open.

A sound from behind her made Kimberly turn fast enough that she almost lost her balance. There stood what appeared to be a surf bum with a blood-stained crowbar in one hand, and Kimberly's framed family photo in the other.

"How could you love this man?" the beach bum cried in disbelief, pointing at her unconscious husband with the end of his weapon. "I've loved you since the moment I saw you crossing the street when you were taking your daughter to school. My love is deeper than anything this guy could have ever offered you. I'll be a better father to your little girl than he would have ever been."

The stranger then grinned sheepishly, standing there in his flip-flops and worn clothing, his sun-stained skin peeling, long hair with curls swaying as he tossed her family picture—shattering it upon the wall. Kimberly screamed as the man advanced to grab her arm.

On the man's hand was Jeff's old, enchanted ring.

THE KINGDOM OF VUDOR AND
THE DEMON OF HOLLOW'S KEEP

THIS JESTER IN A CROWN.

Young Wesley and his father had ventured as far East as any dare go. Wesley's father, a merchant, made a humble living by ferrying spices from kingdom to kingdom. You could say he was well-educated and well-traveled. Young Wesley, however, was just coming of age, and as such joined his father on this trip to assist, learning the family business as the days went by.

On one particular stop for the evening, the father and son found themselves on the eastern rim of their business territory—this was as far as young Wesley had ever traveled with his father. As their wagon and horses slowed to a halt, Wesley gazed out on the eastern horizon. As his father hitched their horses to a tree nearby, Wesley could see the peaks and valleys in the distance from their position on the edge of Wellshire Crest. The land looked barren and forsaken spread out before him, all seemed as if covered in shadow. There were dark clouds in the distance around the mountains that rose to the east. Wesley's imagination struck in this moment, imagining the mountains as stone guardians of the unknown beyond. Wind gusted past young Wesley and sent a shiver up his spine.

"Father, can we get a fire going? I can't help but feel it will be a trifle cold this evening." the young boy queried.

The temperature was dropping quickly. Wesley's father nodded in agreement, and the two of them built a fire more suited to a larger company of men, but all the more toasty and enjoyable on this cold overlook. After a simple hot meal of bean stew and cabbage, Wesley spoke up, inquiring about the barren wasteland that lay before them.

"Father, what happened to the people in the old kingdom of Vudor? Why do so many avoid going this far east?"

The merchant fell silent and shifted his gaze from the flames of their warm fire to the frigid cold mountains to the east. After a few moments of silence, his gaze met young Wesley's.

"As to your second question, nothing but death waits for anyone in the territory beyond those peaks."

"And to my first question?" the young Wesley asked, curious as to what had happened.

Wesley's father looked down at the earth beneath his boot, picked up a handful of dirt, and let it slowly pass through his fingers. Letting out a large sigh, he replied: "The old kingdom of Vudor was destroyed by both a mad king and a powerful demon. The eastern lands are best forgotten. Their tale is one of arrogance and selfishness; a people who sought salvation in the fortunes of a fool they made their king. A king who empowered a great evil for his own gain. And a people who embraced the unspeakable for the sake of their king."

As the wind whipped around Wellshire Crest, no amount of crackle from the fire could drown out the sound of a moan, emanating just beyond the deep ravines at the feet of those stone guardians—those ice peaked mountains that created a natural barrier to Vudor. The frigid breeze of night set upon their camp. With no light source except the popping fire before them and the expanse of stars overhead, the merchant then began telling young Wesley of the fall of the Kingdom of Vudor.

The Kingdom of Vudor was once a pinnacle of innovation, filled with men of virtue. Even the poorest in the kingdom were the envy of other kingdoms, as the noble minds had a philosophy of goodwill for all within their borders. King after king had served the people faithfully and generously. It was said other leaders in the lands to the west placed their joint prosperity in the leadership of Vudor, for it was said, "Upon the throne of Vudor other kingdoms look for guiding light."

Vudor was also known for its excellence across many trades. The most amazing sorcerers, alchemists, warriors, blacksmiths, poets and studied scholars were among its citizens. The Knights of Bothemiere had even managed to train wild dragons to assist in their defense of Vudor. It used to be that you could see the watchtowers lit just beyond the peaks to the east; and in the sky above you would perchance find a dragon patrolling the perimeter of their lands. It was a wonder to see—a true marvel of achievement.

All of their leadership, talent, philosophies, and worldviews pooled over time in Vudor, creating a truly unique kingdom that was simply one-of-a-kind. Those with less opportunity—the young and the old from other kingdoms—flocked to Vudor to join such an exemplary society. The people of Vudor were known to be compassionate and of good heart. Most people, from nobility down to the common man, would consider service to others before themselves.

But it wasn't always to be.

It was winter in the Kingdom of Vudor, and the cold crept into the grand hallways of the King's castle, not unlike the skeletal hand of death itself. A great sickness overcame the King that season, and he ultimately passed away as he slept into the night. When the kingdom awoke the next day, never had such great mourning filled the land.

"Whatever shall we do? What shall now become of our beloved lands?" many cried out upon hearing the news.

You see, the King did not have an heir.

Men of ambition had rather little say in these matters without noble backing. Outside of the royal guard, all knights and troops were pledged to the great noble houses. Naturally, the nobility was going to decide the next in line for the throne. Many an influential knight had considered taking the throne by force, but few could gather enough men without financing to challenge the royal guard—much less the remaining noble houses. It's both fortunate and unfortunate that this was the case for the Kingdom of Vudor: fortunate because it kept order and avoided bloodshed; unfortunate because *wealth* was the real power that directed who could ascend to the throne.

The people of Vudor were at peace with this reality. Nobility in the kingdom was rumored to have considerable virtue, for how else were they so wise as to acquire their wealth and status? Most simply went along without question.

The nobilities' leadership had worked exemplary thus far in Vudor's history, bringing the kingdom great prosperity! Why question it now?

And so it was. The noble houses of Vudor had extensive wealth that had been amassed over generations. Protecting their wealth and position during this transition became of utmost importance. Infighting among the nobility would not suit the future of their lands well, and it came to be decided that who better to be king than the most financially successful person among the nobility, the Grand Duke of Auree.

The Duke of Auree was a descendant of a noble house, known for growing their vast fortune over generations in the trade and export of the finest commodities on behalf of the crown. Most in the nobility hoped their position in the kingdom would one day reflect the prestige and influence of the Grand Duke. If any in the nobility were to be a steward of their collective wealth and possessions by leading the kingdom, the Grand Duke of Auree was perceived to be the perfect choice.

The Grand Duke had the allegiance of the wealthy due to his enchanting personality, not to mention his entertaining and rather lavish parties. He commanded the endearing respect of the people—for he would often sponsor championship tournaments throughout the kingdom. The Grand Duke could often be seen celebrating his great tournaments with the common peasants during tours of his popular "warrior pits." The Grand Duke had somehow managed to be both an elite in the nobility and was seen as having a kindred spirit with the common man.

Once the noble houses all agreed to pledge allegiance to the Grand Duke of Auree as their new king—a sigh of relief swept across the lands of Vudor. No bloodshed would come of a new claim to the throne, and all that had made the kingdom glorious would be preserved and protected for the next generation.

All was as it should be, or so it seemed at the time.

The new King was thrilled to begin his reign and ushered in celebrations throughout the kingdom to commemorate the occasion. The nobility was pleased, as the King honored all existing agreements and claims to property within Vudor. In addition, the King quickly set about improving the castles and fortresses, adorning them with beautiful ornamentation such as gold and precious stones. Upon the following spring, the King gathered his royal guard and paraded village to village, just to meet his subjects and grace them with a chance to hear from their new ruler.

Oh, how the golden trumpets would blast upon his arrival!

Banners blew in the warm breeze of his stirring proclamations, and many were taken by just how charming their new monarch appeared to be.

There was, however, quite the darker truth stirring beneath appearances. The "Great" Duke of Auree, you see, had inherited the majority of his wealth and prestige through his bloodline. While generations of his forefathers had worked tirelessly to protect the family wealth, the Duke had instead spent almost all of his inheritance and was, in fact, a *fraud*. He had cheated the crown out of taxes, falsified records, and lied to just about every person in the kingdom in order to save face. Had it not been for the prior King's untimely death, the "Great Duke" was certain to be found out and beheaded, as his debts and lies came to light.

Thankfully for the Duke of Auree, both the reputation of his bloodline, and his propensity to lavish gifts upon the other noble houses, kept all suspicion away. When the nobility offered the crown, the Duke didn't see his directive as a holy responsibility to guard the kingdom, rather, he saw a solution to his debts: he could both pilfer the vast riches of the kingdom, and obtain the ultimate authority to protect his own interests. With the noble houses' unquestioning loyalty, and his popularity among his subjects, even if someone was to raise the specter of accountability, the Great Duke as King could easily spirit away any and all dissent—silencing his opposition.

For three long years, the King dug deep into the pockets of the kingdom to augment his own shrinking wealth. As the gold began running low, the King indebted the kingdom to other kingdoms through lines of credit. Soon, the King began asking his advisers for budgetary cuts to make. When the King didn't receive favorable advice, he replaced his advisors with the first fool who would reinforce his own point of view. Soon, the dragons were released from captivity, many noble armies were disbanded, outposts were abandoned—all so as to redirect the wealth of the kingdom, allowing the King more personal spending power.

The masses that migrated across the lands to join in Vudor's rumored fortunes—those who wished to become subjects of the crown—began being imprisoned and blamed for work shortages, as well as the overall financial state of the kingdom. As expected, all dissent was quickly snuffed out by the order of the King. No one dared question the King on these matters, and the King's plan to wield royal power for his own fortune worked beautifully. The King and all nobles in his favor had become extraordinarily wealthy while they leeched the riches of Vudor. All was going according to the King's plan, or so the King thought.

There was, however, one problem not yet brought to the King's attention.

The Demon of Hollow's Keep.

———

Long before the foundations of the Kingdom of Vudor, there were divisions among those lands. Smaller kingdoms were scattered across what would become Vudor, often waging war against one another. One such kingdom, the Kingdom of Yugom, had built an incredible solution to ward off incoming forces who desired to wage war. While most castles were built on hillsides with fortified towers to affront a siege, the Kingdom of Yugom built in the reverse: a castle beneath the earth, carved out of an endless web of caves underground, complete with hidden alternate routes to safety throughout the lands.

They named the place *"Hollow"*—for you could hear the air crying out as it moved hurriedly throughout the darkness of the cavern-built castle. The castle had a keep, and while traditional keeps were fortified towers that rose high above their protective walls—Hollow's Keep descended into practically an abyss. This keep was a labyrinth of treasures, with quarters built to house a king and his armies for several months during a long siege, if need be. There were even large caverns with fresh bodies of water to draw from.

Hollow's Keep was the ultimate unseen fortress of security—nearly impossible to find, navigate, much less sack. Opposing armies would be better served attempting to starve out the inhabitants, but by the time they even considered such moves, the forces of Yugom within the castle could simply use the hidden underground routes to flank, cutting off any invading forces.

So, how did the Kingdom of Yugom fall?

Simple arrogance.

Yugom chose to ride out and meet their foes directly on the battlefield. They were caught up in the great battle of Rasklot and swiftly defeated during the initial fighting. Over time, the hidden routes to and from Hollow's Keep were forgotten, and those who attempted to navigate the graven depths did so at their ultimate peril.

Soon, Hollow's Keep passed into legend as its secluded location became overgrown and lost to navigators of the landscape. Centuries passed, and eventually all kingdoms to the east of these great mountains united into the Kingdom of Vudor, all ruled by one throne and one crown.

IT IS SAID THAT THE VILE SEEK DARKNESS
TO CRAFT THEIR DEEDS.

A demon passing through those lands happened upon the keep and realized his great fortune: there could be no place on earth as deep or as dark as this submerged fortress. Needing neither food nor water, the demon took up residence in Hollow's abandoned depths. There he waited and practiced his dark arts. As generation after generation grew old, Hollow's Keep passed into a faded tale told by children, and the demon was able to grow in both might and magic—undisturbed by mere mortals for quite some time.

As fate would have it, in the third year of the new King's reign over Vudor, a band of thieves stumbled across one of the overgrown entrances that led to Hollow's Keep. These men of the dagger traversed the darkened pathways most would not attempt to navigate—seeking a den for their treachery—and perhaps hoping to stumble upon some long-forgotten treasures of the legendary kingdom of Yugom. You can imagine their shock when, after locating the Keep, they were confronted with the *current inhabitant*.

The demon wasted no time in making short work of the thieves. Rather than slaughter them, he played a rather peculiar dark magic trick: the demon at once possessed the leader of the outfit, and then through powers unbeknownst to men of that age, enchanted the other men to profess their loyalty to him.

Now taking the appearance of human form, the demon realized that this was an entertaining moment worth seizing! The demon could now put his dark arts to the test on humanity itself, through the might of these ruffians. There was little risk to him personally: for if the mortal body he now inhabited was to be killed, he could just as easily take another, and if boredom set in, he could always retreat to his palace of the depths. At once, the demon set to the task of planning the evil work to follow.

Speaking softly in the darkness of the Keep, barely lit by their torches, the demon instructed his men.

"In all tales of glory warriors long to reside, your might will be unparalleled. You will bring the people to their knees. All will either pledge allegiance to my sovereign dark spirit, or they will be cut down by you, my forces. For if you pierce their skin with your blade, you shall enchant them to follow my lead, but if any of them resist our allegiance, you shall drive your swords into their chest—and take their heads as a warning for others to tremble in fear. The death you bring will be swift and merciless. We shall ascend to rule over these lands, and even the mountains shall tremble under our wrath!"

And so it was. To those the demon had enchanted, he granted an unnatural power of strength and speed. The demon and his men emerged from Hollow's Keep, and thus began their reign of terror among those that crossed their path.

I t was not long before tales of horror from the villages reached the grand halls of the King. Vudor, it seems, was facing an unspeakable evil—and the people were crying out for something to be done.

The King stewed on the reports he was getting from scouts all over the kingdom. He sat with his advisors and discussed tactical options.

How does one fight a man with the strength of three men? And why were so many of his subjects either joining the invasion forces or being slaughtered?

The reports bewildered the King.

Despite these events, and somewhat ironically, the King was more troubled that his lavish parades and great feasts were to be canceled, rather than that his subjects were under a great threat.

"Send a garrison of troops to the farthest village west; I want to put down this petty rebellion before word spreads of a weak King!" the King commanded.

A garrison was henceforth sent to the small village of Porto. When the troops arrived, they found many heads from the village on spikes. The village was completely burned to the ground, and not a living person remained.

Where did the rest of the villagers go?

Just as the troops were ready to turn back and report on their findings, the shrill sound of screams came from all directions—the troops found themselves surrounded. By *villagers*. The people closed in on the royal troops, and a bloodbath began. The people threw themselves at the troops, and the knights cut them down, villager by villager, wave after wave.

One villager got close enough to slice a knight's hand, and in a moment of shock, the knight turned on his own fellow troops and began attempting to down his brethren. More and more of the troops started to turn on one another, and the battle would have been lost had it not been for a retreat of the remaining troops to a hillside to the east. You see, there was a set of royal archers stationed hidden behind that hill, and as the troops retreated, the archers were able to lay waste to the valley of wretched that pursued. When the fighting was over, the survivors could not believe their eyes.

Who, or what, could have driven these villagers—nay, our very own men—to turn on us so!? Something must have bewitched this place! We must bring news of these events to the King at once!

When the troops returned and informed the King, the King was very pleased.

"What great fortune!" the King shouted with glee. "What great fortune that my mighty warriors laid waste to this threat! All in the Kingdom must celebrate!"

The King's military advisors attempted to rein the King's excitement in. They advised that clearly this matter of security needed further investigation, as neither the leader of this uprising had been caught, nor had the reasoning behind the villager's actions been made known.

"Nonsense," the King jovially retorted, "this invasion has whittled down to nothing, and soon, *just like magic*, most will forget it ever happened. On with our planned feast!"

Both the military advisors and the nobility were deeply concerned by the King's attitude toward this threat, but how could they sway the King? They knew that at a moment's notice they would be tossed out of the grand halls if they lost favor with the crown. And so, all remained silent, hoping to trick the King through dropped hints and suggestions on how best to handle the situation, while aiming to remain in the King's favor.

As time went on, more and more territories within the Kingdom of Vudor fell to the Demon of Hollow's Keep and his enchanted masses. As reports came in, the King was furious—not at the news of his kingdom in flames, but at the mere suggestion that this threat existed at all. The King denied all reports coming from across the countryside, and blamed foreign kingdoms for planting false reports that made him look weak. The King claimed other kingdoms were attempting to start a panic among his subjects.

"The Kingdom of Vudor is of great honor!" The King proclaimed to his subjects. "Our ears shall not be deceived by these serpent tongues, those jealous of our prosperity! We have soundly defeated this so-called 'foe' many seasons back. Let it be known by decree of the King that anyone who speaks these rumors is a traitor to the crown. Speak not on these things further, for it will not go well with you in so doing!"

And thus, the reports of destruction stopped coming into the King's grand halls. The King's subjects fell silent, and many chose—despite evidence to the contrary—to believe their King.

The Demon of Hollow's Keep could not contain his laughter when he was brought word of these happenings.

"How could this fool, fat on his throne, really believe these things? Surely, he must have a death wish—that his subjects place his head upon their spike before I place it upon mine? That he would grip his kingdom so tight as to drain its blood before I claim its corpse? *What foolish madness.* I do wish this was a tad more difficult—pity me that I spent so long developing my skills in darkness, only to need but a spoonful to trounce this jester in a crown."

———

The demon and his troops swept the lands of Vudor. Those who did not flee either joined the demon or were beheaded. Slowly but surely, the demon and his masses closed in on the King's castle.

On one particular evening, as the King looked out on the horizon past the safety of his walls, he could hear the drumbeat of the demon's bewitched. Fear swallowed the King whole, for he had not admitted this possibility to himself all this time—that this threat could even exist. The King considered taking his royal guard and fleeing to the north, leaving the castle and its inhabitants to fend for themselves.

"Your majesty," a worn voice quietly arose from behind. "The sorcerers have created a spell that will protect whoever ingests this potion. Specifically, you will be shielded from being placed under the control of the dark spirit and from being put to death by the hands of the supernatural."

The sorcerer hobbled on his cane and outstretched his paper-thin hand, withered by age. In it was a vial of an unknown liquid.

"So, you and those silly magicians finally came up with something of value!" the King scoffed.

"Indeed, we have," the sorcerer assured, "and we can make more if you buy us time. We need another few weeks to gather ingredients, but we could protect much of the kingdom once production begins."

The King took the vial, placing it in his robe, and then with a nod sent the old man on his way. Turning to face the drums beating in the distance, the King ordered his guard to lock the gates of the castle and to prepare for battle.

The ensuing battle occurred in the dead of night. Rain beat down on the castle as lightning ripped through the sky. The gates could only hold for so long, and soon the demon and his army made their way into the throne room. Outnumbered and clearly outmatched, the King ordered his royal guard to stand down.

"Let's have a diplomatic discussion—you and I." the King said slyly to the demon.

The demon was intrigued. He could easily lay waste to what remained of the King's men and take the throne for himself, right then and there. But, given his immortality, entertainment and curiosity were of more interest than pure conquest at this moment.

What could the King possibly be up to?

"Indeed," the demon cackled, "it is time we should have a talk!" The demon smiled and then looked to the doorway behind the throne room. "Your chambers then? I would have invited you over to my place, but it's a bit of a… downer."

The demon grinned ear to ear, clearly enjoying his own humor and wit.

When the King and the demon were finally alone, the King made a proposal. "What if I were to let you roam my lands, untouched, and allow you to keep all those you desire, and kill my subjects as you please?" the King spoke, as he inspected the jewels on his rings.

The demon sat down in a nearby chair, howling with laughter. "You amaze me, dear King. I've been around since the dawn of time itself, and what a rare treat it is to be surprised. You're a nasty little creature, aren't you? *Thank you for that.*"

The demon paused for a moment to look the King over.

"So, let's say I play your little game, and I leave you, your men, and this castle alone for the time being. What then? To what end? What is in it for *you*?" the demon questioned.

"Power and wealth," the King replied, "and being the greatest King to ever rule over Vudor. That my line of succession never leaves these halls, and that songs will be sung of my wisdom."

The demon couldn't believe the arrogant stupidity of these things.

Was this King really so foolish? This King would surely die by the hand of his own subjects if he allowed a demon to destroy the kingdom's lands unchecked. No, this must be a trick.

The demon had stopped being entertained by the hubris of this fool, and now it was time to finish the evil work he had begun. The demon grabbed his sword from its hilt and grazed the King's cheek with the blade.

"You now belong to me." the demon hissed. "It's a cruel trick that you'll be ordering your subjects to the slaughter at my direction, instead of your cowardice. But fear not, your legacy will conclude the same."

"I think you've misjudged the situation." the King smirked. "You have no power here against me. I am the Great King of Vudor! If you leave my castle, it's because I'll allow it!"

And at once, the King pulled his sword and moved to stand before the exit to the room.

"Strike me if you can." the King chided.

The speed and power with which the demon swung his blade toward the King's skull was not unlike the crack of a whip. The demon, however, was horrified to find that his lethal blow could not land on the King—for it was as if some unseen force stopped his blade from impact. The demon tried again and again, but no matter the effort, no blows landed.

Furious, the demon threw his blade out the chamber window.

"As I said, you may leave if I allow it."

The King grinned. He raised his blade to meet the chest of the demon.

"You do understand how this works, right?" the demon replied. "Strike this flesh down and I'll simply take another man. You'll cut down all who are within these walls before you rid yourself of me. Make no mistake, I don't plan on leaving. I'm here for your throne."

"It sounds like we are at an impasse, dark spirit of the Hollow."

The King sheathed his blade.

"Now, about my proposal?"

Seeing that indeed he had no better alternatives, the demon leaned against the stone wall, listening.

"I will allow you to kill and claim those who you wish in this kingdom. You will not touch my interests, but the peasantry is yours."

As the King paced, he added, "Many kingdoms lie to our west, and they would be well worth your time if this pursuit of yours continues to entertain."

"And what do *you* get out of it?" the demon hissed.

"Power. Wealth. Fame. I now own the recipe for a potion that prevents your dark powers from being able to harm. My kingdom, nay, all the kingdoms will need such an assurance. The potion will be sold at a very high profit, and only to those who align with my interests. Those that pay will thrive, and those that don't, well…"

Silence filled the room. Then the demon walked toward the King, and without saying a word, he nodded, passing the King and then taking his men outside of the castle walls.

The deal had been struck.

As the Kingdom of Vudor began to rebuild, the King had his men travel the lands proclaiming that there was nothing to fear from these invaders, that in fact they were loyal, humble servants of the King. The people were ordered to not live in fear—that they should go on with their lives just as before.

Once a limited amount of the potion had been made, the King tightly controlled its supply. Word eventually got out that the King was withholding a magical elixir that could beat the supernatural forces at play. Many noble houses rose up in protest, wondering why such a powerful magic would not be employed by the King to save the kingdom.

But the King would not relent.

All sorcerers who shared the truths of the magic potion with the common man were expelled from the King's court and shamed as enemies of the crown. The King then employed alchemists to spread word of magical jewelry that one could wear to ward off the invaders if they happened upon your village. (These jewels, obviously, did not work, nor did they actually help protect the people. They were, however, a tightly controlled commodity by the King and made the crown and loyal noble families considerable wealth from the peasantry.)

The King sent a message to the demon, asking for his aid in the battle over the minds of his subjects. The demon, all too thrilled with the way things were going, gladly provided some from his innermost circle to assist the King. The King made these agents of the demon High Priests of the Kingdom of Vudor. The High Priests of Vudor then swayed public opinion and divided the kingdom against itself, eventually leading to internal violence. Zealots rose up under the teachings of the priests, and they began attacking any in the nobility that tried to honor the old ways of Vudor. If any in nobility spoke ill of the King, the zealots would make them pay dearly by revoking their positions of authority, and at times threatening their very lives.

Eventually, the Kingdom of Vudor fell into ruin. As death and destruction ravaged their lands, the people grew violent, and the kingdom collapsed under its own oppressive weight. It's been said of those people:

"Their graves were already dug; all that was required of Vudor's populous was to but climb into them."

The subjects of Vudor were absorbed in the lies of their King—many remained in utter denial, and many more fell to the demon. The King was left with no united people to rule over and died alone as he clung to the remains of a once great kingdom. The riches of the Kingdom of Vudor were spent and squandered. The noble houses either fell to the demon or split up into warring nomadic forces.

To this very day, zealots of the late King still roam those lands—preaching violence and hatred of any who reject his foolish beliefs.

The Demon of Hollow's Keep led his great masses over the frozen peaks and into the barren valley beyond. As his army of evil marched toward the west, other kingdoms had heard of the terrors and tragedy of Vudor. Not willing to fall in the same manner as those to the east, their sorcerers concocted potions to keep their subjects safe from the demon's great evil. These kingdoms armed themselves with the dragons Vudor had long abandoned, and when the demon marched his troops into the valley beyond the peaks, the west was waiting to meet him. Dragons rained such fire upon those troops of death that the ice melted from those towering peaks, mixing with the blood of the demon's fallen forces, boiling their bones in the flames from the beasts of the sky.

The demon soundly lost his campaign to conquer other kingdoms and lands: for our kings were not foolish—instead they chose to heed the warning and wisdom of their advisors.

The demon is said to have retreated to Hollow's Keep; most likely licking his wounded pride to this very day.

W esley's Father looked past their now dwindling campfire toward the peaks to the east. "I'm sure the Demon of Hollow's Keep is waiting until the world forgets. Just long enough for him to have another go at it, all over again."

The wind continued whipping past Wellshire Crest. After a moment of quiet reflection between the father and son, young Wesley spoke.

"Maybe he's just waiting for another fool to come along wearing a crown."

O' JOSEPHINE

HAPPINESS IS YOURS FOR THE CHOOSING.

O' Josephine.

Without you, these walls are barren.

I stand alone in the home we built, waiting for you to haunt these halls. Why did you leave me in such haste, without so much as a goodbye? My days are filled with sorrow, my nights, a restless slumber.

Oft as I'm just to sleep, I make out a blurry vision of your approach—beckoning me to join you for one last dance. I now lie awake, staring at the ceiling of our bedroom. If the sound of music filled this dwelling once again, would your soul descend and join me?

I shall put a record on.

Odd that such a sharp instrument, this needle, be required to produce the loveliest of melodies. Not dissimilar to your passionate way of presiding; your presence brought out the most beautiful refrains. What a life we had.

How empty my life has become, O' Josephine.

I hear a noise upstairs. I am disappointed to find it was only the sound of the house shifting under the weight of my sorrows. Come back to me, O' Josephine! Make haste, as my soul is stretched thin and cannot bear another moment without your love.

As I walk alone through our home, I happen upon a mirror. I've heard rumors that a mirror can become a window to our very soul. How I would love to trespass through your window and be together like when we were young.

Which of these mirrors leads to you?

O' Josephine

I've long thought of joining you versus awaiting your return. If I but drink a sweet poison, you and I could be reunited in an instant, yet my remaining time on earth would be forfeit. Are not my remaining hours already forfeit without you at my side?

I ponder such questions more and more.

Time moves slowly now. The hour is late. Clock hands seemingly create the sound of echoes rather than that of forward movement. I keep the drapes drawn over our windows, as nothing of beauty is to be seen outside, and nothing but horror to be seen within. A crow made permanent residence of our entry eave, constantly bemoaning a warning to those that would listen.

I should have listened. But what is it to truly hear?

Rain begins pattering softly upon our roof. Fitting for my tears of agony without you. Soon the thunder rattles the glass of our windows, and I'm certain of your anger by the ferocity of the drops now pounding down. I would be angry too, robbed of our love and life together.

I am angry.

I see the drapes aflutter and realize I've somehow left a window open. What an oversight! As it is shut, I make out what could be you, standing in our garden. Lightning flashes, and my vision of you is gone.

Shall I leave the front door unlocked, just in case?

O' Josephine.

If I light a candle, will you find your way back here—to this place? To but see your shadow upon a corner of our home would be more than enough to break my loneliness. I remember lighting the candles for our dinners. What precious moments those meals were. I and my storytelling, you and your laughter.

I shall go and set the table for the event of your return.

As I pull plates from the cupboard, I am reminded your skin was like that of fine China. So fair and delicate. So full of beauty. So easily broken. Why did we choose to quarrel over such arbitrary perceptions? Shouldn't our love have been enough for everlasting happiness? Why must my will always be bent to that of your own? Why couldn't you take no for my answer?

I hear a faint version of your laughter down the hall. I do not mind your footsteps upon our floor, or the sway of the chandeliers as you toy with me and move unseen throughout our home.

You have always been welcome here with me.

I have prepared a delicious meal for two tonight. I pour you the finest of wines, if only you would but be seated and enjoy it with me. Alas, there is but an empty chair across from mine. I sense your spirit with me in this moment, spurning my invitation to dine, without regard to the efforts I've made to welcome you home.

Do you know how difficult it was to find a true clairvoyant? At what length I went to extend an offer for you to join me tonight?

I see that you've knocked away your glass.

This behavior is not unlike when your temper used to flair in life. Ours was that of a passionate love and, as is often the case, with great passion came great outbursts, especially when a lack of understanding arose between us.

Now you've gone and thrown the food off the table as well.

I'm trying my best here to apologize and seek forgiveness. Can we but rekindle our love? Though the flame of your life has been snuffed out, the smoke from your life's wick can fill these precious halls. We can yet embrace each other once more! You'll remain at my side until my time to depart this mortal plane; then together we shall depart for the hereafter—our hearts joined forever.

Happiness is yours for the choosing.

Countless noises emanate from the kitchen. As I enter to find all objects in disarray, I can't help but once again apologize for the distance between us and how I long for your spirit to reside in peace and love alongside that of my own. Being dead clearly has struck an emotional chord with you, and I don't begin to claim to understand what it's like in your situation.

A knife is pulled by your unseen hand from a pile of silverware now lying on the floor, then thrown across the room—and is now stuck firmly in the door frame beside me.

That's fair.

O' Josephine

I was the first to wield the kitchen knife in the heat of our last argument. You kept screaming at me, swinging hands that used to embrace me, but in the moment were used as weapons.

I only stabbed you in defense.

I'm coming to a better understanding of your perspective. You believe it's my fault for stabbing you so many times. But how could you not see that those actions were the only way to bring about a peaceful quiet in our relationship?

I never intended to kill you, just to quiet your anger.

I see my explanation has brought about a stillness in our midst.

Do you not understand the lengths I went through to keep you at my side? I wept for days after our last argument. I laid next to you in our bed, hoping you would apologize. I got nothing but a cold shoulder and spiteful silence from your lips. Soon, I realized you had dug into your position and there was nothing I could do.

So, I buried you.

Until I became so utterly lonely.

Upon further reflection, I decided the best way to continue our love was by placing your body within the walls of our home, so that you may feel its warmth and so you would always be with me, despite the distance our last fight created.

Hear me, O' Josephine! Stop with your violent retribution—taking your anger out on our possessions and home. Quiet your moans and your incessant slamming of doors, your throwing of objects!

O' Josephine!

Without you, these walls are barren.

THE DOOR

TO LIVE IS
BETTER.

1

Ted Moffit pulled into the clearing, flanked by mountain peaks and forest all around. When his engine turned off, the sounds of nature resumed a tranquil state. Other than a light wind and birds chirping, no sound of human origin could be discerned. Ted closed the door of his vehicle, taking it all in.

Nature. Quiet. Solitude. This is what I've been seeking.

Ted glanced over his highly equipped 4x4, complete with all the overlanding and survival gear one could imagine.

Ted smiled under the warm sun as his pride swelled. He had made it this far out with nothing more than a few latitude and longitude coordinates, his packed 4x4, a GPS device and some helpful tips from other overlanding types on social media. Ted had been highly invested in finding a secluded camp location, especially one hidden from most in the hobby. Far away from public campgrounds and accessible roads, Ted was finally alone—with no cell signal.

A vacation of pure, unadulterated peace.

Ted quickly got to work. First, finding a downed tree that had naturally met its end (at least a year ago by the looks of it), Ted pulled his chain saw from the 4x4 and began cutting. A short time later, the tree was carved up and ready to be split into firewood. He loved the manual labor in all of this; with no noises to speak of except his chopping and the sound of the wind through the trees, Ted soon had a large pile of wood ready to keep himself warm during his stay. After forming a fire pit out of stones from a nearby stream, Ted lit a small fire and began setting up camp. His pop-up tent raised from his vehicle rollbars with ease, dropping a small ladder to the ground. Ted also pulled an awning from his roof rack and reinforced it with some rope and tent pegs. A propane grill was added, as well as a small canvas chair.

This whole configuration was sure to be the perfect base of operation and rest for the coming week. Ted planned to hike in various directions across the area, exploring as he went, and then return to this clearing each evening for dinner and sleep. As the sun set and dinner sizzled on the grill, he pulled a drink from his cooler and sat down next to the fire. A hawk flew overhead, and Ted sat in silent wonder, thankful he was no longer reachable by phone, and that by contrast, he could now slow down enough to take this sight in.

The evening became night, and the fire slowly cooled to embers. Turning in under a sea of stars, Ted climbed the ladder to his elevated tent. Pulling his sleeping bag over his shoulders, he stared at the night sky from behind the transparent netting.

A sky full of stars.

Ted's mind connected each bright point, creating imaginary figures and faces—from mythical gods of the past, to the faces of friends and family no longer with him. He stared into the night sky for what seemed like hours, but were more likely just minutes, until he eventually lost consciousness.

───

Ted gripped the wheel of his sedan as Shannon's small convertible swung wildly into his lane. Ted's mother was in the passenger seat screaming, and Ted threw all his might on the brake pedal. Shannon looked into Ted's headlights, helpless and terrified, from her driver's side door—now directly in front of him.

Try as he might, Ted was unable to stop soon enough to avoid impact.

2

Ted awoke to sunshine and the sound of a nearby creek bubbling. The birds were already at work for the day, singing their songs, completely unaware of the nightmare Ted had just escaped.

Nature is better. Quiet is better. To live is better. Life is better.

Ted arose and prepped his food rations for the day. He threw together a small pack of cheese and summer sausage, a knife and cutting board, some crackers, and a bottle of yellow mustard for a light lunch. He liked to keep his meals simple when out hiking. Additionally, he packed a few emergency supplies and his GPS device. Ted started out east from camp, crossing the small stream nearby, and then continued through the woods. As he was hiking, his mind returned to his dreams.

My dreams keep getting worse. Maybe I need to get used to them?

The forest to the east was steep, and the terrain was rough. Ted became exhausted by the incline. The route was muddy, steep, and uneven. Being as there were no trails to keep track of, Ted constantly checked his GPS to verify he had not veered too far one way or another. The dense nature of the forest going this direction choked the light from the sky. The hours passed by, and Ted realized he had better head back soon. The uncomfortable possibility of hiking this uneven terrain downhill in the dark toward his camp motivated him to avoid taking too many breaks.

Ted made it back with just enough time to wash his boots and gear in the nearby stream. Wild deer approached while he did these things, curious about this newcomer.

Nature is better. Quiet is better. To live is better. Life is better.

Sitting by the fire that evening, Ted whittled down a stick with a pocket knife his late father had given him. The wood and golden handle read "Teddy" and was one of his most prized possessions.

His father had passed of Leukemia not long after gifting it to him.

Ted worked away at the branch in the firelight, planning a handcrafted walking stick to sand and finish when he got back home after this trip. While carving, Ted's mind wandered to his mother and Shannon.

Will I ever find peace?

Ted felt in his soul, if he was ever to find peace, it would be out here. The evening became darker as clouds rolled in, hiding the stars from the sky. He put out the fire, put his equipment and supplies under the 4x4's awning, and climbed into his sleeping bag—zipping the entrance to his tent behind him.

Ted lay smelling the fresh scent of rain while droplets bounced on the top of his shelter. A forceful downpour eventually gave way to a lighter, pitter patter of drops, creating a rhythm of sorts that lulled him to sleep.

S hannon looked up from her cola, across the picnic table at Ted. She turned and smiled warmly at his mother. The sun was setting, and Shannon was glowing with excitement.

Ted's mother had tears in her eyes, filled with happiness in this moment.

Sure, Ted had another two years of college left. They knew finances would be tight. The question of marriage would have to come later, as had been explained. But her son had found love! And Shannon was a wonderful, sweet girl.

Ted's mother couldn't resist hinting that she always wanted a girl in the family, a daughter to go shopping with. Or grandkids, for that matter.

"Mom, we're just moving in together, you know, to save money on campus housing, right? Let's wait on the wedding date and baby shower."

Ted's voice was filled with humor and shock that his mother was taking this so well.

Since his father's passing, his mom had been a tad bit needy. If Ted was on break from school, his mom always asked for him to come back home and help her tend to the house. In reality, these requests were to provide her company, mainly so she didn't feel so alone after his father's death. It was a pleasant surprise to see her take the news of Ted's next big life decision—a more serious relationship with Shannon, paired with a new living arrangement—so positively.

Shannon blushed as Ted's mother placed a hand on her arm, exclaiming, "Praise the Lord, we are just adding to the family!" Shannon had also been a bit nervous about this moment, but clearly Ted's mother was in her corner—she had nothing to worry about. *Except maybe pressure to make some grandkids,* she thought, laughing to herself when trying to think of what a miniature Ted would look like one day.

The meal ended, and Shannon slid into her bright yellow convertible, ready to head back to the college campus. Ted opened the door to his old sedan, letting his mother get seated before closing her door and entering the vehicle himself. As he went to back up, Shannon rolled past, waving as she drove away. Ted followed in pursuit, as they would be on the same stretch of freeway for some time.

Ted and Shannon had developed this playful habit when driving where they would blow kisses or use sign language for "I love you" when passing.

Such a moment occurred.

One last time.

3

Ted gasped as he awoke, the images fresh in his mind. Tears rolled down his cheek as he wept silently. He realized he was shaking and needed to exit his tent and get some fresh air. The morning breeze was crisp, fresh from the showers that had swept the area. He cooked some eggs over the fire, slicing up veggies to make an omelet of sorts. Birds sang out, and Ted shook the morning panic attack off, steadying himself with all his therapist had taught him through his mindfulness exercises.

Nature is better. Quiet is better. To live is better. Life is better.

Ted gathered his supplies for the day, this time heading south toward what appeared to be a set of mountainous cliffs. After about two hours of hiking, the forest began to part and reveal their base.

Too steep here. Going to have to search for a way up.

Ted looked for about an hour until he found a somewhat less steep embankment that, by crawling on all fours, allowed him to reach a small plateau overlooking where he had hiked. With an eye on the horizon behind him, Ted took a swig from his water bottle. Try as he might, he could not make out the clearing where his camp was located. He glanced at his wristwatch. To avoid nightfall on the hike back to his camp, Ted figured he had about a half hour before he needed to head back.

Turning toward the mountain cliffs behind him, he decided now was as good a time as any to relieve himself on the shrubs lining the slope of the cliff. Ted walked toward a patch of trees and brush that was nearest his position, and, having barely unzipped his pants, felt immediately like something was off about the environment surrounding him.

There was a stillness that felt highly unnatural. No birds or wind, no small crickets, nothing of note but an eerie silence. Ted quickly zipped his pants back up and fastened his belt, checking his surroundings as he did so.

The sound of something metallic being unlocked broke the silence.

"Hello, anyone there?" Ted's voice rang out.

No answer came.

Ted searched the brush, pushing deeper into the tree line skirting the cliff. Just beyond, Ted found what seemed impossible against the rocky formation: a lone door on the side of the mountain.

The doorway was not that of an old barn, an old shed, or some handmade cabin. Nor was this door dragged to the cliff and left to rot, leaning against the stone as some abandoned oddity. No; this was a door more like what you would find in any suburban home: the door was painted pristine white, complete with polished bronze hardware. The door was literally embedded into the side of the stone cliff, looking not a day older than brand new.

Everything about the door seemed out of place. The moss from the rocks of the cliff left the door untouched. Not a speck of dirt, grime, water stain, spider web or bugs appeared on the door. Other than the shaded tree line, nothing grew up in front of the door, and no weeds or other shrubs blocked it. There was no path to speak of; clearly no foot traffic disturbed the ground enough to create the perception of one.

Just a perfect, pristine white, modern suburban door with polished bronze hardware installed on the side of a mountain, in the middle of nowhere.

Ted's mouth was agape with amazement and wonder.

How did this get here?

His mind immediately flew to irrational fears of what could lie beyond the door—all based on some of the popular television shows he had been consuming.

Hidden government facility?

A cartel marijuana grow?

Ted had a few epiphanies during the moments he stood staring at this discovery. The door was expertly placed into the side of the mountain. The craftsmanship was exquisite and clearly intended as an entry point. In addition, this location was remote—near impossible to stumble upon. Ted had driven on mainly BLM (Bureau of Land Management) and private land. It took Ted over two hours off the nearest main road to arrive at this location. His camp was far from any GPS coordinates for previously used overlanding campsites.

It was clear he must be the only person to have ever stumbled across this doorway. Nobody was intended to find this, except whoever put it here. And Ted was *alone*. His cell signal range ended well before finding his camp location—worse, nobody knew where he was or where to look for him. He had planned this as a complete getaway off the grid. His coworkers only knew he was gone for vacation. *Nobody* knew of his whereabouts.

If something did happen to me here, nobody would even come looking.

At this thought, a small shiver went down his spine.

Ted stood for a while in silence, contemplating his next move. This was a huge, exciting—if not dangerous find. Whatever adventure Ted was looking for hiking alone in the wilderness, he had most certainly found it. The doorway beckoned to be opened, and yet, he could not pull together the courage to approach the door any closer.

Too much of a risk. Could be trouble. Double back and think this over.

He listened to his gut and quietly backpedaled to the edge of the small plateau. After carefully making his way down the embankment, he noted his GPS coordinates and continued onward at a hurried pace. About three hours later, he found himself back at his campsite.

Ted looked over his equipment to see if there were any signs of someone having been there while he was away. Other than his own footprints, he found no evidence of someone else disturbing his camp.

Slowly letting his guard down, Ted began thinking of what could come next. He decided camp lights and a campfire would be too risky—possibly alerting whoever owned the doorway of his continued presence in the area. Ted settled for a small propane heater that night for warmth, and just a granola bar for dinner. As he tried to sleep, regret flooded his mind about not having the courage to open the door and find out what was on the other side.

I need to man up. This is the discovery of overlanding legend! What am I going to do, go home with a story about how I found something amazing and then ran away, afraid to even investigate? I need to go back.

Ted, as he lay in his sleeping bag, deduced the safest option would be reconnaissance. He must check the surrounding area and verify that he was alone, in fact, to make sure he wasn't about to stumble into a dangerous situation.

I should bring the drone. That way, I can check the area from the sky and make sure all is clear. I'll also bring my backpacking tent, portable sleeping bag and food rations. Maybe I can just observe the area a bit before I try the door, just to be sure it's safe.

Ted realized this plan could be overkill—maybe the door was just some private shed someone built, or something just as boring.

But why there?

And why is the door in perfect condition?

Curiosity filled Ted as he pondered the possibilities.

It took until the wee hours of the morning, but finally, sleep quieted his mind.

The small yellow convertible pulled in parallel next to Ted's sedan on the freeway. Air blew through Shannon's hair as the vehicles cruised at the speed of highway traffic. She pulled her glasses down, winked, and then shouted, "I LOVE YOUUU" to Ted.

Shannon blew a kiss, then sped past, moving forward in her lane.

Without warning, a large semi-truck popped a tire and swerved at her. The truck hit her convertible broadside, sending a yellow flash into Ted's traffic lane. Shannon's vehicle came to a stop after connecting head on with the shoulder, leaving her driver side door in Ted's path.

Shannon looked up at Ted's fast approaching headlights in terror.

4

Ted awoke in a pool of his own sweat. He had a racing pulse and a headache. *Nature is better. Quiet is better. To live is better. Life is better.*

The horrific images from his dreams never seemed to let up. Ted almost dreaded going to sleep, as he knew the nightmares would just keep plaguing him. He had only recently approached his doctors for help in this area, and they had recommended therapy. The counseling was working somewhat, as he didn't tense up when driving anymore. And going from a small, old sedan, to a huge 4x4 made Ted feel a lot taller, bigger, and safer on the roads. However, none of these things really stopped the nightmares—just mainly the daytime PTSD.

Can't change the past.

Ted quickly swept aside his memories and regrets, choosing instead to prepare himself for the investigation of the doorway on the mountain.

Maybe this discovery is a good thing. Something else to focus on, something new.

Ted began packing and planning his approach.

If I was to get hurt or go missing, there needs to be a way for someone to find me.

Ted wrote down the GPS coordinates of where he was headed, tucking the note into his 4x4 glove box. Ted collected his pocketknife, unfinished walking stick, and a small revolver from a locked compartment under his passenger seat.

Not that I hope to use a gun. Just insurance against the worst. Who knows what to expect?

Ted made excellent time retracing his steps to the base of the ridge where the doorway plateau would be overhead. Taking cover under some trees in the area, he deployed his aerial drone. Thankfully, it was equipped with thermal imaging; by flying it above, he would not only get an eagle-eye view of any camps or development in the proximity, but also the heat signatures of any people. Ted sent the drone up and stared intently at his control screen, waiting for any clue as to who, or what, could be in the surrounding area.

Ted found *zilch*. The drone swept back and forth over the mountainside, and nothing stuck out. Even more unexpected, Ted decided to fly the drone as close as possible to the plateau brush where he saw the door, and the camera found no door at all.

Impossible.

Ted assumed he hadn't put the drone exactly in the right place. Certain that there was no one nearby, he climbed the embankment and made his way to the tree line that shaded yesterday's discovery. As Ted approached, the clear sound of metal unlocking could be heard.

Sure enough, there before him was the door.

Ted approached with caution. The doorknob looked as if it had just been polished, his reflection shone perfectly in its brass as he reached for it. He took a deep breath, turned the knob, and slowly pulled the door open.

The door revealed a hallway.

Not too long, not too short. White painted walls with various family photos hung, as well as a perfect white carpet floor. A small table with a lamp was located at the end of the hallway. The scent of lavender filled Ted's nose. To him, this hallway was representative of any typical suburban home. He stood facing a brand-new door, in the middle of nowhere, leading to a brand-new hallway inside of a mountain. The absurdity of it made him giggle slightly, if not nervously.

Let's do it. Let's find out where this hallway goes.

Ted entered the doorway.

Concerned with clearly leaving any signs that he had been here; he removed his hiking boots and placed them atop his backpack on the edge of the hallway just inside the door. Now in his socks, Ted felt more confident walking along the spotless carpet. Passing photos of a young family and their kids, it was surreal walking toward the end of this hallway, in what began to feel more and more like a house. As Ted made his way, a slight breeze drifted through the hall from the plateau and edged the door closed.

Probably for the best, I don't want to advertise too much.

As he reached the end of the hallway, Ted ascertained that he indeed was inside what appeared to be a suburban home—complete with a living room, kitchen, staircase, and multiple bedrooms. After confirming nobody was around and that there were no security cameras or other elements that might tip off the homeowners to his presence, Ted began to inspect the place more thoroughly. The house didn't just feel picture perfect; it was picture perfect.

Almost like a model home that was staged for a realtor showing.

Ted searched room to room. A home gym. Fully stocked bathrooms. A playroom for the kids, full of toys neatly put away. A master bedroom, living room, dining room—all designed with tasteful modern furniture. As Ted opened the fridge in the kitchen, to his amazement it was stocked with fresh food, and upon glancing at the expiration dates, he noticed that everything had been purchased recently… if not yesterday or today.

It was at about this moment that Ted perceived something he had overlooked.

Sunlight was pouring in through the skylights.

That's impossible. It must be artificial. I'm inside a mountain.

He ran to a window and pulled up the shade, only to find a small side yard, a fence line, a neighbor's home, and indeed *the sky itself.* Ted began calculating his current reality. From what he knew, he was supposed to be inside a mountain. It was one thing to carve out a model home inside a mountain and artificially light it. It was a completely other thing to add neighboring homes and a sky.

Ted retraced his footsteps back to the original hallway and walked toward the door he had entered through. The sight of his boots and backpack brought assurances that this was not some trick of the mind, or a part of a mental break down. Ted grabbed the bronze doorknob and turned it, giving the door a shove.

The door swung open to reveal the plateau and the forest beneath, under a moonlit sky.

What the hell? How is this possible?

Ted checked his watch. He had only been inside for about an hour—given his day so far, that would put the time around two in the afternoon. Sure enough, his watch confirmed this.

Is there a solar eclipse I wasn't aware of?

Ted put his shoes back on and quickly walked out on the Plateau where he could get a better view. Sure enough, this was no solar eclipse, just a full moon on a starry, warm night.

A warm night? That's odd too. I was nearly freezing last night.

Ted glanced back at the open door, daylight still flooding the hallway of the model home inside the mountain. A minute passed, and try as he might, Ted couldn't reconcile everything he was experiencing. What sounded like the howl of a coyote echoed off the plateau, and he decided to head back into the home to continue his investigation.

He closed the door behind himself and once again took his shoes off. After leaning his walking stick against the wall, Ted grabbed a water bottle from his bag and drank. Placing it back in his bag, he set out to explore more of this place. Finding the front door to the home, Ted opened it and was immediately hit with the warm glow of the sun. The sunlight felt good on his skin, and as his eyes adjusted to the brightness, he could not believe what lie before him.

There in front of Ted was a typical suburban street, surrounded by a typical suburban neighborhood.

How could something of this magnitude even be done?

Ted turned around and faced the home that served as his entrance to this place.

Blue sky above and behind. Even on the other side of the house?

Ted quickly went around back, hopped the gate to the backyard, and was met with a swimming pool and an outdoor kitchen. A warm, gentle breeze blew. An inflatable designed to look like a pink flamingo floated whimsically across the undisturbed surface of the pool.

How is it all of this exists!?

By Ted's calculations, the door where he entered the hallway would have been located at the back of the house—putting where he was standing the exact spot the plateau should be, and the rear of the home exactly where the cliff wall should have been. But there were no doors on the backside of the home, only a sliding glass door that led into the main living area.

Ted gave the sliding door a try, and to his surprise, it was already unlocked. He walked through the house, and after approaching the hallway door again, deduced the door should open to the backyard. But he had just confirmed that *no door* was present on the backside of the home!

Ted once again opened the perfectly pristine white door in the hallway to reveal the plateau he had just come from, albeit a bit colder outside than last he was out there, with daylight pouring over the woods. He closed the door again and returned to the outdoor patio, tossing himself in a poolside lounger.

This is a scientific impossibility. How could two different, real physical locations exist in the same place?

The sun felt warm on Ted's skin, and a fatigue swept over him. The warm breeze gently drifted through the backyard. As he was considering all the implications of the doorway, fatigue set in, and Ted fell asleep.

Ted found himself hearing his mother's scream. He quickly turned to see his mother, fear in her eyes, as a yellow flash entered his lane of traffic. Ted threw all of his might onto the brake pedal. Shannon looked on, helpless and terrified, directly in front of him.

Smash. Roll. Smash. Roll. Smash.

Ted looked to his right and found his mother bleeding from the blunt force trauma of the accident. She was shaking in shock; the blood running down her face as she took one final look into the eyes of the son she loved. She whispered, "Momma loves you Teddy," as Ted grabbed her hand and squeezed it, attempting to reassure her that it would be alright.

Seconds later, his mother was gone.

Ted somehow managed to crawl out of his sedan, blood running down his cheek. He staggard with a limp towards a growing number of onlookers that were checking to make sure everyone was ok. Against the backlit headlights of his wrecked sedan, Ted's silhouette looked like an approaching zombie.

Nervous strangers asked if he was ok while they dialed emergency services on their phones.

In the distance, Ted could hear the sirens and see the colors of strobing lights approach. As Ted shambled toward Shannon's yellow convertible, he could see that his sedan had crushed the driver side door and windshield. Ted could not find Shannon in the wreckage, but he already knew her fate.

Ted fell to his knees sobbing, then collapsed on the pavement as an ambulance arrived.

5

Ted awoke, lurching forward after what only seemed like a few moments unconscious. The inflatable flamingo in the pool beside him was such a contrast to the memories he had just relived in his dream. He had not intended to doze off, but, due to exhaustion, he must have.

To live is better. Life is better. Is it better?

He was beginning to get another migraine. And his stomach churned and gurgled out of hunger. Ted returned to his bag and grabbed his lunch, deciding to eat it while sitting on the front porch of the home. As Ted ate, he watched the street, but nobody drove by. Nobody even *walked* by. Ted had seen no other living person on this side of the doorway: no kids playing, no neighbors mowing their lawn, no traffic—just silence.

It occurred to him that there were cars present in the neighborhood, all parked neatly in the driveways of the houses on the block. Ted noted that the neighborhood had an oddly reminiscent feeling of the Americana of old. American flags were flying from nearly every home on the street, and there was this weird feeling of perfection that was rampant through all the home facades. It was visually comparable to an overbearing homeowner's association, or something to that effect. It was as if this place was a model town, and every lot here had the perfect home, lawn, and car.

It's like Doomtown from the Nevada Test Site, minus the mannequins.

Ted recalled an unfrequented history he had learned in college—a nasty slice of American pie, if you will. The U.S. government, back in the 1950s, had built a small town in Nevada to use as a nuclear bomb test site. Unfortunately, nobody predicted fallout from such an activity would end up killing Americans in other parts of the state. This neighborhood felt to Ted like a modern take on it, albeit fully developed and without the dressed-up department store dummies.

Yep, it feels like Doomtown.

Nature is better. Quiet is better.

Ted thought of the mindfulness exercise from his therapy sessions.

Nature indeed was better. Quiet doesn't exactly feel better, specifically in this place.

He decided his next task ought to be checking out the other homes in the vicinity. Ted fetched his walking stick and put his boots back on. There was no point in pretenses; if someone knew he had been here, then so be it. As Ted looked through neighboring windows, he found what became a consistent theme: all new homes, similar décor choices, and alternate home layouts. He decided to knock on a few front doors. Nobody ever answered.

Eventually, Ted decided to test the neighborhood for activity by being a nuisance. He would create a ton of noise, and if people started emerging, he would bolt back inside and out the hallway door—fleeing to the safety of the woods. If no one emerged, then these other homes were possibly free for the exploring.

Ted stood in the middle of the neighborhood street and called out to see if anyone would respond. When that didn't yield any results, he once again knocked on a few nearby doors. After continued silence, he walked to the original home containing the doorway back to the forest. He stared at the pristine vehicle in the driveway and chose to escalate his attention-seeking technique. He whipped his walking stick at the driver's side window—shattering it completely. The explosion of the window glass was strangely therapeutic for Ted, who had become less at ease the longer he was alone here.

No car alarm sounded.

Frustrated, he reached into the vehicle and pounded away at the horn of the car, yelling about how "late his wife was for their evening dinner."

Ted was humored by this bit of fun, but was really hoping someone would emerge to ask him to cut it out.

Nobody came.

Nobody opened their doors, much less looked out their windows. Not even one set of blinds in the neighborhood opened, and once he stopped with the horn, no sounds of traffic could be heard approaching at all.

Ted was clearly alone in this neighborhood.

He decided to try the neighbor's front door. To his surprise, it was unlocked. Ted entered the home, his small revolver hidden in the event he needed it. As he searched the home, it all felt very familiar, if not an alternate layout of the home he already knew. One big difference of note was that there was no hallway or door that led to anywhere unusual in this home. Ted repeated this exploration, home by home, throughout the neighborhood. All homes he searched were similar. Very clean. Brand new. Alternate layouts. Stocked fridge. No hallways with doors leading back to the woods.

After about the sixth home he entered, Ted had a startling discovery. On a credenza, there was a picture frame. It was an all too familiar family—the family from the photos in the original home he had entered this place through.

What the?

Ted began thinking his first impressions were correct.

This was a little too perfect. A little too staged.

He checked the next home over, and sure enough, all photos within were of the same family.

Ted walked back toward the house he had entered the neighborhood through.

This place doesn't add up.

He approached the driveway and stopped by the vehicle, frozen in disbelief.

The vehicle's window had been cleaned up and repaired.

Not a piece of shattered glass remained.

So, I'm not alone after all.

An unexpected voice came from behind.

"No fucking way! Could this be Ted!?"

6

Ted spun around as he nearly had a heart attack. He held a defensive arm up, swinging his walking stick, as if expecting an attack to launch from behind him. Ted came face to face with two individuals: a young man and woman about his age—both in hiking apparel and ball caps.

"Whoa, whoa there. We didn't mean to startle you. We're hikers out exploring, just like yourself."

The sudden newcomer looked at his female traveling companion for reassurance, and she looked at Ted, nodding in solemn agreement. The young man continued the introduction.

"This is Kara, and I'm Ethan. We've been out in the area hiking. Are you Ted Moffit?"

Ethan pulled a newspaper clipping with a photo and held it up, comparing Ted's features.

"We've heard stories of your disappearance. During our camping trip, we decided to search the area for you. We found your campsite and the GPS coordinates in your glove box. That led us here… wherever *here* is."

Ethan then looked down both sides of the neighborhood, half expecting a car to drive by at any moment.

Kara chimed in.

"This place is so wild; I wonder how this is all done. There must be holographic technology used to simulate the sky. I mean, we're inside of a mountain!"

Ethan grimaced at Kara, looking nervous.

Kara gave a strict glance to Ethan that had undertones Ted couldn't quite catch. Kara returned her gaze to Ted and continued.

"I can totally see why you would want to stay in this place, whatever it is. You are Ted, correct? I'm pumped we found you. Talk about solving a mystery."

Ted paused a moment before he spoke.

"Well, you've found me. What is all this about you solving a mystery by finding me? I've literally been on vacation for three days."

Ted began slowly taking steps backward, toward the house.

I might be in danger, and these two might not be who they claim to be. Are they stalling to keep me here?

Ted casually checked the position of his gun tucked in his waist under his shirt. The cold metal touching his skin made him feel more prepared for whatever could come.

Kara noted Ted's movements and apprehension.

"Three days? Ted, it's been *ten years* since there were reports of your disappearance. You've become somewhat of a legend. You were so far off the grid, your profile was so low, that nobody ever found your camp, until we did, yesterday."

Now Ted knew this whole conversation was bullshit. He had left the note with GPS coordinates this morning in the 4x4, so there was no way Kara's story checked out. And even if an additional day had passed, which would, he supposed, explain the nighttime scene he experienced the last time he checked the plateau, the impossibility of a decade passing cemented Ted's conclusion.

These two are involved in whatever this place is and could want to harm me.

Ted's mind raced to his belongings inside the home.

That's when Ted noticed his bag slung over Ethan's shoulders.

They have stolen my supplies so they can keep me here!

Ted advanced toward the pair of strangers, motioning to his bag with the unfinished walking stick.

"Mind if I get my things back?"

Ethan pulled the bag off his shoulders, extending it in his hand toward Ted. As Ted moved forward to take the bag, Ethan dropped it and instead grabbed the walking stick and wrest it from Ted. In a quick maneuver, Ethan knocked Ted to the ground and then attempted to pin him down, all the while Kara yelled for Ethan to stop.

Ethan, while working to pin Ted to the ground, grumbled about needing to drag Ted to the authorities, if need be, to claim a reward.

"He's a missing person for a decade and has clearly lost his damn mind. It's better for him this way: they'll get him professional help, and we'll be famous for finding both him and this place. We're the only ones out here—Kara, will you just get me the rope so I can tie his hands, *please!*"

Kara stood immobile for what seemed like a few seconds. As Ethan yelled for help again, Kara quickly pulled a rope from her backpack. As he attempted to tie Ted's wrists behind his back—Ted seized his moment. Ted rolled furiously and kicked, throwing Ethan off balance, just long enough for Ted to rise to his feet and pull out the pistol he had been hiding. Immediately realizing the danger of the moment, Ethan raised his hands and stepped back. Kara slid behind Ethan. Ethan pointed to Ted's pistol and spoke slightly out of breath.

"It's not worth it. You've proved your point. We'll just go. If you want to be lost forever, that's your business." Turning to Kara over his shoulder, he muttered, "You were right. This reward isn't worth all this effort. The fame of finding him will do us nothing if we end up dead."

Kara shot back. "We could end up dead. All because you are an asshole who loses his cool. I never even cared about the stupid reward."

Ted motioned with the pistol to the end of the block.

"Walk. I want you to walk to the end of the street and stay there until the sun goes down."

Ethan and Kara walked quickly toward the end of the block and rounded the corner. Ted watched until they were out of his sight. With the two now gone, he grabbed his pack and checked its contents. His sleeping bag, tent, and other assorted items were still there. Ted slung the pack over his shoulder and quickly went inside.

Once inside, Ted secured the external doors by locking all the deadbolts, and cautiously searched room to room. Thankfully, there was nobody else present in the home. Desiring to put some distance between himself and the two strangers, he thought it best to gather supplies from the fridge, refill his water bottles, and head back out to the plateau where he could hike back to his camp.

214

The skylights indicated the sun was about to set.

My would-be kidnappers will soon come back to this place looking for an exit.

After rushing to pack his bag, Ted stood at the end of the hallway, staring at the door that started this whole experience.

Through the walls, Ted could hear a disturbance coming from somewhere within the neighborhood.

What could those two be up to now? Enough of this bullshit. I'm getting out of here.

Ted turned the knob and swung the door open.

7

Ted was taken aback by the instant frigid nature of the air on the other side. It was early daylight, possibly morning, and the ground in front of the door brought with it a new challenge: snow. It had snowed on the plateau.

Dammit. Seriously?

Ted shook his head and realized this was going to be a very cold trek, compared to his previous luxurious day in sunny suburbia on the other side of the door. He considered turning around and getting some rest in the home.

But what about the uproar that just started in the neighborhood? Would those two attempt to tie me up again? Nah, I'd rather not find out. They could be a part of whatever that place is.

Pushing himself to his physical limits, Ted descended the now-ice-ridden embankment below the plateau. White snow glistened in the shade of the forest as winter creatures scurried past to their respective dens. It felt like the journey took twice as long, but Ted eventually found himself back at the clearing and his camp.

All was not well.

Ted's year old 4x4 looked like it had weathered for a decade under the elements. The windows were all shattered, and his rooftop tent had long been rotting away. The combination of mold and chewed fabric on his tent told him that his entire setup was unsalvageable. His other supplies were still present; however, they had been clearly disturbed and searched through. Whoever did this was lazy enough to leave his supplies in their weatherproof bags with the zippers open, thus exposing these items to the elements. Not to give up too quick, Ted attempted to start his vehicle, but the effort was clearly in vain. Everything was in ruin. Ted spent the next few moments trying to make sense of his surroundings.

How is it possible, in less than a day, all my possessions have deteriorated at such an alarming rate? And the snow? Could Ethan and Kara have been right? Has a decade really gone by?

Ted walked to the stream near his camp and bent down, splashing water on his face. The water was frigid. As Ted paused, continuing to think things over, he gazed down and caught his own reflection on the surface of the water.

The face that stared back at him was just as he remembered.

I'm not any older. How is it that my camp has aged?

Ted trekked into the forest west of his camp location, covering his tracks by using a piece of brush as he went. He would be safest there; if he didn't set a fire, his new location could remain covert enough to get some sleep. Ted erected his backpacking tent and a small compact sleeping bag for warmth from his pack. He rolled his pack into a makeshift pillow and then settled in for some rest. This day had been so chaotic and draining.

Ted's head barely hit the edge of his bag before he was out cold.

The courtroom was packed, and Ted sat emotionless as the judge handed down the verdict. The trucking company owed Ted and Shannon's family 5 million dollars in damages for the accident. The accident that claimed both Ted's past and his future. His heart and his soul.

With no family left to console him, Ted sat alone as others congratulated and comforted Shannon's parents as the room emptied. The last one remaining in the room besides Ted was Shannon's father. He quietly approached and sat down beside Ted.

"You know we don't blame you, right? It's… an unspeakable pain, losing the heaven you had on this earth, to what feels like the cheap promise of a heaven in the hereafter."

Ted remained silent as he wrestled with his emotions.

"I know we would rather have our Shannon. All this, and the money…" her father's voice drifted off into a crack. Shannon's father wiped a tear from his eye. Regaining his composure, he continued.

"… All the money… it's just a penalty for a mistake that cost our loved ones their lives. The money doesn't right the wrong, heal the pain, or replace the loss. It does, however, give us an opportunity to move forward. A means to pay off old debts. A means to buy the *chance*, not the *promise*, of a better tomorrow. Not necessarily a tomorrow that is better than before the accident. Just one that's better than *today*."

Shannon's father let another moment pass—as he himself searched for the words to bring Ted some comfort.

"We love you like a son. I beg you—forgive yourself for what was clearly not your fault. Our family hopes you find peace. And I hope that one day you will find some small bit of heaven, like our dear Shannon, here on earth again. Take this verdict, the money, and begin a new path with your life."

Shannon's father then touched Ted's shoulder softly before standing up and leaving the courtroom. Ted sat silent and numb for quite some time, listening to the building's central air conditioning.

Alone.

8

Ted raised his head up, leaving a small puddle of drool on his makeshift pillow. His neck was sore from sleeping so hard.

What time is it? What day is it? Was all that insanity yesterday a dream?

Checking the sky, Ted confirmed it was now the following morning. Rising slowly due to the cold, Ted took extra time to gather his things and pack them back into his bag.

Ted made his way back to his camp. Confirming the worst of his fears, Ted watched from the edge as the wind blew shreds of torn, rotten canvas from what was his rooftop tent.

I'm going to need to get help.

Ted knew he was far from any main roads via his 4x4. On foot in the snow, Ted knew the trip back was near impossible with the supplies he had. On the other hand, Ted could go back to the door, and back to the sunny neighborhood. There would be plenty of food and supplies there, but Ethan and Kara could also be waiting to ambush him. Not that being taken to civilization would be such a bad thing, but the assumption was too large for Ted.

Better to enter civilization on my own terms and confirm what they claimed.

An idea struck Ted that he hadn't thought of yet. Ethan and Kara, *if* they were who they claimed to be, would have a mode of transportation nearby. Ted began heading north, assuring himself he could always turn back if his search came up empty. It wasn't long before a newer vehicle, much newer looking than anything Ted had seen before, was found parked down the snow-covered trail about a half mile away. It was obscured by snow, but with a shape unmistakably foreign to these woods. Ted approached, found the handle, and tried the door. Astoundingly, it opened with ease and a slight popping sound.

The vehicle chimed as Ted climbed into the driver's seat. It was clear nobody had been inside for quite some time; yet the interior was pristine and clean. Ted noticed a start button and pressed it. The vehicle came to life, greeting him with a holographic "welcome" projected upon the dash. There was a strange sign-in process before he could operate it, but thankfully there was a "guest" user mode—no key seemed to be required. Ted was presented with an auto-mated driving option or a manual one. He chose the automated option, then selected the nearest town from the menu screen.

Drive time: 3 hours.

The journey was long, but the vehicle handled surprisingly well without any of his input. When he arrived, Ted instructed the vehicle to park at a café so he could grab a bite to eat. Soon Ted found himself seated in a small diner, bustling with activity. He ordered some pancakes and eggs and waited for what felt like forever, as his stomach growled in hunger. As the meal was dropped off at his table, Ted asked the server if they had the newspaper from today. The waitress left, then returned with today's edition, placing it neatly on the edge of the booth. Ted took a sip of his coffee and then dared to check the date on the paper.

It had indeed been over *twelve* years.

As unbelievable as this revelation was, nobody could have staged this. Ted read through the entire paper. Politics, world events, financial markets, sports— all were a far cry from the world as it was when Ted found the door just two days ago. In the single day Ted had spent on the other side of the hidden door, twelve years had passed by. Ted ate his meal, dwelling on what to do next. All his credit cards were obsolete—thankfully he had brought cash with him while camping, so Ted was able to pay for his meal with what the waitress called "vintage money."

As he exited the restaurant foyer, Ted saw a bulletin board with various handbills posted. His eyes narrowed in on a set of posters. All of them were typeset with a large lettering of MISSING at the top. Ted quickly found an image of himself on one poster, along with a computer-generated facsimile of what he would look like at 35.

Not quite that old yet. In fact, I haven't physically aged a day over 23.

Ted chuckled to himself about how odd the aged picture of himself looked.

But this means Ethan and Kara were telling the truth; I have been missing.

Ted looked at the reward listed, realizing it indeed was a nice sum of money.

Do I get the money if I turn myself in?

Another poster caught his eye. In it, below the MISSING title, were both Ethan's and Kara's photos. Ted checked the date on their disappearance, comparing it to the date he had just seen on today's paper.

A difference of over two years! So, they must have just entered through the door when they ran into me.

Now it was all making sense. However it happened, time passed considerably faster on this side of the door.

To Ethan and Kara, they had only been on the other side for maybe an hour, but to the real world, it was over two years. I had only been inside the door for about six hours, but to the real world, it has been twelve years. By that calculation... every 5 seconds anyone spends on the other side of the door, an entire day here has flown by!

And that's when Ted remembered that he locked Ethan and Kara out of their only exit back. And he most likely had their vehicle. Despite their attempt to force him to come back here, Ted felt it would be cruel to allow them to needlessly lose more of their lives to time, as he had.

Shit. I must go back. I've got to warn them. They were telling the truth, and they have no idea what they have gotten themselves into. Hopefully they can recover their lives from two years missing, unlike my life, which is now twelve years long past. Everyone I know probably moved on with their lives a long time ago, and I can't leave these two to the same fate.

For Ethan and Kara, Ted knew his time away would be mere seconds from when he left through the door. Ted purchased some food supplies and instructed the automated vehicle to take him back to his campsite coordinates. As his vehicle navigated the route, Ted went in and out of consciousness. He was so tired, yet unable to fully rest, as the automatic vehicle technology still left him feeling uneasy.

Ted once again found his decaying camp remains, and then journeyed on foot to the plateau where the door was hidden. Once more, the clear sound of metal unlocking could be heard. He was once again greeted with the white, pristine, suburban door with polished brass hardware—untouched by the elements surrounding it.

Ted took a deep breath, then opened the door and entered the familiar hallway.

9

Ted could hear a woman's screams emanating from the front door of the home. Ted raced down through the home toward the pounding on the front door.

"Help me please, somebody help!"

The woman's voice sounded like Kara.

Ted unlocked the front door as a scraped and bloodied Kara lunged inside, screaming for Ted to shut the door and lock it again. He moved instinctively fast, and as he did, he caught a fleeting glimpse of what Kara had been so terrified by.

Running toward the home were what appeared to be tall, shadowy figures with huge claw-like limbs and glowing eyes.

Ted slammed the door shut and locked the front door. Kara cried, clearly injured, terrorized out of her mind. Ted quickly helped Kara move into the hallway by the door that led to the plateau. Kara needed a moment to gather herself, and so Ted sat opposite Kara, their backs against the pristine white walls, as Ted trained his revolver down the hallway. Ted hoped that whoever, or whatever, had been chasing Kara would not break into the home. For moments, they sat in pure silence and terror as Kara covered her mouth and silently cried.

Nothing.

No movement nor attempts to gain entry to the home could be heard. Kara, regaining her composure after some time, explained to Ted what happened.

———

"You should have just given him the bag." Kara was livid after having a gun pulled on her. "So what if there is a reward for finding him? Pulling a stunt like that was so, so very stupid, Ethan. We could have been killed or seriously hurt. Over what, *money?*"

Ethan knew she was right. His desire to claim the reward had gotten the best of him, and his knee-jerk reaction in trying to force Ted to come back with them was poorly thought through. Even if he had been successful in tying Ted up, would he have been able to get him to hike down a cliff and through a forest all the way back to their vehicle?

"I'm sorry. I got carried away and decided to make the first move—that guy looked like he was ready for a fight from the moment we introduced ourselves."

"No duh, he was looking for a fight; you sure as hell gave him a reason for one. We're lucky he didn't pull that trigger."

Kara walked ahead of Ethan, leaving him behind. Ethan caught up and faced her, placing his hands on Kara's shoulders, and looked apologetically into her eyes. Kara flung her hands up and shoved Ethan back a foot, then placed one hand on her forehead while seating the other on her hip as she paced back and forth. They had just rounded the corner out of sight from Ted, and this moment seemed as good as any to make her disapproval of Ethan known.

"Your actions put us at too much risk." Kara scolded. "I'm all about adventure and exploration, but this hiking trip is over. We're going to wait until the sun has fully set, and then we're getting the hell out of here. Hopefully, that guy will let us back through the hallway door and isn't standing there—barricading the exit and guarding it with his gun! If we get out of this alive, we're not going to speak a damn word of this discovery, or this experience, to anyone we know. And you and I are going to need some space. I need time to consider our relationship and if it's even worth salvaging. *You got that?*"

Ethan nodded, taking the moment to catch his breath and evaluate Kara's level of anger. He knew they were on rocky footing as of late, but had hoped this adventure would bring them closer together, instead of driving them further apart. Of course, he now knew that the odds of their relationship lasting much longer were very, very small. Kara seemed more distant now than she had ever been. And unmistakably, he knew he was at fault for this.

The sun sank beneath the horizon line over the neighborhood. Kara motioned to Ethan that it was time to go once dusk began, and Ethan followed. The two rounded the corner and began walking back toward the home they entered this place through. Once they made it about halfway down the street, a chorus of screams pierced their ears, originating from what felt like all directions. Just as suddenly as it occurred, the screams stopped, and the neighborhood returned to eerie silence.

"What the fuck was that?" Ethan asked aloud.

Kara, visibly shaken, glanced back toward Ethan. As Ethan tried to think of something comforting to say in the moment, his gaze drifted from Kara's eyes to a shadow moving in one of the neighboring yards. The shadow looked to have glowing… *eyes?* Before Ethan could make heads or tails of the shape, it moved toward them. Within moments, hundreds of similar shadows began sprinting, climbing, and crawling toward their position. The screams resumed, and Ethan grabbed Kara's arm, then began a full sprint toward the home containing their exit.

The shadow creatures were *much faster* than Ethan and Kara.

Intuiting that their sprint would be clearly overtaken by the creatures, Ethan yelled for Kara to run, placing himself between the onslaught of shadows with glowing eyes and Kara. As the shadows closed in on Ethan, their figures morphed into 8-foot beasts with long, lanky limbs, fingers and claws. Despite his best efforts, Ethan's punching and kicking were no match for the evil pursuing him.

Ethan was killed within seconds of the creatures catching him.

Kara screamed as she glanced over her shoulder and witnessed Ethan being torn to shreds. A shadow creature quickly came up on her left and its claws sliced into her side, fresh blood pouring from the wound. Kara happened to have a knife attached to her, and she whipped it out of its sheath, plunging it into the creature's eyes. The shadow figure let out a screech that froze the activity of all the others, buying Kara precious moments to reach the front door of the home.

Kara tried the front entrance, only to find it locked. As she screamed in terror, pleading for anyone in earshot to help, Kara beat on the door with the desperation of a person who knew their life was about to end.

Ted flung the door open just long enough for Kara to lunge inside and warn him to seal the entry.

10

H ad Ted been a moment later to unlock the door, Kara explained she would have been killed, just as Ethan was.

Kara sat, visibly disturbed and in shock, across from Ted as he absorbed this information. She had cuts and various shallow lacerations all over her body and clothing—clearly from the creatures he had just witnessed outside in the street.

Ted never broke his gaze away from the end of the hall, his arm outstretched with the revolver, ready to fire at the slightest movement. He was processing everything as best he could, having just accepted that he lost twelve years of his life exploring a random neighborhood hidden in a mountain. A hidden neighborhood that during the daytime was picturesque while stealing years of your life, but by nightfall contained shadow creatures that want to kill you.

"We need to leave." Ted spoke, his voice full of resolve. "We can formulate a plan on the other side of the door, but we need to move *now*." Kara nodded and Ted again helped her to her feet—all the while still aiming his gun down the hallway. The pair exited through the door and closed it tightly behind them.

The plateau was warmer than before and sunny. Green grass replaced the previous snowy landscape. It was about mid-day by the looks of it.

Ted finally relaxed a bit.

I wonder how much time has passed. A few months?

Time was in their favor, as every second the creatures took reaching the door would be hours for Ted and Kara on this side. They braced the door closed with a few nearby branches. The branches wouldn't stop those things if they were determined to get through, but they would at the very least give Ted and Kara a warning signal while they were within earshot.

After securing the door, Ted helped Kara down the side of the cliff, and deep into the tree line surrounding the base. Ted did his best to dress Kara's wounds with what little supplies they shared between their bags. Thankfully, Kara was not critically injured in any way, and other than the shallow cuts and torn clothing, she was in good enough shape to walk.

Together, they hiked back to the location of Ted's camp. The camp had clearly aged a bit more since the last time Ted laid eyes on it, but because it was already in bad shape, not much had changed. Ted made a small fire and Kara wept, clearly emotional about what happened to Ethan.

"I know Ethan was being a dick when he attempted to tie you up. He was always so impulsive. It's what I hated about him." Kara spoke through tears, looking at Ted as he listened. "Can you forgive me for being a part of that moment? I was afraid, unsure of what the right thing was once he got into an altercation with you. We were so far out here and alone; I was afraid for my safety. It doesn't excuse what I did, but I hope we can trust each other. Obviously, we've both been through hell and back today."

Ted put his jacket around Kara's shoulders. He understood the impossibility of the situation. Ted did his best, explaining what he had come to understand about the door and its relationship to time. He covered everything: how he found the door, his experiences in the neighborhood beyond the door, and his trip leaving the area and returning to society after his encounter with Kara and Ethan.

"So, you're saying that while it was a mere hour for Ethan and I on the other side of the door, *two years* have passed on this side?"

Kara's eyes were wide open in shock, their glassy surface flickering with the firelight.

Ted confirmed Kara's conclusion.

"And when you exited the doorway, while to you it was a couple of days here, it was only *seconds* you were missing on the other side of the door?" Kara asked.

Ted shook his head in agreement yet again.

Kara continued, "It's a good thing you came back for us, or I would have been a goner. If you'd have taken another few days, a week or a year to come back, you would have found my fresh corpse instead of me pounding on the door. As unbelievable as all this time stuff is, it becomes a hell of a lot more believable when you've already been chased and nearly killed by shadow creatures."

Kara laughed nervously.

"It's good that you've kept your humor in all this. As someone who's also suffered great tragedy and loss, it's the hallmark sign that maybe you'll be okay after all."

Ted moved closer to Kara and put his arm around her.

Kara leaned her head on Ted's shoulder and the two of them sat silently in the ruins of Ted's original camp.

The sky was full of stars and the two shared the sole sleeping bag Ted had packed. Kara and Ted stared up into the open night sky, both thankful to be alive and not alone.

Nature is better. Quiet is better. To live is better. Life is better.

11

The following morning, Ted and Kara devised a plan. They agreed that it would be awkward reentering civilization together after all this time, and that many would have questions, some of which could eventually lead to the discovery of the door. With evil and dangers waiting on the other side, the two agreed they should do whatever was possible to destroy the doorway.

Remembering that during his searches, he found the garage in the home had a full spare gasoline tank, Ted floated the idea of soaking the hallway in gas, closing the door, and then lighting the whole thing on fire. At the very least—this would burn down the home on the other side and hopefully seal off the entrance on this side, most likely through rubble. Kara agreed with the merits of the plan, but was worried about the creatures. It would only have been seconds since they left the hallway, and there was great risk that they could be attacked by reentering the doorway.

They bounced ideas back and forth, one involving Ted going inside while Kara stayed on the plateau, but that idea fell flat on the realization that if Ted got into trouble, years could go by before Kara would know it. They also discussed possibly getting supplies from the nearest town, but they deduced that would potentially expose them to more risks: days of hiking with heavy supplies, while possibly allowing someone to discover their identities in the meantime. It was concluded and agreed upon that going back through the door together was the best way to end this nightmare once and for all. Once the home burned, it would hopefully prevent anyone else from ever accessing the doorway.

Ted and Kara hiked back to the plateau. An unlocking sound could be heard. The door remained undisturbed—all branches bracing the door were still in place. After clearing them away, Ted and Kara opened the door and entered the hallway.

All was silent. The hallway wall and carpet that had been previously stained with blood from Kara's injuries was back to its brand new, immaculate condition. Ted held his pistol and motioned for Kara to quietly follow him. The two clung to the wall as they moved through the pristine, picture-perfect home.

Quiet is better. To live is better.

As Ted and Kara entered the garage, careful to not make the slightest of noises, Ted glanced out of the small windows cut into the garage door. There, in the street, stood hundreds of silhouette creatures, eyes glowing, unmoving, and silent. On the ground in the neighbor's yard lie the knife Kara had stabbed a shadow creature with during her escape. And but a bit farther down the street lie the body of Ethan, among hundreds of shadow creatures with glowing eyes.

All were facing the home Ted and Kara were in.

All were completely still.

Ted quickly moved to assist Kara in collecting the gasoline can from the garage. If they were going to do this, they needed to move *fast* and *silent*. The two made their way back to the hallway and began pouring gasoline along the hallway walls and white carpet. Taking time to splash and fully soak the doorway that began all of this—Ted and Kara returned to the plateau. It was hot and dark outside.

Ted lit a match, then tossed it into the hallway.

The hallway immediately went up in flames with a fury. White carpet turned to black, flames jumped the walls and began burning the family photos decorating them—the pictures edges curling past the shattering glass of their frames as the fire ravaged the hallway. Ted slammed the door shut, only to see flames burst from the seams of the frame and envelop the perfect white door. As the polished bronze handle began to glow and tarnish under the constant heat of the blaze, Kara and Ted could hear screams coming from the other side of the door—not unlike those that Ethan and Kara had experienced after dark in the neighborhood.

Just as sudden as the screams had begun, they suddenly ceased in unison.

Ted and Kara watched in disbelief as the door crumbled into bits of wood and ash still aflame, falling to the plateau floor. Behind the door, a rocky cliff face was revealed—not the hallway that was previously located on the other side. Ted and Kara stood in place, watching until the final embers of the burned door had gone out.

Nothing was left of the door, or the world it contained, but a small pile of ash.

12

Ted and Kara slowly but surely found their way back into society. Having experiences of the hidden neighborhood in common, Ted and Kara developed a deep relationship and an unconditional love for each other over time. They ended up getting married and quietly rebuilt the lives they had forfeited to the unspeakable place beyond the door.

Ted and Kara made sure to keep a low profile, both used assumed names and earned a living through a business they had built in a very small town. A few years after all of these events, Ted and Kara welcomed a daughter into their world. As she grew, their daughter brought them great joy and happiness.

It was when their daughter turned 5 that the unimaginable occurred.

Ted had been working in their garage on a project when Kara screamed in horror. Ted's fight-or-flight kicked in. Running to meet his bride, Ted found Kara pressed against their daughter's bedroom wall.

A metallic unlocking sound was audible.

Kara pointed at the adjacent wall.

Ted came into a full understanding of why Kara had screamed.

There, on his daughter's bedroom wall, stood a pristine white door with a polished bronze handle.

Ted ran to the door and flung it open.

A familiar hallway stood before Ted. It was as if their fire had never been set. All photos hung on the wall in the same places, untouched by flame. At the end of the hallway was a table and a lamp.

And there, in the middle of the pristine white carpet, lay Kara's bloody knife, plunged into his daughter's teddy bear.

From beyond the hallway, hundreds of screams arose.

The Door

THOSE DOWN DEEP

NOT SO GOOD AT HIDING.

ADVENTURE OUTPOST ISLAND

Harvey Happ, a real estate mogul, petitioned and lobbied the U.S. Government to build a dam on Ash Creek in order to create a manmade lake. As Happ was of significant wealth, there was no politician he couldn't buy, representative whose ear he could not bend, or opposition he couldn't silence in service to his plans for the creation of a lake that would *just so happen* to border his expansive vacation home. The location was ideal, as forests and even a snow-capped mountain would tower over the body of water once created. Happ purchased all of the land surrounding the site. He made a deal with the government to sell most of it to the state for pennies on the dollar—on the condition that they name the lake after him and turn the land into a state park.

The dam was built in 1945, and the resulting body of water was named Harvey Happ Lake, or Happ Lake for short. A state park surrounding it was eventually established, and not long after, generations of campers and day-trippers would make memories in its waters.

It would be an understatement to say that Harvey Happ was a visionary. One of the many outcomes he planned for was the depth of the lake, and upon initially surveying the land, he realized that if he built his vacation home on a certain hill, that as the dam filled the lake, his property would transform from a hilltop into an island. In this way, Harvey Happ was a genius of planning: once the lake was filled, Happ had his own private island home complete with its own dock for the use of his family as well as his various business dealings.

It was a shame then, that in 1949 tragedy struck the Happ family. Four years after having built his own island paradise within a manmade lake, Harvey

Happ was reported to have returned to his island home from a business trip, only to find his wife and children missing. Authorities searched the island, the waters, and the surrounding state park, but no trace of Harvey's family was ever found. Eventually, the search was called off, and Harvey was left to isolation and despair—to live alone on the island estate within the lake bearing his name.

Or so the public *assumed* would be the outcome. Harvey's ensuing actions, however, raised the public's brow of suspicion over these events as time passed. Harvey Happ went on to court various celebrities from the moving pictures, almost immediately dating various starlets, as if he was skipping the grieving process entirely. This drove the press to speculate whether Happ had in fact played some role in the disappearances of his family, and although these events became the talk of gossip columns, very little actual evidence in the case of the missing Happs ever came to light. And so, life for Harvey Happ went on as his wealth saw fit.

In the summer of 1953, Harvey Happ was engaged to be married to the lovely Rosetta Silverstine of Hollywood fame. The two decided to evade the press by taking some time at Happ's island estate and were witnessed on multiple occasions by locals together on the lake in Happ's boat, enjoying the summer. As fate would have it, toward the end of that summer, tragedy struck once again.

Harvey's boat was found adrift and abandoned in the lake, and while their possessions were in the vessel, neither Harvey nor Rosetta could be located anywhere nearby. Authorities searched the Happ property and island, but to no avail. Happ and Silverstine's disappearance rocked papers near and far. Two weeks afterword, a body washed ashore, and it was confirmed to be that of Ms. Silverstine's. The coroner noted that Rosetta had markings consistent with strangulation, but decided to keep those details from the press at the time, as they potentially could create a public panic. The nation mourned as one of Hollywood's sweethearts and brightest stars was to never perform again. Speculation and rumors as to what may have happened spread throughout America. Harvey Happ's disappearance was never solved.

Eventually Harvey Happ's island estate was acquired by the government and incorporated into the state park. In 1959, Happ island was renamed to Adventure Outpost Island—the buildings given a cheery makeover and cabins were added to create a scout themed camp retreat for children. Brightly colored canoes adorned the estate docks, and the island became known for being the single best childhood camp experience in the nation. Waitlists grew for the opportunity—even just the chance—to enroll children for a summer on the island.

Happ Lake saw some of its happiest summers as Adventure Outpost Island grew in popularity and prestige. That ended abruptly in July of 1977, as Happ Lake's haunted past began to catch up with its present.

A troop of scouts set out from the island dock in a canoe. They were to circle the island while observing wildlife, eventually returning to their daily activities back at camp after their morning on the lake.

The troop never returned.

As dusk began to set in, the remaining troops of scouts launched a search and rescue operation on the lake in an attempt to aid their peers. Eventually, the missing troop's canoe was located in a cove on the perimeter of the lake. When law enforcement aided in the search, divers were brought in to look for any clues, all while park rangers scoured the surrounding landscape. The following morning, the divers found the bodies of the twelve scouts, all drown about 40 feet from the shore—their bodies stuck in the mud floor of the lake.

The authorities tried to make sense of the drownings. The best reasoning they could muster for this senseless tragedy was that the scouts must have gone for a swim, with one or two eventually having some trouble. When fellow scouts came to their aid, all of them must have been overcome due to the current—unable to stay above water. The scout canoe most likely drifted beyond their reach, and as none were wearing life jackets, the troop drowned. What underscored this tragedy even further: the canoe was aptly equipped with life jackets—had they been worn, this tragedy would have never happened.

Parents cried in horror as they were told the news that they would never see their children again. Anger over the tragedy filled the surrounding lake community. Allegations about a lack of oversight and misuse of funds filled local papers. The public outcry over the incident was enormous, and it forced the state to shutter the popular summer scout program.

Adventure Outpost Island sat undisturbed and untouched for quite some time. Scout canoes, once brightly colorful, faded in the sun, some sinking from the dock while others eventually washed ashore due to neglect and weather patterns in the winter—a painful reminder of the events that had led to the island's closure. The abandoned buildings became overgrown and lost to time.

Happ Lake would continue to see tragedies in the ensuing years, despite the closure of the scout program. A family swimming on a holiday weekend. A pair of kayakers. Young children. Adults. The inebriated. The sober. The careless. The careful. Those who didn't know how to swim well, as well as those who, in fact, *did*. Over the next forty years, Happ lake would go on to claim *fifty-six souls* beneath its deceitfully beautiful waters.

Outside of the lake waters, Adventure Outpost Island was another danger altogether. Buildings had begun to fall apart. Teens looking for trouble began visiting the island at their own peril. Graffiti encompassed the abandoned buildings. Seances were rumored to be held in the old master bedroom of Harvey Happ, now blackened by a fire that was clearly started by trespassers. The final straw for locals was a couple of teens, who, after overdosing on drugs while on the island, washed ashore.

Residents demanded the government sell Adventure Outpost Island to a developer with a plan or prevent public access to it. Due to the history of the lake and the sheer magnitude of the cleanup operation needed, a buyer was increasingly difficult to find, and the state settled for the next best option: erecting a chain-link fence around the perimeter of the island and posting signage warning would be trespassers away.

And so, Adventure Outpost Island sits alone on this lake, to this very day, behind a prison of its own making… waiting to claim its next victim…

2

"What a load of horseshit."

Robby broke his gaze from Darren, who had been telling the story, to Chad, who interrupted the silence with this colorful outburst. Across the campfire, Jessica and Cassey exchanged glances and giggled at Chad's rebuff of the tale. Darren scowled as Chad decided to continue.

"You're telling me that while some rich dude was getting it on with an actress, everyone just assumed—because he found happiness—that he murdered his family? Then when he and his new girl both likely drown in an accident—and on an unrelated note—a bunch of goodie-two-shoes kids from a rich kids camp drown some years later, we're all supposed to assume THAT is the reasoning for why this lake is *haunted*? People drown all the time everywhere from stupid stuff. My uncle drowned in his own swimming pool last year because of a heart attack. Should I be worried my aunt's diving board is now cursed?"

At this, Jessica and Cassey howled with laughter, Cassey shooting her cola out of her nose, while Jessica failed miserably at trying to blot the drink from her friend's shirt. Robby laughed as well, and even Darren had to crack a smile witnessing Cassey blast soda out of her nostrils.

Darren returned his gaze to Chad and responded, "If you ever manage to land a backflip, you *should* be worried your aunt's diving board is now cursed, as nothing short of the supernatural could propel your fat ass to land that move."

More laughter ensued from the teens around the fire. Chad flashed a grin at Darren, acknowledging the sick burn, and held up the bird in response. Darren tipped an invisible hat toward Chad, and all were in relatively good spirits.

"Well, since none of you are too concerned about the haunted history of the lake, you all wouldn't be afraid of a little adventure of our own on the island, right? It's getting late, and I packed all the supplies we would need."

Darren unzipped a few large duffle bags he had stashed nearby, revealing their contents: a pair of inflatable rafts, oars, various flashlights of all shapes and sizes, and a pair of bolt cutters–clearly meant for slipping through the chain-link fence currently wrapping the island.

Robby pointed and laughed.

"For a guy who just told ghost stories about people drowning, you clearly forgot the life jackets."

"Not to worry, you all don't believe in ghosts and haunted lakes, do you?"

Darren had a huge grin, all but begging for one of them to admit they bought his tale.

Chad wasn't about to give Darren the pleasure.

"Nah, my man, you're so full of shit. If you drown, it will be because you already let out all your hot air!"

Darren smiled and returned the bird.

The girls, however, were not laughing as much—instead, they were processing the fact that the boys were really planning to break into a restricted island and wanted them to tag along.

"Um. So just so we're clear, you're serious about going to the island tonight?" Cassey asked. "Couldn't we get like, caught or something? I don't want a record, and my parents would murder me."

"—And…" Jessica added, "What about shady types? Didn't those kids wash up on shore after doing drugs over there? What if we, like, run into some druggo who freaks out after running into us?"

Darren continued organizing the contents laid out from his duffle bags.

"Don't you girls worry, we'll protect you. Besides, Chad is as big as a tank and could take two dudes with his bare hands."

"Hell yeah." Chad cheered as he smirked and flexed.

The girls discussed to the side of the boys, who had already enthusiastically began inflating the rafts. After a consensus was reached, the two returned.

"We'll go," Cassey informed, "as long as I get to ride with Darren and Chad, and Jessica gets to ride with her undying love, Robby."

Jessica scowled and smacked Cassey on the arm, then the two giggled a bit.

Robby had known Jessica was interested in him for some time. He wasn't sure what to make of it. On one hand, Jessica was attractive, and had been a good friend of his since they were young children. On the other hand, Robby had his eyes on another girl from his algebra class and was a bit indecisive on what to do about his crush. Robby was torn and needed more time, unwilling to commit to any official direction at this moment.

Robby played it dumb and smiled at Jessica and Cassey, replying with, "Ah, give Jess a break. She knows she's safer with me. Chad moves a bit too slow!"

More banter and playful conversation ensued among the group as they prepared their rafts. The group then set out on Happ Lake, paddling in the dark through chilly waters toward the now shuttered island.

3

Adventure Outpost Island sat in stark contrast against the clear night sky. Snowcapped mountains towered over the moonlit lake, and only the sounds of nature and that of a slight breeze filled the group's ears as they rowed. The warm air was offset by the deep, chilly waters of Happ Lake, and patches of fog roamed the surface as they crept toward the old scout dock.

Darren's raft was the first to reach the dock, and soon after, Robby's raft followed. As to not leave anything to chance, the group lifted the rafts out of the water and placed them on the dock for safekeeping, rather than tie them up. The group then proceeded to the infamous archway at the end of the dock that would mark their entrance to the abandoned island.

An old, wooden arch with peeling paint read:

AD ENTUR OUT OST IS AND
(Some of the large, wooden letters had fallen away.)

And beneath the wooden lettering swung a sign, surprisingly less weathered and somehow still intact, significantly altered by graffiti:

Here we dedicate ~~Adventure~~ MURDER Outpost Island to the joyful ~~memories~~ LOSS of childhood, the pursuit of ~~adventure~~ GREED, and the spirit of the ~~American pioneer~~ CORRUPT. May all who pass through this gate be filled with ~~hope~~ FEAR for what tomorrow may bring, and a ~~love~~ RESPECT for ~~nature.~~ THOSE DOWN DEEP.

Below the aged archway stretched an average-looking chain linked fence that continued to span the entire perimeter of the island. Posted on the fence was a sign that read:

DANGER | NO TRESPASSING

This island has been classified as a danger to the public due to unstable structures and a lack of proper maintenance. Funding has not been approved for the state scout program in many years. This state-owned property is hereby closed to the public. All trespassers will be met with fines as well as possible prison time. Do not enter these premises.

YOU HAVE BEEN WARNED

And in pen scrawled below the sign text someone added:

YES, YOU HAVE.
FEAR AND RESPECT THOSE DOWN DEEP.

Robby, after reading the signage and warnings aloud, frowned, and put his hands in his pockets. "Maybe we shouldn't do this. It seems more likely to me one of us will get hurt falling through some flooring or something, rather than be arrested for trespassing."

The girls both nodded in agreement.

Darren and Chad turned and rolled their eyes. They began hiding behind each other, clearly poking fun at him. After the jokes had played out, Darren became more serious and spoke up.

"Dude, we didn't come all this way to chicken out. Not on my watch. You are all about to have the best summer adventure of your lives, and I'm here to make sure of it."

And with that, Darren and Chad began creating an opening in the chain-link fence with the bolt cutters.

4

Once through the newly created opening in the fence, the group chose to walk further up the overgrown path before turning their flashlights on, hoping to avoid being caught on this midnight expedition. Out of view from the shore, they used their flashlights to explore the surrounding cabins and camp. Other than broken windows, rotting furniture, some caved in cabins, and a few signs directing campers from clearly happier days—there really wasn't much of interest.

It was at this point that Chad suggested they search for and explore the old Happ mansion. Ultimately, everyone agreed, as they had already come this far. The group began searching for maps or signage that could direct them further. A few moments later, Cassey came upon a sign that pointed the way to the residence, and not long after, they found themselves standing at the foot of the historic home.

The Happ mansion sat isolated in a spirit of foreboding.

Harvey's estate had fallen into a despair that was exhibited not only by its abandoned and uninhabited state, but also by the overall mood and aura the building gave off. The mansion was a juxtaposition of elegant opulence while mother nature's roots and vines broke through the walls and windows. Trees grew into the interior as well, and certain portions of the structure had collapsed due to unmitigated natural growth and an overall weathering of the building.

The overgrowth and state of the residence made it look as if the very tentacles of mother nature twisted up and grasp the home, seemingly with the desire to claw back the estate from its perch atop the lake.

Robby stared in awe at the base of the decrepit structure.

"We're all going to get laid after telling tonight's story. We could make a pact to make up literally anything about this night. As long as we are all in on it, nobody will ever question us when school is back in session."

Chad and Darren gave each other a high-five while Cassey elbowed Jessica, smirking.

Jessica was not impressed with this moment and rolled her eyes.

"So—what are you all going to claim happened tonight? Just so we can align our stories?"

Chad was not about to miss a moment to control the narrative.

"We planned to do this for WEEKS, and then, because of a full moon… and the unrelated anniversary of the island closing… that, uh, so happened to be… TONIGHT—we broke into the island and entered the Happ mansion."

Seeing that this story was gaining buy-in, Chad continued, in an overly excited and bombastic tone.

"Then we were chased out by the tap-dancing ghost of none other than Rosetta Silverstine, singing her hit Broadway musical number HARVEY I CAN'T BREATHE."

Laughter exploded infectiously throughout the group.

Chad continued to spin his tale.

"Robby was scared so shitless that he PASSED OUT and Jessica had to carry him back to the rafts alone in the dark! And Darren, Cassey, and I had to fend off the zombie hordes of undead drug addicts to BARELY ESCAPE with our lives."

At this, Chad took a bow.

Jessica slow clapped, while Cassey and Darren patted Robby on the back in reassurance.

Darren smirked.

"Exactly how it went down."

"We're all in agreement." added Cassey, winking at Robby.

Robby shook his head.

This was not the tale he wanted circulating back on campus.

244

5

The group eXplored the main floor of the mansion cautiously. The home was robbed of most of its valuables, other than a few damaged items lying about. Almost no furniture remained, most glass windows were broken, and all doors were removed. The only elements that testified to the once greatness of the property were the crown molding, woodwork on the trim, and ornamentation around various fireplaces. After the main floor search turned up nothing of interest, Chad and Cassey decided to explore the top floor while Darren, Robby and Jessica volunteered to check out the basement.

Darren took the lead, with Jessica and Robby in tow. The basement had a staircase that descended into the dark, flooded lower level of the estate. As beams from their flashlights searched the chamber, Darren was the first to submerge himself waist high into the murky waters. Jessica stopped short and wondered aloud if snakes could be present, refusing to go further the more she thought about the matter.

They understood the natural dangers before them enough. Neither Darren nor Robby wanted to linger. Robby and Darren reassured Jessica that they would be back momentarily, as curiosity compelled them to see what could be found within the bowels of the historic home. Darren set his wristwatch for five minutes as a way of keeping the pair accountable and asked Jessica to watch the time. If they were not back in ten minutes, Jessica was to go and wait at the entrance to the home and get help from the others.

Jessica sighed with regret for coming on this adventure, as Robby and Darren continued into the basement's dark corridors until the light from their flashlights were no longer visible.

Jessica sat alone, waiting and praying for their quick return.

6

C had and Cassey made multiple attempts to reach the second floor. Most staircases had fallen into such shambles that entire sections were impassable, due to either objects that had fallen onto the stairs, or sections of the stairways missing entirely—collapsing themselves under the rot that had set in.

In one area of the mansion, Cassey realized that the trunk and branches of a tree intruded into the home in such a way that, if climbed, they could reach a second-floor balcony.

Chad was not exactly thrilled that his part of this exploration turned into scaling up a tree onto God knows what kind of platform, all the while hoping the second story floor wouldn't cave in given the shape of the mansion. Not wanting to appear frightened, Chad offered to climb the tree first. After a few branches gave way and almost falling once or twice, Chad finally made it to the balcony.

"What do you see up there?" Cassey asked.

Chad swept the upstairs with his flashlight. Considerably more possessions and furniture were located on this floor, no doubt preserved due to the inaccessibility of the stairways. The beam from his light reflected off a golden framed mirror located on the wall, as well as other golden touches such as sconces that had long since given up their welcoming glow. Antique chairs were knocked down from where they used to sit by a fireplace, and moonlight shone from a slightly open door, beckoning Chad to further explore the upstairs hallways.

"Jackpot." Chad answered. "Come on up! Let's see what treasures this home still contains."

Cassey was both considerably more athletic and nimbler than Chad, and it showed as she effortlessly scaled the tree and reached the second floor. Chad lent Cassey his hand as she crossed the balcony railing.

Suddenly, the railing gave way and fell to the first floor, shattering on impact and sending explosive echoes throughout the abandoned estate. Chad moved quickly to pull Cassey toward himself and keep her safe from a potential fall.

Cassey embraced Chad, thankful for the security his large arms offered in the close call of this moment, resting her head upon Chad's chest as she caught her breath. An awkward glance ensued, and she resumed her independent stance while Chad also felt the need to guard himself through playing the moment off with some humor.

"Why are you trippin' Cassey? We've got no time for your suspense. Fat guy is the first to go in all scary movies, remember?"

Chad grinned while pointing an accusatory finger in Cassey's direction.

"And also, no more trying to be the first to die in this story. Clearly, that role is mine. You must wait your turn, friend."

Cassey nodded, thankful for humor to break the tension, if just for a moment.

In her own head, Cassey considered the situation, admitting to herself that this abandoned home was indeed perilous and full of dangers. In some ways, she wanted to get the heck out of here, get back to the rafts, and be done with this adventure. Yet another part of her was exhilarated. Her near-death ascent to the second floor ignited a hunger within Cassey to face this moment and explore onward.

When, if ever, would I get a chance to do something like this again?

Just think of the stories we will tell.

Cassey turned her flashlight toward the partially open doorway.

"I'm good. Let's do this. It's time to see where this door goes. I want a souvenir from Harvey Happ—considering his home nearly killed me—*that bastard.*"

Chad nodded, chuckling, and the two began walking toward the exit.

7

Robby and Darren missed their self-imposed deadline.

Jessica yelled down into the dark to see if the guys were alright. After multiple unreturned calls to her friends, chills ran down her spine. She knew she had waited long enough. Jessica quickly made her way back upstairs as agreed and walked out the front doorway of the mansion.

As she crossed the threshold of the entrance to the decrepit estate, a hand shot out from the dark interior and grabbed the back of her clothing, pulling her back inside.

———

"What the hell?"

Darren was clearly confounded.

Robby agreed with Darren's audible concern.

"Yeah dude, I have no clue where we are. I swear we were only a hallway or two over from where we left Jessica. None of this looks familiar."

Ideas of hidden treasures that had filled their heads proved foolish: almost nothing other than moldy, water filled rooms and corridors existed in the depths of this basement.

And now, they were lost.

Darren's wristwatch alarm beeped. They needed to get back to Jessica before she went and gathered help, possibly leading the others into this wet, hellish maze. The pair had followed the walls and felt they were going in circles, with no visible way out.

After a few more passes, Robby spotted what seemed like an opening that they had previously overlooked. To their amazement, an undiscovered room with a spiral, iron staircase lie before them.

Darren sighed with relief.

"Better than nothing. We'll get upstairs and double back to grab Jessica and the others."

Robby shone his flashlight around the newly discovered room.

"Assuming they themselves don't end up lost down here before we reach them."

Just then, the sound of a splash echoed through the room.

Both Darren and Robby turned and pointed their flashlights toward the source of the sound. A rat went swimming by, and as gross as this fact was, the pair were relieved to know the source of the sound.

Just past the rat, Darren's flashlight caught what appeared to be writing etched on the brick wall before them. The handwritten scrawl read:

THOSE DOWN DEEP INVITE YOU TO JOIN THEM.

Robby and Darren exchanged a nervous laugh, and quickly decided the adventure was over for the night, as they had both seen enough. They were thoroughly creeped out. The pair moved quickly toward the staircase that ascended in the middle of the room. As both Darren and Robby climbed the stairs out of the waters of the basement, a new sound filled the space: bubbles of air coming from the same location as the rat previously splashing about.

The pair froze, once again pointing their flashlights toward the source of the sound. A small dark object was becoming exposed at the surface of the water. Slowly, a figure emerged from the water, resembling that of a child in a nightgown, with soaking wet hair covering its face. The figure's small boney hand reached up and ran its fingers through its wet hair, as if to brush the tangles out.

Then, a small child's voice arose.

"Mommyyyyy. New friendsssss."

8

I t took effort, but eventually Chad and Cassey were able to shift the balcony hallway door ajar just enough to slide through the opening.

Vines had grown all over the walls, and it looked as if the Happs had built a courtyard garden in the center of the home. This discovery better explained how nature had so easily invaded other areas of the house. The balcony hallway was protected by a roof that opened directly over the courtyard beneath it. Although the overgrowth had consumed much of the first floor, the remaining balcony hallways were left mostly untouched. Artworks still hung undisturbed, furniture and sitting areas were still placed throughout the halls, and other than the east wall and obvious exposure to elements over the years, the second floor remained as it had existed in previous eras.

Chad and Cassey searched the halls, room by room, for anything that seemed of interest. They found a child's playroom with various porcelain dolls strewn about, what looked to be a study, various guest bedrooms, and even an old music den with a cello still upright in its stand waiting to be played once more. It wasn't until they approached a portion of the hallway near the east wall that appeared to have been burned that their excitement peaked.

"This must be it." Cassey wondered aloud.

"Christ, someone really did catch this place on fire. Were seances really held in there?" Chad asked, now with more of a worried tone. "I half expect to see an old hag fling open the charred door and fly around on a broom."

"Only one way to find out…"

Cassey's voice trailed off as she reached for the doorknob.

The door swung open with ease, but the squeal it made when doing so echoed through the abandoned halls, leading Cassey and Chad to exchange an alarmed glance.

This indeed was Harvey Happ's master bedroom. Oddly enough, no furniture in the room had burned—most items were only covered with soot from the fire.

The floors, walls, and ceilings were black from the burn damage, while the draperies were clearly a loss—their tattered, charred remains blowing along with the cobwebs from the passage of night breeze through the busted windows lining the room.

The moonlit sky illuminated enough of the area to reveal that, in addition to the burn damage, various items had been moved about to clear a spot on the floor for a ceremony of sorts. Candles, wax, and etchings on the blackened floor made the case that although the rest of the second floor was left untouched, this room in particular saw quite a bit of activity over the years.

Cassey picked up a photo frame and wiped the ash and dust away, revealing an old photograph of Harvey, his wife and three children.

"Two boys and a little girl. She must have been about six. How sad for the kids. This island must have been magical to live on."

Cassey then placed the photo frame back where she found it on the nightstand.

Chad rummaged through a couple of wardrobes and found a coat with something heavy in the pocket. He pulled the object out, only to find a flash of gold.

"What do you have there?" Cassey asked as she approached.

Chad shone his flashlight on the object in question. Rectangular in shape, the discovery turned out to be an old lighter. When Chad turned it over, he found it was engraved.

"Harvey Happ Investments," he read aloud.

"Aha!" Cassey said, snatching the lighter from Chad. "My souvenir from Mr. Happ himself! Our tales will now have proof, and everyone *but Robby* will get laid."

Chad was about to object as he had found the lighter, however, Cassey's joke about poor Robby had him cracking up enough that he decided not to protest. Chad instead gave Cassey a high-five, acknowledging the sick burn on their mutual friend.

The two continued to share a few laughs about how Robby looked when they turned his idea around on him earlier.

They stopped when suddenly a *new* voice of laughter could be heard coming from behind the master bathroom door.

Jessica screamed as she turned to face whoever pulled her back into the doorway. Her pulse racing, Jessica found herself in disbelief when she found *nobody behind her.*

As she panned the room with the beam of her flashlight, the batteries suddenly seemed to die and her light went dark. After a few smacks, Jessica began to tremble as her torch was of no use anymore.

Giggles arose. A shadow moved at the end of the entryway foyer.

"Come find ussss…" a small voice whispered from the other end of the room.

"Come playyyy…" a second voice added from another direction.

"Cassey? Chad? This isn't funny." Jessica's voice quivered, nearly cracking into a cry. "Please, let's leave this place."

Giggles from the dark corners of the room continued.

9

D arren dropped his flashlight in terror at the sight of the little girl approaching their staircase in the water. Pushing Robby aside, Darren rushed for
the top of the staircase. Robby was not far behind.

The pair reached a doorway that had been latched closed for quite some
time. It took both of them immense effort to slide the rusted bolt out of the
locked position after all these years. A wall swung open once the bolt broke
free, and both boys rushed out of the stairwell. Down the hall, they could
see Jessica standing at the entrance to the home, and as the pair ran toward
her, she screamed.

The hallway door between them slammed shut.

Darren turned just in time to witness the wet, boney child emerge from the
basement stairway passage.

Robby and Darren began ramming the hallway door. Eventually, one of
Robby's kicks caused the door frame to splinter and give way, allowing for
an escape route.

But Jessica was now *gone.*

Robby and Darren entered the main foyer of the Happ mansion, their eyes
darting back and forth as they yelled for Jessica.

Now multiple children's laughter filled their ears from all directions.

A small, boney hand tagged Darren.

"Now you're it."

And with that, Robby's flashlight went out. Darren was swept off his
feet in an instant. Robby turned to hear Darren scream and disappear into
the darkness of one of the other rooms, dragged at an impossible speed by
two small figures.

Just then, the little girl from the basement appeared behind Robby.

She looked toward him and raised a boney finger to her skeletal lips.

"Shhhhh. We're supposed to hide now."

Then the girl giggled and skipped off deeper into the darkened home.

Jessica cried out a warning as the two shadows moved quickly to close the hallway door. Seeing she had no other alternatives—except to flee or remain vulnerable to what would no doubt come next—Jessica sprinted from the entrance of the home, back through the abandoned remains of the island. She had made it about halfway back to the dock when pain set into her chest from running so hard that she began to feel lightheaded.

Jessica found a nearby cabin and ducked into it, hiding underneath what appeared to be an old desk. Above the desk was a busted window. She sat silently, catching her breath through tears, hoping to hear one of her friends headed back to the docks.

Moments passed. Eventually, the sound of scraping arose, ever so quietly, on the night breeze. Curious, Jessica found a small crack in the cabin wall and looked for the source of the sound.

Outside, a ghastly woman sauntered onward, slowly dragging tangled strands of algae and dead branches in her dress. The woman's voice gargled and cracked a question on the wind.

"Where are you? The children are waiting."

The woman froze in front of the cabin where Jessica was hidden. She turned and looked at Jessica, as if she could see right through the cabin wall.

The woman laughed.

"Not so good at hiding."

10

A t first, it was *one* voice of laughter. As the master bathroom door opened, it became a *chorus* of laughter.

Chad and Cassey stood frozen as a procession of cloaked and veiled women wearing various emblems emerged from the darkness of the bathroom and took their place in a semi-circle, facing the two intruders. Unable to see their faces, Chad and Cassey assumed these were the individuals responsible for the ceremonial etchings and candles around the room. As the master bath doorway was located next to the hallway exit, the two friends had their back against the open windows.

Chad assessed the situation quickly, and immediately concluded a jump from the window to escape was out of the question—they were far too high up, and this side of the home bordered a cliff, so a fall would certainly prove fatal.

"So sorry, we didn't know anybody was around." said Cassey, her voice quivering apologetically. "We'll be leaving right away."

A scream arose through the mansion. The voice sounded like Jessica's. Robby and Darren could be heard shouting as well.

A cloaked figure spoke above the terrified screams of their friends.

"No. You shall not. Your time has already passed."

Cassey and Chad exchanged a glance, knowing what must be done.

The pair made a dash past the cloaked women toward the exit. As they did this, sinister laughter filled the room.

A skeletal hand reached out and grabbed Cassey's arm.

Chad turned and batted it away.

In an instant, the cloaked figures collapsed into bone and ash, their robes burning away into a flash of flame and smoke, leaving nothing but marks where they once stood.

But the cloaked figures' laughter remained.

Not only remained.

It GREW, echoing down the hallways and rooms of the home.

Chad and Cassey sprinted for the balcony where they had entered this section of the mansion. Upon arriving at the collapsed balcony and tree, they made a grave discovery.

Their own bodies lie at the bottom of the first floor.

Chad had not, in fact, saved Cassey from her fall.

Cassey had instead accidentally dragged Chad down with her once the balcony railing collapsed. The two lie peacefully upon each other in a pool of blood, a portion of the railing impaling both their midsections.

Cassey looked at Chad from the balcony and let out a tearful sob, and Chad drew her close.

"Now you understand." a small voice spoke from behind.

The pair turned to find a small girl, soaking wet, running her skeletal fingers through her hair.

"Will you play with me?"

———

Darren wrestled powerlessly as the two small boys dragged him away at unnatural speed. Darren realized he was being taken against his will and didn't have the strength to fight against what was happening to him. The last thing he remembered as his head hit a doorframe was shouting for Robby's help before he blacked out.

Clearly considerable time had passed since, as the light from dawn poured into the home through the windows. Darren stood, feeling a sharp pain in his head, but otherwise in good shape. Making sure to remain quiet, Darren crept along the walls of the home until he made it to the entrance. He bolted out the front door and didn't stop running until he reached the docks where they left the rafts.

One raft was missing.

Some of us got away last night. Darren thought, relief pouring over him.

Time to get off this island myself.

Darren took one step onto the dock and was met with searing, unimaginable pain. He pulled back, and, after a few moments recovering, attempted to move onto the old wooden dock again toward the remaining raft. Once more, his effort was met with a level of pain that was unbearable. Pulling away this time, he was startled by a pat on the back.

"Play it cool, dude. Happens to the best of us. The water is reserved for *those down deep*."

A couple of teens stood on the island shoreline. One of the group sized Darren up and then spoke.

"First time trying to leave, huh? Well, the good news is we have plenty of space at the mansion, and the Happ family is more than welcoming. Before long, you'll be just another guest of the family."

Darren looked puzzled and remained speechless.

Another of the group chimed in.

"He clearly doesn't get it."

The teen approached Darren and slugged him in the arm.

"You're dead, bro. Welcome to the island."

11

Robby ran as fast as he could away from the Happ mansion. He knew this meant Darren was left to those things, and whatever that ghost of a little girl was. But he didn't care. He needed to get the hell away from here. He hoped Chad, Cassey, and Jessica would be waiting for him at the docks—but prepared himself in the event that he alone escaped this island of spirits.

Just as Robby rounded the corner, about halfway to the docks, he came face to face with a new danger.

A crypt-like woman was focused on a nearby cabin.

Robby froze in place but for a moment. The woman turned, her ghastly face somehow drawing a smile from rotten flesh and bone.

"Shall you join my family here as well? Some of your friends have made our acquaintance—they eagerly await your arrival. The invitation is open to *both* of you."

The woman turned back toward the cabin.

Just then, Jessica burst through a side window.

Robby ran around the backside, avoiding the woman.

"I decline your invitation!" Robby yelled at the skeletal wraith woman, as he sprinted away.

The woman smiled and placed her hands on what was left of her boney hips, hidden beneath her tattered clothing.

The undead woman did not pursue Robby and Jessica further.

Robby didn't stick around to figure out why.

———

Robby eventually caught up with Jessica as they both ran toward the docks. "Cassey? Chad?" Robby asked, slowing their pace once it appeared they had reached the rafts.

Jessica shook her head and sobbed.

"Never saw them. But that skeleton woman claimed she already has our friends! What about Darren? Wasn't he with you?"

"They took him." Robby answered, defeated. "I barely escaped."

Jessica and Robby got into one of the two rafts and began paddling back toward their camp on the main shore of the lake. Relief began to fill the pair as they crossed the calm lake in the dead of night. Soon, the main shore appeared through the mist, and help was but a few minutes away.

The surface of the lake was suddenly disturbed.

A boney hand reached up out of the calm waters and grabbed Jessica's arm, pulling her into the lake. Jessica resurfaced a few yards away from Robby, unmistakably being swept back into the deep of Happ Lake's waters.

Robby shouted for Jessica to swim faster as she flailed, attempting to make it back to their inflatable raft. Just as it seemed she would make it, Jessica turned in horror and screamed aloud.

"MY ANKLE!"

Robby watched Jessica's terrified face disappear beneath the surface of the misty moonlit water. Robby held his paddle as a weapon and waited for what felt like an eternity.

After a long pause, Robby put down the paddle and sat down in the raft.

Not even a bubble of oxygen resurfaced.

Robby was left to the eerie silence of crickets and a slight wind blowing across the lake.

After a few moments gathering his wits, Robby paddled to the shore. Robby ran past the campsite fire pit where this nightmare began, and into his car—where he drove to the nearest ranger station for help.

12

Jessica woke to the mid-day sun shining down on the sandy beach on the north side of Harvey Happ Island. She was soaking wet, cold, and coughing up lake water. A child's hand extended in an offer to help Jessica to her feet.

"Ma'am, are you in need of some help? We could be of service."

Jessica took the child's hand and found a young boy wearing a uniform with a handkerchief and various patches. Behind him were a group of children, all about the same age, all just as eager to come to her aid. Jessica realized she was looking at the long dead troop of scouts who had drowned all those years ago. She knew she should be frightened, however, in the moment, she could sense a tenderness in the boys.

"Thank you very much for your help. I'm a bit disoriented."

"We understand. The whole thing leaves you feeling silly and not quite yourself." the boy replied, motioning to his troop.

Soon a blanket was brought forth and placed lovingly over Jessica's shoulders, and the troop built a small, makeshift fire in the sand to provide her warmth.

"We've been waiting for a long time to come to the aid of others. Do you know how hard it is to earn merit badges when you are dead?"

The troop exchanged knowing glances and nodded in agreement.

And so, Jessica sat for hours with the troop of boys, listening to their stories, and learning of the fate that had become her own. After some processing and grief, the troop of boys comforted Jessica in her distress and sent a messenger back to the main house. Minutes later, Darren, Chad and Cassey appeared and embraced their friend in a tearful reunion, as the troop applauded this moment of happiness. As the sun began to set, the friends stood together, watching the amber reflection upon the lake. Jessica and Cassey offered up a prayer that wherever Robby was, hopefully he could find peace.

As the sun disappeared behind the mountains, a small girl approached.

"Our family looks forward to you joining us for dinner."

13

The dining table was set, and the mansion had taken on a surreal form: no longer were elements of the home in disrepair or overgrown—the mansion looked to have returned to its former glory.

Golden and ornate, framed artworks once again lined the walls, sconces were now lit with a warm glow, furniture was staged, a feast was prepared, and everyone looked rather lively—that is, like their former selves before death. The Happ children ran, playing tag throughout the room.

The fifty-six souls who had drowned in the lake were present, including the troop of young boys who looked all too interested in the food before them. The overdosed teen junkies were here as well, standing socially awkward in a corner of the room. A group of cloaked and veiled women stood behind the head of the banquet table. And at the head of the table was none other than Mrs. Happ herself.

A fork tapping a champaign glass gathered the attention of those in attendance. Mrs. Happ then spoke.

"Greetings, guests and family. Welcome to our little get together this evening."

Rosetta Silverstine protested from the other side of the room.

Mrs. Happ raised a glass, toasting Rosetta in jest.

"Always one for drama. And the audience loves her for it."

Laughter filled the room. Once the laughter subsided, Mrs. Happ began to explain the purpose of the night's festivities.

"Now to business. As you all know, we have some new souls joining us this evening."

The room parted as all those in attendance clapped, revealing the presence of Darren, Chad, Jessica, and Cassey at the dinner.

"What you may not be aware of is that tonight we have something to celebrate. A young man named Robby, friend to our newest guests, declined my invitation to this very dinner. He will most certainly put in motion events that will finally set the history of our family right."

And with that, the room erupted in applause. Darren, Chad, Jessica, and Cassey looked at each other with great concern—unsure of what was to come next.

At Mrs. Happ's direction, the cloaked women opened a door to the side of the dining hall and dragged a person—tied to a chair with a bag over their head—toward the end of the banquet table. Mrs. Happ took a bow and then gleefully raised her voice above the crowd.

"May I present the dishonorable guest of the evening, my husband, Mr. Happ himself!"

The room once again erupted in cheers as the bag was pulled from the person's head. Sure enough, there Harvey Happ sat, bound and gagged, and disheveled—clearly not enjoying his portion of the afterlife.

"Now that was to be *my husband*! You *undying flapper*!" Rosetta Silverstine accused above the cheers.

Mrs. Happ smiled and winked at her imprisoned husband, then addressed the room. "Rosetta is just jealous she didn't get to enjoy my possessions very long."

More laughs and applause ensued.

Darren leaned over and whispered to Chad, just loud enough for Jessica and Cassey to hear.

"Well, at least you got the ghost of Rosetta Silverstine right in your story. Too bad we didn't live to tell the tale."

Cassey's eyes rolled in disapproval, while Jessica put her head in her hands, clearly in disgust.

Chad quipped back, never one short of words.

"That's not even the worst of it. Robby is going to get laid *after all*. He is the only one who survived with a story."

Jessica glared at Chad, while Cassey and Darren exchanged a humored glance.

14

Divers found Jessica's body early on. Robby spent days going over his story with the authorities while law enforcement combed over the island, eventually stumbling upon the bodies of Darren, Chad and Cassey in the decaying Happ residence. Although Robby was treated as a prime suspect in the deaths of his friends, psychologists attested to his mental state of believing what he claimed to see, and with no real evidence other than that of trespassing, Robby was released from custody with a small fine.

Robby went on to college after finishing high school, eventually getting laid, and tying the knot not long after the lucky girl became pregnant. Robby never told his bride, or eventual children, about the events at Happ Lake—instead choosing to avoid all bodies of water by relocating to a small desert town in a very dry Arizona.

The additional deaths on Happ Island were the last straw for the U.S. government. The island structures were demolished and cleared away, and even the state park surrounding the lake was transitioned to become a wildlife refuge. A newer, state-of-the-art reservoir for local water was built, and Harvey Happ Lake was drained.

As the water receded, two barrels were found at the deepest points of the lake.

Harvey Happ's skeletal remains were found nearby the barrels, perfectly preserved in the fast-drying mud of the now obsolete lake bearing his name.

One barrel contained the three skeletal remains of Harvey's children.

The other barrel contained the skeletal remains of Mrs. Happ, mysteriously holding some of Rosetta Silverstine's jewelry and a shred of ripped clothing in her hands.

CHILLING TRACKS: THE PLAYLIST
MUSIC THAT SPIRITED THESE TALES

The Hauntings of Mirestone

Easy Lover | Neon Arcadia, N A T I V E S, Emma Rowley

The Train to Nowhere

Quanto costa morire | Francesco De Masi

The Woman in the Darkness

Ghost | VHS Collection

Growl

Mirrorball | Young the Giant

When the Fire Goes Out

Midnight | Coldplay

LISTEN ON SPOTIFY

Free Overnight Delivery

Severed | The Decemberists

The Antique Wingback

i love you | Billie Eilish

On Dealing with Intruders

Haunt Me | Samsa

Bumble the Clown

Madhouse | Allan Rayman

The Spell

Let It Die | Ellie Goulding

**The Kingdom of Vudor
and the Demon of Hollow's Keep**

Vanities | Charlotte Gainsbourg

O'Josephine

Josephine | RITUAL, Lisa Hannigan

The Door

Place Your Debts (TW Walsh Remix) | Jimmy Eat World

Those Down Deep

Haunting | Halsey

ACKNOWLEDGMENTS

Many individuals were subjected to draft versions of the tales in this book. A huge thank you goes out to my extended family and friends who shouldered the burden of glancing at these stories while in development. I'd also like to thank my wife for all of her support in encouraging me to create this work. I can't thank her enough for the feedback and affirmation she brought to my initial manuscript, and her steadfast belief that this book was something I was meant to write.

I'd like to thank my editor Alexis Henry, as without her help, this book would have been a terrifying fright. I'd also like to thank Amber Bizworth as she and the team at Think Deep Press committed to bringing this collection of tales to the public's eye. I understand that they had to deal with some unfortunate events at their old office—apparently when the design team was handling my artwork for this book. I'm thankful everyone is safe and enjoying their new office space. Somehow, despite the fire, we were still able to meet our deadlines for publishing. I'm forever grateful to Think Deep Press for their efforts in this regard.

A huge thank you goes out to any readers who choose to leave me a review for this book. It's not easy to compete in a world saturated with content. Your support and feedback are the lifeblood of my ability to continue bringing haunted tales to you. If I am to be a successful author, it's going to be because of you, the fans, and your enthusiasm for my stories.

ABOUT THE AUTHOR

Rip Graven lives in Portland, Oregon, where he devotes a large portion of his time to interviewing spooks and writing down their stories.

This is his first work of fiction.

For more information please visit:
talesbyripgraven.com

To reach out to Rip Graven directly, please email:
rip@talesbyripgraven.com

HAUNTED BY THIS BOOK?

TRY THE <u>FREE</u> AUDIO VERSION, EXCLUSIVELY AVAILABLE AS A PODCAST.

tales by rip graven .com

Newsletter Sign Up

The Official Running Chills Audiobook Podcast

Running Chills: The Playlist

Exclusive Patreon content such as:

A complete issue of *Haunter's Monthly Magazine*

(and the return of *Ghastly Gossip!*)

Exclusive Running Chills merch

Behind the scenes access

...and more!

Made in the USA
Middletown, DE
07 November 2024

64001341R00155